The Filigree Ball by Anna Katherine Green

Anna Katharine Green was born in Brooklyn, New York on November 11th, 1846.

Anna's initial ambition was to be a poet. However that path failed to ignite any significant interest and she turned to fiction writing. She published her first—and most famous work in 1878—'The Leavenworth Case'. Wilkie Collins praised it and it sold extremely well.

It led to Anna writing 40 novels and to becoming known as 'the mother of the detective novel.'

In helping to shape the genre she brought many other innovations including a series detective: her main character was detective Ebenezer Gryce of the New York Metropolitan Police Force, but in three novels he is assisted by the nosy society spinster Amelia Butterworth, another innovation and a prototype for Miss Marple, Miss Silver and others.

She also invented the 'girl detective': in the character of Violet Strange, a debutante with a secret life as a sleuth. Anna's other innovations included the now familiar dead bodies in libraries, newspaper clippings as "clews," the coroner's inquest, and expert witnesses. Yale Law School once used her books to demonstrate how damaging it can be to rely on circumstantial evidence.

Her career was now well advanced and she was much admired.

On November 25, 1884, Green married the actor and stove designer, and later noted furniture maker, Charles Rohlfs, who was seven years her junior. They had three children; Rosamund, Roland and Sterling.

Although Anna was a progressive she did not approve of many of her feminist contemporaries, and was opposed to women's suffrage.

On November 25, 1884, Anna married the actor and noted furniture maker, Charles Rohlfs, who was seven years her junior. They had three children; Rosamund, Roland and Sterling.

Anna Katharine Green died on April 11, 1935 in Buffalo, New York, at the age of 88.

Index of Contents

THE FILIGREE BALL

BOOK I

THE FORBIDDEN ROOM

CHAPTER I

"THE MOORE HOUSE? ARE YOU SPEAKING OF THE MOORE HOUSE?"

For a detective whose talents, had not been recognized at headquarters, I possessed an ambition which, fortunately for my standing with the lieutenant of the precinct, had not yet been expressed in words. Though I had small reason for expecting great things of myself, I had always cherished the hope that if a big case came my way I should be found able to do something with it something more, that is, than I had seen accomplished by the police of the District of Columbia since I had had the honor of being one of their number. Therefore, when I found myself plunged, almost without my own volition, into the Jeffrey Moore affair, I believed that the opportunity had come whereby I might distinguish myself.

It had complications, this Jeffrey-Moore affair; greater ones than the public ever knew, keen as the interest in it ran both in and out of Washington. This is why I propose to tell the story of this great tragedy from my own standpoint, even if in so doing I risk the charge of attempting to exploit my own connection with this celebrated case. In its course I encountered as many disappointments as triumphs, and brought out of the affair a heart as sore as it was satisfied; for I am a lover of women and—

But I am keeping you from the story itself.

I was at the station-house the night Uncle David came in. He was always called Uncle David, even by the urchins who followed him in the street; so I am showing him no disrespect, gentleman though he is, by giving him a title which as completely characterized him in those days, as did his moody ways, his quaint attire and the persistence with which he kept at his side his great mastiff, Rudge. I had long since heard of the old gentleman as one of the most interesting residents of the precinct. I had even seen him more than once on the avenue, but I had never before been brought face to face with him, and consequently had much too superficial a knowledge of his countenance to determine offhand whether the uneasy light in his small gray eyes was natural to them, or simply the result of present excitement. But when he began to talk I detected an unmistakable tremor in his tones, and decided that he was in a state of suppressed agitation; though he appeared to have nothing more alarming to impart than the fact that he had seen a light burning in some house presumably empty.

It was all so trivial that I gave him but scant attention till he let a name fall which caused me to prick up my ears and even to put in a word. "The Moore house," he had said.

"The Moore house?" I repeated in amazement. "Are you speaking of the Moore house?"

A thousand recollections came with the name.

"What other?" he grumbled, directing toward me a look as keen as it was impatient. "Do you think that I would bother myself long about a house I had no interest in, or drag Rudge from his warm rug to save some ungrateful neighbor from a possible burglary? No, it is my house which some rogue has chosen to enter. That is," he suavely corrected, as he saw surprise in every eye, "the house which the law will give me, if anything ever happens to that chit of a girl whom my brother left behind him."

Growling some words at the dog, who showed a decided inclination to lie down where he was, the old man made for the door and in another moment would have been in the street, if I had not stepped after him.

"You are a Moore and live in or near that old house?" I asked.

The surprise with which he met this question daunted me a little.

"How long have you been in Washington, I should like to ask?" was his acrid retort.

"Oh, some five months."

His good nature, or what passed for such in this irascible old man, returned in an instant; and he curtly but not unkindly remarked:

"You haven't learned much in that time." Then, with a nod more ceremonious than many another man's bow, he added, with sudden dignity: "I am of the elder branch an live in the cottage fronting the old place. I am the only resident on the block. When you have lived here longer you will know why that especial neighborhood is not a favorite one with those who can not boast of the Moore blood. For the present, let us attribute the bad name that it holds to—malaria." And with a significant hitch of his lean shoulders which set in undulating motion every fold of the old-fashioned cloak he wore, he started again for the door.

But my curiosity was by this time roused to fever heat. I knew more about this house than he gave me credit for. No one who had read the papers of late, much less a man connected with the police, could help being well informed in all the details of its remarkable history. What I had failed to know was his close relationship to the family whose name for the last two weeks had been in every mouth.

"Wait!" I called out. "You say that you live opposite the Moore house. You can then tell me—"

But he had no mind to stop for any gossip.

"It was all in the papers," he called back. "Read them. But first be sure to find out who has struck a light in the house that we all know has not even a caretaker in it."

It was good advice. My duty and my curiosity both led me to follow it.

Perhaps you have heard of the distinguishing feature of this house; if so, you do not need my explanations. But if, for any reason, you are ignorant of the facts which within a very short time have set a final seal of horror upon this old, historic dwelling, then you will be glad to read what has made and will continue to make the Moore house in Washington one to be pointed at in daylight and shunned after dark, not only by superstitious colored folk, but by all who are susceptible to the most ordinary emotions of fear and dread.

It was standing when Washington was a village. It antedates the Capitol and the White House. Built by a man of wealth, it bears to this day the impress of the large ideas and quiet elegance of colonial times; but the shadow which speedily fell across it made it a marked place even in those early days. While it has always escaped the hackneyed epithet of "haunted," families that have moved in have as quickly moved out, giving as their excuse that no happiness was to be found there and that sleep was impossible under its roof. That there was some reason for this lack of rest within walls which were not without their tragic reminiscences, all must acknowledge. Death had often occurred there, and while this fact can be stated in regard to most old houses, it is not often that one can say, as in this case, that it was invariably sudden and invariably of one character. A lifeless man, lying outstretched on a certain hearthstone, might be found once in a house and awaken no special comment; but when this same discovery has been made twice, if not thrice, during the history of a single dwelling, one might surely be pardoned a distrust of its seemingly home-like appointments, and discern in its slowly darkening walls the presence of an evil which if left to itself might perish in the natural decay of the e place, but which, if met and challenged, might strike again and make another blot on its thrice-crimsoned hearthstone.

But these are old fables which I should hardly, presume to mention, had it not been for the recent occurrence which has recalled them to all men's minds and given to this long empty and slowly crumbling building an importance which has spread its fame from one end of the country to the other. I refer to the tragedy attending the wedding lately celebrated there.

Veronica Moore, rich, pretty and wilful, had long cherished a strange liking for this frowning old home of her ancestors, and, at the most critical time of her life, conceived the idea of proving to herself and to society at large that no real ban lay upon it save in the imagination of the superstitious. So, being about to marry the choice of her young heart, she caused this house to be opened for the wedding ceremony; with what result, you know.

Though the occasion was a joyous one and accompanied by all that could give cheer to such a function, it had not escaped the old-time shadow. One of the guests straying into the room of ancient and unhallowed memory, the one room which had not been thrown open to the crowd, had been found within five minutes of the ceremony lying on its dolorous hearthstone, dead; and though the bride was spared a knowledge of the dreadful fact till the holy words were said, a panic had seized the guests and emptied the houses suddenly and completely as though the plague had been discovered there.

This is why I hastened to follow Uncle David when he told me that all was not right in this house of tragic memories.

CHAPTER II

I ENTER

Though past seventy, Uncle David was a brisk walker, and on this night in particular he sped along so fast that he was half-way down H Street by the time I had turned the corner at New Hampshire Avenue.

His gaunt but not ungraceful figure, merged in that of the dog trotting closely at his heels, was the only moving object in the dreary vista of this the most desolate block in Washington. As I neared the building, I was so impressed by the surrounding stillness that I was ready to vow that the shadows were denser here than elsewhere and that the few gas lamps, which flickered at intervals down the street, shone with a more feeble ray than in any other equal length of street in Washington.

Meanwhile, the shadow of Uncle David had vanished from the pavement. He had paused beside a fence which, hung with vines, surrounded and nearly hid from sight the little cottage he had mentioned as the only house on the block with the exception of the great Moore place; in other words, his own home.

As I came abreast of him I heard him muttering, not to his dog as was his custom, but to himself. In fact, the dog was not to be seen, and this desertion on the part of his constant companion seemed to add to his disturbance and affect him beyond all reason. I could distinguish these words amongst the many he directed toward the unseen animal:

"You're a knowing one, too knowing! You see that loosened shutter over the way as plainly as I do; but you're a coward to slink away from it. I don't. I face the thing, and what's more, I'll show you yet what I think of a dog that can't stand his ground and help his old master out with some show of courage. Creaks, does it? Well, let it creak! I don't mind its creaking, glad as I should be to know whose hand— Halloo! You've come, have you?" This to me. I had just stepped up to him.

"Yes, I've come. Now what is the matter with the Moore house?"

He must have expected the question, yet his answer was a long time coming. His voice, too, sounded strained, and was pitched quite too high to be natural. But he evidently did not expect me to show surprise at his manner.

"Look at that window over there!" he cried at last. "That one with the slightly open shutter! Watch and you will see that shutter move. There! it creaked; didn't you hear it?"

A growl—it was more like a moan—came from the porch behind us. Instantly the old gentleman turned and with a gesture as fierce as it was instinctive, shouted out:

"Be still there! If you haven't the courage to face a blowing shutter, keep your jaws shut and don't let every fellow who happens along know what a fool you are. I declare," he maundered on, half to himself and half to me, "that dog is getting old. He can't be trusted any more. He forsakes his master just when—" The rest was lost in his throat which rattled with something more than impatient anger.

Meanwhile I had been attentively scrutinizing the house thus pointedly brought to my notice.

I had seen it many times before, but, as it happened, had never stopped to look at it when the huge trees surrounding it were shrouded in darkness. The black hollow of its disused portal looked out from shadows which acquired some of their somberness from the tragic memories connected with its empty void.

Its aspect was scarcely reassuring. Not that superstition lent its terrors to the lonely scene, but that through the blank panes of the window, alternately appearing and disappearing from view as the shutter pointed out by Uncle David blew to and fro in the wind, I saw, or was persuaded that I saw, a beam of light which argued an unknown presence within walls which had so lately been declared unfit for any man's habitation.

"You are right," I now remarked to the uneasy figure at my side. "Some one is prowling through the house yonder. Can it possibly be Mrs. Jeffrey or her husband?"

"At night and with no gas in the house? Hardly."

The words were natural, but the voice was not. Neither was his manner quite suited to the occasion. Giving him another sly glance, and marking how uneasily he edged away from me in the darkness, I cried out more cheerily than he possibly expected:

"I will summon another officer and we three will just slip across and investigate."

"Not I!" was his violent rejoinder, as he swung open a gate concealed in the vines behind him. "The Jeffreys would resent my intrusion if they ever happened to hear of it."

"Indeed!" I laughed, sounding my whistle; then, soberly enough, for I was more than a little struck by the oddity of his behavior and thought him as well worth investigation as the house in which he showed such an interest: "You shouldn't let that count. Come and see what's up in the house you are so ready to call yours."

But he only drew farther into the shade.

"I have no business over there," he objected. "Veronica and I have never been on good terms. I was not even invited to her wedding though I live within a stone's throw of the door. No; I have done my duty in calling attention to that light, and whether it's the bull's-eye of a burglar—perhaps you don't know that there are rare treasures on the book shelves of the great library—or whether it is the fantastic illumination which frightens fool-folks and some fool-dogs, I'm done with it and done with you, too, for to-night."

As he said this, he mounted to his door and disappeared under the vines, hanging like a shroud over the front of the house. In another moment the rich peal of an organ sounded from within, followed by the prolonged howling of Rudge, who, either from a too keen appreciation of his master's music or in utter disapproval of it,—no one, I believe, has ever been able to make out which,—was accustomed to add this undesirable accompaniment to every strain from the old man's hand. The playing did not cease because of these outrageous discords. On the contrary, it increased in force and volume, causing Rudge's expression of pain or pleasure to increase also. The result can be imagined. As I listened to the intolerable howls of the dog cutting clean through the exquisite harmonies of his master, I wondered if the shadows cast by the frowning structure of the great Moore house were alone to blame for Uncle David's lack of neighbors.

Meantime, Hibbard, who was the first to hear my signal, came running down the block. As he joined me, the light, or what we chose to call a light, appeared again in the window toward which my attention had been directed.

"Some one's in the Moore house!" I declared, in as matter of-fact tones as I could command.

Hibbard is a big fellow, the biggest fellow on the force, and so far as my own experience with him had gone, as stolid and imperturbable as the best of us. But after a quick glance at the towering walls of the lonely building, he showed decided embarrassment and seemed in no haste to cross the street.

With difficulty I concealed my disgust.

"Come," I cried, stepping down from the curb, "let's go over and investigate. The property is valuable, the furnishings handsome, and there is no end of costly books on the library shelves. You have matches and a revolver?"

He nodded, quietly showing me first the one, then the other; then with a sheepish air which he endeavored to carry of with a laugh, he cried:

"Have you use for 'em? If so, I'm quite willing, to part with 'em for a half-hour."

I was more than amazed at this evidence of weakness in one I had always considered as tough and impenetrable as flint rock. Thrusting back the hand with which he had half drawn into view the weapon I had mentioned, I put on my sternest sir and led the way across the street. As I did so, tossed back the words:

"We may come upon a gang. You do not wish me to face some half-dozen men alone?"

"You won't find any half-dozen men there," was his muttered reply. Nevertheless he followed me, though with less spirit than I liked, considering that my own manner was in a measure assumed and that I was not without sympathy—well, let me, say, for a dog who preferred howling a dismal accompaniment to his master's music, to keeping open watch over a neighborhood dominated by the unhallowed structure I now propose to enter.

The house is too well known for me to attempt a minute description of it. The illustrations which have appeared in all the papers have already acquainted the general public with its simple facade and rows upon rows of shuttered windows. Even the great square porch with its bench for negro attendants has been photographed for the million. Those who have seen the picture in which the wedding-guests are shown flying from its yawning doorway, will not be especially interested in the quiet, almost solemn aspect it presented as I passed up the low steps and laid my hand upon the knob of the old-fashioned front door.

Not that I expected to win an entrance thereby, but because it is my nature to approach everything in a common-sense way. Conceive then my astonishment when at the first touch the door yielded. It was not even latched.

"So! so!" thought I. "This is no fool's job; some one is in the house."

I had provided myself with an ordinary pocket-lantern, and, when I had convinced Hibbard that I fully meant to enter the house and discover for myself who had taken advantage of the popular prejudice against it to make a secret refuge or rendezvous of its decayed old rooms, I took out this lantern and held it in readiness.

"We may strike a hornets' nest," I explained to Hibbard, whose feet seemed very heavy even for a man of his size. "But I'm going in and so are you. Only, let me suggest that we first take off our shoes. We can hide them in these bushes."

"I always catch cold when I walk barefooted," mumbled my brave companion; but receiving no reply he drew off his shoes and dropped them beside mine in the cluster of stark bushes which figure so prominently in the illustrations that I have just mentioned. Then he took out his revolver, and cocking it, stood waiting, while I gave a cautious push to the door.

Darkness! silence!

Rather had I confronted a light and heard some noise, even if it had been the ominous click to which eve are so well accustomed. Hibbard seemed to share my feelings, though from an entirely different cause.

"Pistols and lanterns are no good here," he grumbled. "What we want at this blessed minute is a priest with a sprinkling of holy water; and I for one—"

He was actually sliding off.

With a smothered oath I drew him back.

"See here!" I cried, "you're not a babe in arms. Come on or— Well, what now?"

He had clenched my arm and was pointing to the door which was slowly swaying to behind us.

"Notice that," he whispered. "No key in the lock! Men use keys but—"

My patience could stand no more. With a shake I rid myself of his clutch, muttering:

"There, go! You're too much of a fool for me. I'm in for it alone." And in proof of my determination, I turned the slide of the lantern and flashed the light through the house.

The effect was ghostly; but while the fellow at my side breathed hard he did not take advantage of my words to make his escape, as I half expected him to. Perhaps, like myself, he was fascinated by the dreary spectacle of long shadowy walls and an equally shadowy staircase emerging from a darkness which a minute before had seemed impenetrable. Perhaps he was simply ashamed. At all events he stood his ground, scrutinizing with rolling eyes that portion of the hall where two columns, with gilded Corinthian capitals, marked the door of the room which no man entered without purpose or passed without dread. Doubtless he was thinking of that which had so frequently been carried out between those columns. I know that I was; and when, in the sudden draft made by the open door, some open draperies hanging near those columns blew out with a sudden swoop and shiver, I was not at all astonished to see him lose what little courage had remained in him. The truth is, I was startled myself, but I was able to hide the fact and to whisper back to him, fiercely:

"Don't be an idiot. That curtain hides nothing worse than some sneaking political refugee or a gang of counterfeiters."

"Maybe. I'd just like to put my hand on Upson and—"

"Hush!"

I had just heard something.

For a moment we stood breathless, but as the sound was not repeated I concluded that it was the creaking of that far-away shutter. Certainly there was nothing moving near us.

"Shall we go upstairs?" whispered Hibbard.

"Not till we have made sure that all is right down here"

A door stood slightly ajar on our left.

Pushing it open, we looked in. A well-furnished parlor was before us.

"Here's where the wedding took place," remarked Hibbard, straining his head over my shoulder.

There were signs of this wedding on every side. Walls and ceilings had been hung with garlands, and these still clung to the mantelpiece and over and around the various doorways. Torn-off branches and the remnants of old bouquets, dropped from the hands of flying guests, littered the carpet, adding to the general confusion of overturned chairs and tables. Everywhere were evidences of the haste with which the place had been vacated as well as the superstitious dread which had prevented it being re-entered for the commonplace purpose of cleaning. Even the piano had not been shut, and under it lay some scattered sheets of music which had been left where they fell, to the probable loss of some poor musician. The clock occupying the center of the mantelpiece alone gave evidence of life. It had been wound for the wedding and had not yet run down. Its tick-tick came faint enough, however, through the darkness, as if it too had lost heart and would soon lapse into the deadly quiet of its ghostly surroundings.

"It's it's funeral-like," chattered Hibbard.

He was right; I felt as if I were shutting the lid of a coffin when I finally closed the door.

Our next steps took us into the rear where we found little to detain us, and then, with a certain dread fully justified by the event, we made for the door defined by the two Corinthian columns.

It was ajar like the rest, and, call me coward or call me fool—I have called Hibbard both, you will remember—I found that it cost me an effort to lay my hand on its mahogany panels. Danger, if danger there was, lurked here; and while I had never known myself to quail before any ordinary antagonist, I, like others of my kind, have no especial fondness for unseen and mysterious perils.

Hibbard, who up to this point had followed me almost too closely, now accorded me all the room that was necessary. It was with a sense of entering alone upon the scene that I finally thrust wide the door and crossed the threshold of this redoubtable room where, but two short weeks before, a fresh victim had been added to the list of those who had by some unheard-of, unimaginable means found their death within its recesses.

My first glance showed me little save the ponderous outlines of an old settle, which jutted from the corner of the fireplace half way out into the room. As it was seemingly from this seat that the men, who at various times had been found lying here, had fallen to their doom, a thrill passed over me as I noted its unwieldy bulk and the deep shadow it threw on the ancient and dishonored hearthstone. To escape the ghastly memories it evoked and also to satisfy myself that the room was really as empty as it seemed, I took another step forward. This caused the light from the lantern I carried to spread beyond the point on which it had hitherto been so effectively concentrated; but the result was to emphasize rather than detract from the extreme desolation of the great room. The settle was a fixture, as I afterwards found, and was almost the only article of furniture to be seen on the wide expanse of uncarpeted floor. There was a table or two in hiding somewhere amid the shadows at the other end from where I stood, and possibly some kind of stool or settee; but the general impression made upon me was that of a completely dismantled place given over to moth and rust.

I do not include the walls. They were not bare like the floor, but covered with books from floor to ceiling. These books were not the books of to-day; they had stood so long in their places unnoted and untouched, that they had acquired the color of fungus, and smelt— Well, there is no use adding to the picture. Every one knows the spirit of sickening desolation pervading rooms which have been shut up for an indefinite length of time from air and sunshine.

The elegance of the heavily stuccoed ceiling, admitted to be one of the finest specimens of its kind in Washington, as well as the richness of the carvings ornamenting the mantel of Italian marble rising above the accursed hearthstone, only served to make more evident the extreme neglect into which the rest of the room had sunk. Being anything but anxious to subject myself further to its unhappy influence and quite convinced that the place was indeed as empty as it looked, I turned to leave, when my eyes fell upon something so unexpected and so extraordinary, seen as it was under the influence of the old tragedies with which my mind was necessarily full, that I paused, balked in my advance, and well-nigh uncertain whether I looked upon a real thing or on some strange and terrible fantasy of my aroused imagination.

A form lay before me, outstretched on that portion of the floor which had hitherto been hidden from me by the half-open door—a woman's form, which even in that first casual look impressed itself upon me as one of aerial delicacy and extreme refinement; and this form lay as only the dead lie; the dead! And I had been looking at the hearthstone for just such a picture! No, not just such a picture, for this woman lay face uppermost, and, on the floor beside her was blood.

A hand had plucked my sleeve. It was Hibbard's. Startled by my immobility and silence, he had stepped in with quaking members, expecting he hardly knew what. But no sooner did his eyes fall on the prostrate form which held me spellbound, than an unforeseen change took place in him. What had unnerved me, restored him to full self-possession. Death in this shape was familiar to him. He had no fear of blood. He did not show surprise at encountering it, but only at the effect it appeared to produce on me.

"Shot!" was his laconic comment as he bent over the prostrate body. "Shot through the heart! She must have died before she fell."

Shot!

That was a new experience for this room. No wound had ever before disfigured those who had fallen here, nor had any of the previous victims been found lying on any other spot than the one over which that huge settle kept guard. As these thoughts crossed my mind, I instinctively glanced again toward the fireplace for what I almost refused to believe lay outstretched at my feet. When nothing more appeared there than that old seat of sinister memory, I experienced a thrill which poorly prepared me for the cry which I now heard raised by Hibbard.

"Look here! What do you make of this?"

He was pointing to what, upon closer inspection, proved to be a strip of white satin ribbon running from one of the delicate wrists of the girl before us to the handle of a pistol which had fallen not far away from her side. "It looks as if the pistol was attached to her. That is something new in my experience. What do you think it means?"

Alas! there was but one thing it could mean. The shot to which she had succumbed had been delivered by herself. This fair and delicate creature was a suicide.

But suicide in this place! How could we account for that? Had the story of this room's ill-acquired fame acted hypnotically on her, or had she stumbled upon the open door in front and been glad of any refuge where her misery might find a solitary termination? Closely scanning her upturned face, I sought an answer to this question, and while thus seeking received a fresh shock which I did not hesitate to communicate to my now none-too-sensitive companion.

"Look at these features," I cried. "I seem to know them, do you?"

He growled out a dissent, but stooped at my bidding and gave the pitiful young face a pro longed stare. When he looked up again it was with a puzzled contraction of his eyebrows.

"I've certainly seen it somewhere," he hesitatingly admitted, edging slowly away toward the door. "Perhaps in the papers. Isn't she like—?"

"Like!" I interrupted, "it is Veronica Moore herself; the owner of this house and she who was married here two weeks since to Mr. Jeffrey. Evidently her reason was unseated by the tragedy which threw so deep a gloom over her wedding."

CHAPTER III

I REMAIN

Not for an instant did I doubt the correctness of this identification. All the pictures I had seen of this well-known society belle had been marked by an individuality of expression which fixed her face in the memory and which I now saw repeated in the lifeless features before me.

Greatly startled by the discovery, but quite convinced that this was but the dreadful sequel of an already sufficiently dark tragedy, I proceeded to take such steps as are common in these cases. Having sent the too-willing Hibbard to notify headquarters, I was on the point of making a memorandum of such details as seemed important, when my lantern suddenly went out, leaving me in total darkness.

This was far from pleasant, but the effect it produced upon my mind was not without its result. For no sooner did I find myself alone and in the unrelieved darkness of this grave-like room, than I became convinced that no woman, however frenzied, would make her plunge into an unknown existence from the midst of a darkness only too suggestive of the tomb to which she was hastening. It was not in nature, not in woman's nature, at all events. Either she had committed the final act before such daylight as could filter through the shutters of this closed-up room had quite disappeared,—an hypothesis instantly destroyed by the warmth which still lingered in certain portions of her body,—or else the light which had been burning when she pulled the fatal trigger had since been carried elsewhere or extinguished.

Recalling the uncertain gleams which we had seen flashing from one of the upper windows, I was inclined to give some credence to the former theory, but was disposed to be fair to both. So after relighting my lamp, I turned on one of the gas cocks of the massive chandelier over my head and applied a match. The result was just what I anticipated; no gas in the pipes. A meter had not been put in for the wedding. This the papers had repeatedly stated in dwelling upon the garish effect of the daylight on the elaborate costumes worn by the ladies. Candles had not even been provided—ah, candles! What, then, was it that I saw glittering on a small table at the other end of the room? Surely a candlestick, or rather an old-fashioned candelabrum with a half-burned candle in one of its sockets. Hastily crossing to it, I felt of the candlewick. It was quite stiff and hard. But not considering this a satisfactory proof that it had not been lately burning—the tip of a wick soon dries after the flame is blown out—I took out my penknife and attacked the wick at what might be called its root; whereupon I found that where the threads had been protected by the wax they were comparatively soft and penetrable. The conclusion was obvious. True to my instinct in this matter the woman had not lifted her weapon in darkness; this candle had been burning. But here my thoughts received a fresh shock. If burning, then by whom had it since been blown out? Not by her; her wound was too fatally sure for that. The steps taken between the table where the candelabrum stood and the place where she lay, were taken, if taken at all by her, before that shot was fired. Some one else—some one whose breath still lingered in the air about me—had extinguished this candle-flame after she fell, and the death I looked down upon was not a suicide, but a murder.

The excitement which this discovery caused to tingle through my every nerve had its birth in the ambitious feeling referred to in the opening paragraph of this narrative. I believed that my long-sought-for opportunity had come; that with the start given me by the conviction just stated, I should be enabled to collect such clues and establish such facts as would lead to the acceptance of this new theory instead of the apparent one of suicide embraced by Hibbard and about to be promulgated at police headquarters. If so, what a triumph would be mine; and what a debt I should owe to the crabbed old gentleman whose seemingly fantastic fears had first drawn me to this place!

Realizing the value of the opportunity afforded me by the few minutes I was likely to spend alone on this scene of crime, I proceeded to my task with that directness and method which I had always promised myself should characterize my first success in detective work.

First, then, for another look at the fair young victim herself! What a line of misery on the brow! What dark hollows disfiguring cheeks otherwise as delicate as the petals of a rose! An interesting, if not absolutely beautiful face, it told me something I could hardly put into words; so that it was like leaving a fascinating but unsolved mystery when I finally turned from it to study the hands, each of which presented a separate problem. That offered by the right wrist you already know—the long white ribbon connecting it with the discharged pistol. But the secret concealed by the left, while less startling, was perhaps fully as significant. All the rings were gone, even the wedding ring which had been placed there such a short time before. Had she been robbed? There were no signs of violence visible nor even such disturbances as usually follow despoliation by a criminal's hand. The boa of delicate black net which encircled her neck rose fresh and intact to her chin; nor did the heavy folds of her rich broadcloth gown betray that any disturbance had taken place in her figure after its fall. If a jewel had flashed at her throat, or earrings adorned her ears, they had been removed by a careful, if not a loving, hand. But I was rather inclined to think that she had entered upon the scene of her death without ornaments,—such severe simplicity marked her whole attire. Her hat, which was as plain and also as elegant as the rest of her clothing, lay near her on the floor. It had been taken off and thrown down, manifestly by an impatient hand. That this hand was her own was evident from a small but very significant fact. The pin which had held it to her hair had been thrust again into the hat. No hand but hers would have taken this precaution. A man would have flung it aside just as he would have flung the hat.

Question:

Did this argue a natural expectation on her part of resuming her hat? Or was the action the result of an unconscious habit?

Having thus noted all that was possible concerning her without infringing on the rights of the coroner, I next proceeded to cast about for clues to the identity of the person whom I considered responsible for the extinguished candle. But here a great disappointment awaited me. I could find nothing expressive of a second person's presence save a pile of cigar ashes scattered near the legs of a common kitchen chair which stood face to face with the book shelves in that part of the room where the candelabrum rested on a small table. But these ashes looked old, nor could I detect any evidence of tobacco smoke in the general mustiness pervading the place. Was the man who died here a fortnight since accountable for these ashes? If so, his unfinished cigar must be within sight. Should I search for it? No, for this would take me to the hearth and that was quite too deadly a place to be heedlessly approached.

Besides, I was not yet finished with the spot where I then stood. If I could gather nothing satisfactory from the ashes, perhaps I could from the chair or the shelves before which it had been placed. Some one with an interest in books had sat there; some one who expected to spend sufficient time over these old tomes to feel the need of a chair. Had this interest been a general one or had it centered in a particular volume? I ran my eye over the shelves within reach, possibly with an idea of settling this question, and though my knowledge of books is limited I could see that these were what one might call rarities. Some of them contained specimens of black letter, all moldy and smothered in dust; in others I saw dates of publication which placed them among volumes dear to a collector's heart. But none of them, so far as I could see, gave any evidence of having been lately handled; and anxious to waste no time on puerile details, I hastily quitted my chair, and was proceeding to turn my attention elsewhere, when I noticed on an upper shelf, a book projecting slightly beyond the others. Instantly my foot was on the chair and the book in my hand. Did I find it of interest? Yes, but not on account of its contents, for they were pure Greek to me; but because it lacked the dust on its upper edge which had marked every other volume I had handled. This, then, was what had attracted the unknown to these shelves, this—let me see if I can remember its title—Disquisition upon Old Coastlines. Pshaw! I was wasting my time. What had such a dry compendium as this to do with the body lying in its blood a few steps behind me, or with the hand which had put out the candle upon this dreadful deed? Nothing. I replaced the book, but not so hastily as to push it one inch beyond the position in which I found it. For, if it had a tale to tell, then was it my business to leave that tale to be read by those who understood books better than I did.

My next move was toward the little table holding the candelabrum with the glittering pendants. This table was one of a nest standing against a near-by wall. Investigation proved that it had been lifted from the others and brought to its present position within a very short space of time. For the dust lying thick on its top was almost entirely lacking from the one which had been nested under it. Neither had the candelabrum been standing there long, dust being found under as well as around it. Had her hand brought it there? Hardly, if it came from the top of the mantel toward which I now turned in my course of investigation.

I have already mentioned this mantel more than once. This I could hardly avoid, since in and about it lay the heart of the mystery for which the room was remarkable. But though I have thus freely spoken of it, and though it was not absent from my thoughts for a moment, I had not ventured to approach it beyond a certain safe radius. Now, in looking to see if I might not lessen this radius, I experienced that sudden and overwhelming interest in its every feature which attaches to all objects peculiarly associated with danger.

I even took a step toward it, holding up my lamp so that a stray ray struck the faded surface of an old engraving hanging over the fireplace.

It was the well-known one—in Washington at least—of Benjamin Franklin at the Court of France; interesting no doubt in a general way, but scarcely calculated to hold the eye at so critical an instant. Neither did the shelf below call for more than momentary attention, for it was absolutely bare. So was the time-worn, if not blood-stained hearth, save for the impenetrable shadow cast over it by the huge bulk of the great settle standing at its edge.

I have already described the impression made on me at my first entrance by this ancient and characteristic article of furniture.

It was intensified now as my eye ran over the clumsy carving which added to the discomfort of its high straight back and as I smelt the smell of its moldy and possibly mouse-haunted cushions. A crawling sense of dread took the place of my first instinctive repugnance; not because superstition had as yet laid its grip upon me, although the place, the hour and the near and veritable presence of death were enough to rouse the imagination past the bounds of the actual, but because of a discovery I had made—a discovery which emphasized the tradition that all who had been found dead under the mantel had fallen as if from the end of this monstrous and patriarchal bench. Do you ask what this discovery was? It can be told in a word. This one end and only this end had been made comfortable for the sitter. For a space scarcely wide enough for one, the seat and back at this special point had been upholstered with leather, fastened to the wood with heavy wrought nails. The remaining portion stretched out bare, hard and inexpressibly forbidding to one who sought ease there, or even a moment of casual rest. The natural inference was that the owner of this quaint piece of furniture had been a very selfish man who thought only of his own comfort. But might he not have had some other reason for his apparent niggardliness? As I asked myself this question and noted how the long and embracing arm which guarded this cushioned retreat was flattened on top for the convenient holding of decanter and glass, feelings to which I can give no name and which I had fondly believed myself proof against, began to take the place of judgment and reason. Before I realized the nature of my own impulse or to what it was driving me, I found myself moving slowly and steadily toward this formidable seat, under an irresistible desire to fling myself down upon these old cushions and—

But here the creaking of some far-off shutter—possibly the one I had seen swaying from the opposite side of the street—recalled me to the duties of the hour, and, remembering that my investigations were but half completed and that I might be interrupted any moment by detectives from headquarters, I broke from the accursed charm, which horrified me the moment I escaped it, and quitting the room by a door at the farther end, sought to find in some of the adjacent rooms the definite traces I had failed to discover on this, the actual scene of the crime.

It was a dismal search, revealing at every turn the almost maddened haste with which the house had been abandoned. The dining-room especially roused feelings which were far from pleasant. The table, evidently set for the wedding breakfast, had been denuded in such breathless hurry that the food had been tossed from the dishes and now lay in moldering heaps on the floor. The wedding cake, which some one had dropped, possibly in the effort to save it, had been stepped on; and broken glass, crumpled napery and withered flowers made all the corners unsightly and rendered stepping over the unwholesome floors at once disgusting and dangerous. The pantries opening out of this room were in no better case. Shrinking from the sights and smells I found there, I passed out into the kitchen and so on by a close and narrow passage to the negro quarters clustered in the rear.

Here I made a discovery. One of the windows in this long disused portion of the house was not only unlocked but partly open. But as I came upon no marks showing that this outlet had been used by the escaping murderer, I made my way back to the front of the house and thus to the stairs communicating with the upper floor.

It was on the rug lying at the foot of these stairs that I came upon the first of a dozen or more burned matches which lay in a distinct trail up the staircase and along the floors of the upper halls. As these matches were all burned as short as fingers could hold them, it was evident that they had been used to light the steps of some one seeking refuge above, possibly in the very room where we had seen the light which had first drawn us to this house. How then? Should I proceed or await the coming of the "boys" before pushing in upon a possible murderer? I decided to proceed, fascinated, I think, by the nicety of the trail which lay before me.

But when, after a careful following in the steps of him who had so lately preceded me, I came upon a tightly closed door at the end of aside passage, I own that I stopped a moment before lifting hand to it. So much may lie behind a tightly closed door! But my hesitation, if hesitation it was, lasted but a moment. My natural impatience and the promptings of my vanity overcame the dictates of my judgment, and, reckless of consequences, perhaps disdainful of them, I soon had the knob in my grasp. I gave a slight push to the door and, on seeing a crack of light leap into life along the jamb, pushed the door wider and wider till the whole room stood revealed.

The instantaneous banging of a shutter in one of its windows proved the room to be the very one which we had seen lighted from below. Otherwise all was still; nor was I able to detect, in my first hurried glance, any other token of human presence than a candle sputtering in its own grease at the bottom of a tumbler placed on one corner of, an old-fashioned dressing table. This, the one touch of incongruity in a room otherwise rich if not stately in its appointments, was loud in its suggestion of some hidden presence given to expedients and reckless of consequences; but of this presence nothing was to be seen.

Not satisfied with this short survey,-a survey which had given me the impression of a spacious old-fashioned chamber, fully furnished but breathing of the by-gone rather than of the present—and resolved to know the worst, or, rather, to dare the worst and be done with it, I strode straight into the center of the room and cast about me quickly a comprehensive glance which spared nothing, not even the shadows lurking in the corners. But no low-lying figure started up from those corners, nor did any crouching head rise into sight from beyond the leaves of the big screen behind which I was careful to look.

Greatly reassured, and indeed quite convinced that wherever the criminal lurked at that moment he was not in the same room with me, I turned my attention to my surroundings, which had many points of interest. Foremost among these was the big four-poster which occupied a large space at my right. I had never seen its like in use before, and I was greatly attracted by its size and the air of mystery imparted to it by its closely drawn curtains of faded brocade. In fact, this bed, whether from its appearance or some occult influence inherent in it, had a fascination for me. I hesitated to approach it, yet could not forbear surveying it long and earnestly. Could it be possible that those curtains concealed some one in hiding behind them? Strange to say I did not feel quite ready to lay hand on them and see.

A dressing table laden with woman's fixings and various articles of the toilet, all of an unexpected value and richness, occupied the space between the two windows; and on the floor, immediately in front of a high mahogany mantel, there lay, amid a number of empty boxes, an overturned chair. This chair and the conjectures its position awakened led me to look up at the mantel with which it seemed to be in some way connected, and thus I became aware of a wan old drawing hanging on the wall above it. Why this picture, which was a totally uninteresting sketch of a simpering girl face, should have held my eye after the first glance, I can not say even now. It had no beauty even of the sentimental kind and very little, if any, meaning. Its lines, weak at the best, were nearly obliterated and in some places quite faded out. Yet I not only paused to look at it, but in looking at it forgot myself and well-nigh my errand. Yet there was no apparent reason for the spell it exerted over me, nor could I account in any way for the really superstitious dread which from this moment seized me, making my head move slowly round with shrinking backward looks as that swaying shutter creaked or some of the fitful noises, which grow out of silence in answer to our inner expectancy, drew my attention or appalled my sense.

To all appearance there was less here than below to affect a man's courage. No inanimate body with the mark of the slayer upon it lent horror to these walls; yet sensations which I had easily overcome in the library below clung with strange insistence to me here, making it an effort for me to move, and giving to the unexpected reflection of my own image in the mirror I chanced to pass, a power to shock my nerves which has never been repeated in my experience.

It may seem both unnecessary and out of character for a man of my calling to acknowledge these chance sensations, but only by doing so can I account for the minutes which elapsed before I summoned sufficient self-possession to draw aside the closed curtains of the bed and take the quick look inside which my present doubtful position demanded. But once I had broken the spell and taken the look just mentioned, I found my manhood return and with it my old ardor for clues. The bed held no gaping, chattering criminal; yet was it not quite empty. Something lay there, and this something, while commonplace in itself, was enough out of keeping with the place and hour to rouse my interest and awaken my conjectures. It was a lady's wrap so rich in quality and of such a festive appearance that it was astonishing to find it lying in a neglected state in this crumbling old house. Though I know little of the cost of women's garments, I do know the value of lace, and this garment was covered with it.

Interesting as was this find, it was followed by one still more so. Nestled in the folds of the cloak, lay the withered remains of what could only have been the bridal bouquet. Unsightly now and scentless, it was once a beautiful specimen of the florist's art. As I noted how the main bunch of roses and lilies was connected by long satin ribbons to the lesser clusters which hung from it, I recalled with conceivable horror the use to which a similar ribbon had been put in the room below. In the shudder called up by this coincidence I forgot to speculate how a bouquet carried by the bride could have found its way back to this upstairs room when, as all accounts agree, she had fled from the parlor below without speaking or staying foot the moment she was told of the catastrophe which had taken place in the library. That her wrap should be lying here was not strange, but that the wedding bouquet—

That it really was the wedding bouquet and that this was the room in which the bride had dressed for the ceremony was apparent to the most casual observer. But it became an established fact when in my further course about the room I chanced on a handkerchief with the name Veronica embroidered in one corner.

This handkerchief had an interest apart from the name on it. It was of dainty texture and quite in keeping, so far as value went, with the other belongings of its fastidious owner. But it was not clean. Indeed it was strangely soiled, and this soil was of a nature I did not readily understand. A woman would doubtless have comprehended immediately the cause of the brown streaks I found on it, but it took me several minutes to realize that this bit of cambric, delicate as a cobweb, had been used to remove dust. To remove dust! Dust from what? From the mantel-shelf probably, upon one end of which I found it. But no! one look along the polished boards convinced me that whatever else had been dusted in this room this shelf had not. The accumulation of days, if not of months, was visible from one end to the other of its unrelieved surface save where the handkerchief had lain, and—the greatest discovery yet—where five clear spots just to the left of the center showed where some man's finger-tips had rested. Nothing but the pressure of fingertips could have caused just the appearance presented by these spots. By scrutinizing them closely I could even tell where the thumb had rested, and at once foresaw the possibility of determining by means of these marks both the size and shape of the hand which had left behind it so neat and unmistakable a clue.

Wonderful! but what did it all mean? Why should a man rest his finger-tips on this out-of-the-way shelf? Had he done so in an effort to balance himself for a look up the chimney? No; for then the marks made by his fingers would have extended to the edge of the shelf, whereas these were in the middle of it. Their shape, too, was round, not oblong; hence, the pressure had come from above and—ah! I had it, these impressions in the dust of the shelf were just such as would be made by a person steadying himself for a close look at the old picture. And this accounted also for the overturned chair, and for the handkerchief used as a duster. Some one's interest in this picture had been greater than mine; some one who was either very near-sighted or whose temperament was such that only the closest inspection would satisfy an aroused curiosity.

This gave me an idea, or rather impressed upon me the necessity of preserving the outline of these tell-tale marks while they were still plain to the eye. Taking out my penknife, I lightly ran the point of my sharpest blade around each separate impression till I had fixed them for all time in the well worn varnish of the mahogany.

This done, my thoughts recurred to the question already raised. What was there in this old picture to arouse such curiosity in one bent on evil if not fresh from a hideous crime? I have said before that the picture as a picture was worthless, a mere faded sketch fit only for lumbering up some old garret. Then wherein lay its charm,—a charm which I myself had felt, though not to this extent? It was useless to conjecture. A fresh difficulty had been added to my task by this puzzling discovery, but difficulties only increased my interest. It was with an odd feeling of elation that, in a further examination of this room, I came upon two additional facts equally odd and irreconcilable.

One was the presence of a penknife with the file blade open, on a small table under the window marked by the loosened shutter. Scattered about it were some filings which shone as the light from my lantern fell upon them, but which were so fine as to call for a magnifying-glass to make them out. The other was in connection with a closet not far from the great bed. It was an empty closet so far as the hooks went and the two great drawers which I found standing half open at its back; but in the middle of the floor lay an overturned candelabrum similar to the one below, but with its prisms scattered and its one candle crushed and battered out of all shape on the blackened boards. If upset while alight, the foot which had stamped upon it in a wild endeavor to put out the flames had been a frenzied one. Now, by whom had this frenzy been shown, and when? Within the hour? I could detect no smell of smoke. At some former time, then? say on the day of the bridal?

Glancing from the broken candle at my feet to the one giving its last sputter in the tumbler on the dressing table, I owned myself perplexed.

Surely, no ordinary explanation fitted these extraordinary and seemingly contradictory circumstances.

CHAPTER IV

SIGNED, VERONICA

I am in some ways hypersensitive. Among my other weaknesses I have a wholesome dread of ridicule, and this is probably why I failed to press my theory on the captain when he appeared, and even forbore to mention the various small matters which had so attracted my attention. If he and the experienced men who came with him saw suicide and nothing but suicide in this lamentable shooting of a bride of two weeks, then it was not for me to suggest a deeper crime, especially as one of the latter eyed me with open scorn when I proposed to accompany them upstairs into the room where the light had been seen burning. No, I would keep my discoveries to myself or, at least, forbear to mention them till I found the captain alone, asking nothing at this juncture but permission to remain in the house till Mr. Jeffrey arrived.

I had been told that an officer had gone for this gentleman, and when I heard the sound of wheels in front I made a rush for the door, in my anxiety to catch a glimpse of him. But it was a woman who alighted.

As this woman was in a state of great agitation, one of the men hastened down to offer his arm. As she took it, I asked Hibbard, who had suddenly reappeared upon the scene, who she was.

He said that she was probably the sister of the woman who lay inside. Upon which I remembered that this lady, under the name of Miss Tuttle—she was but half-sister to Miss Moore—had been repeatedly mentioned by the reporters, in the accounts of the wedding before mentioned, as a person of superior attainments and magnificent beauty.

This did not take from my interest, and flinging decorum to the winds, I approached as near as possible to the threshold which she must soon cross. As I did so I was astonished to hear the strains of Uncle David's organ still pealing from the opposite side of the way. This at a moment so serious and while matters of apparent consequence were taking place in the house to which he had himself directed the attention of the police, struck me as carrying stoicism to the extreme. Not very favorably impressed by this display of open if not insulting indifference on the part of the sole remaining Moore,—an indifference which did not appear quite natural even in a man of his morbid eccentricity,—I resolved to know more of this old man and, above all, to make myself fully acquainted with the exact relations which had existed between him and his unhappy niece.

Meanwhile Miss Tuttle had stepped within the circle of light cast by our lanterns.

I have never seen a finer woman, nor one whose features displayed a more heart-rending emotion. This called for respect, and I, for one, endeavored to show it by withdrawing into the background. But I soon stepped forward again. My desire to understand her was too great, the impression made by her bearing too complex, to be passed over lightly by one on the lookout for a key to the remarkable tragedy before us.

Meanwhile her lips had opened with the cry:

"My sister! Where is my sister?"

The captain made a hurried movement toward the rear and then with the laudable intention, doubtless, of preparing her for the ghastly sight which awaited her, returned and opened a way for her into the drawing-room. But she was not to be turned aside from her course. Passing him by, she made directly for the library which she entered with a bound. Struck by her daring, we all crowded up behind her, and, curious brutes that we were, grouped ourselves in a semicircle about the doorway as she faltered toward her sister's outstretched form and fell on her knees beside it. Her involuntary shriek and the fierce recoil she made as her eyes fell on the long white ribbon trailing over the floor from her sister's wrist, struck me as voicing the utmost horror of which the human soul is capable. It was as though her very soul were pierced. Something in the fact itself, something in the appearance of this snowy ribbon tied to the scarce whiter wrist, seemed to pluck at the very root of her being; and when her glance, in traveling its length, lighted on the death dealing weapon at its end, she cringed in such apparent anguish that we looked to see her fall in a swoon or break out into delirium. We were correspondingly startled when she suddenly burst forth with this word of stern command:

"Untie that knot! Why do you leave that dreadful thing fast to her? Untie it, I say, it is killing me; I can not bear the sight." And from trembling she passed to shuddering till her whole body shook convulsively.

The captain, with much consideration, drew back the hand he had impulsively stretched toward the ribbon.

"No, no," he protested; "we can not do that; we can do nothing till the coroner comes. It is necessary that he should see her just as she was found. Besides, Mr. Jeffrey has a right to the same privilege. We expect him any moment."

The beautiful head of the woman before us shook involuntarily, but her lips made no protest. I doubt if she possessed the power of speech at that moment. A change, subtle, but quite perceptible, had taken place in her emotions at mention of her sister's husband, and, though she exerted herself to remain calm, the effort seemed too much for her strength. Anxious to hide this evidence of weakness, she rose impetuously; and then we saw how tall she was, how the long lines of her cloak became her, and what a glorious creature she was altogether.

"It will kill him," she groaned in a deep inward voice. Then, with a certain forced haste and in a tone of surprise which to my ear had not quite a natural ring, she called aloud on her who could no longer either listen or answer:

"Oh, Veronica, Veronica! What cause had you for death? And why do we find you lying here in a spot you so feared and detested?"

"Don't you know?" insinuated the captain, with a mild persuasiveness, such as he was seldom heard to use. "Do you mean that you can not account for your sister's violent end, you, who have lived with her—or so I have been told-ever since her marriage with Mr. Jeffrey?"

"Yes."

Keen and clear the word rang out, fierce in its keenness and almost too clear to be in keeping with the half choked tones with which she added: "I know that she was not happy, that she never has been happy since the shadow which this room suggests fell upon her marriage. But how could I so much as dream that her dread of the past or her fear of the future would drive her to suicide, and in this place of all places! Had I done so—had I imagined in the least degree that she was affected to this extent—do you think that I would have left her for one instant alone? None of us knew that she contemplated death. She had no appearance of it; she laughed when I—"

What had she been about to say? The captain seemed to wonder, and after waiting in vain for the completion of her sentence, he quietly suggested:

"You have not finished what you had to say, Miss Tuttle."

She started and seemed to come back from some remote region of thought into which she had wandered. "I don't know—I forget," she stammered, with a heart-broken sigh. "Poor Veronica! Wretched Veronica! How shall I ever tell him! How, how, can we ever prepare him!"

The captain took advantage of this reference to Mr. Jeffrey to ask where that gentleman was. The young lady did not seem eager to reply, but when pressed, answered, though somewhat mechanically, that it was impossible for her to say; Mr. Jeffrey had many friends with any one of whom he might be enjoying a social evening.

"But it is far past midnight now," remarked the captain. "Is he in the habit of remaining out late?"

"Sometimes," she faintly admitted. "Two or three times since his marriage he has been out till one."

Were there other causes for the young bride's evident disappointment and misery besides the one intimated? There certainly was some excuse for thinking so.

Possibly some one of as may have shown his doubts in this regard, for the woman before us suddenly broke forth with this vehement assertion:

"Mr. Jeffrey was a loving husband to my sister. A very loving husband," she emphasized. Then, growing desperately pale, she added, "I have never known a better man," and stopped.

Some hidden anguish in this cry, some self-consciousness in this pause, suggested to me a possibility which I was glad to see ignored by the captain in his next question.

"When did you see your sister last?" he asked. "Were you at home when she left her husband's house?"

"Alas!" she murmured. Then seeing that a more direct answer was expected of her, she added with as little appearance of effort as possible: "I was at home and I heard her go out. But I had no idea that it was for any purpose other than to join some social gathering."

"Dressed this way?"

The captain pointed to the floor and her eyes followed. Certainly Mrs. Jeffrey was not appareled for an evening company. As Miss Tuttle realized the trap into which she had been betrayed, her words rushed forth and tripped each other up.

"I did not notice. She often wore black—it became her. My sister was eccentric."

Worse, worse than useless. Some slips can not be explained away. Miss Tuttle seemed to realize that this was one of them, for she paused abruptly, with the words half finished on her tongue. Yet her attitude commanded respect, and I for one was ready to accord it to her.

Certainly, such a woman was not to be seen every day, and if her replies lacked candor, there was a nobility in her presence which gave the lie to any doubt. At least, that was the effect she produced on me. Whether or not her interrogator shared my feeling I could not so readily determine, for his attention as well as mine was suddenly diverted by the cry which now escaped her lips.

"Her watch! Where is her watch? It is gone! I saw it on her breast and it's gone. It hung just—just where—"

"Wait!" cried one of the men who had been peering about the floor. "Is this it?"

He held aloft a small object blazing with jewels.

"Yes," she gasped, trying to take it.

But the officer gave it to the captain instead.

"It must have slipped from her as she fell," remarked the latter, after a cursory examination of the glittering trinket. "The pin by which she attached it to her dress must have been insecurely fastened." Then quickly and with a sharp look at Miss Tuttle: "Do you know if this was considered an accurate timepiece?"

"Yes. Why do you ask? Is it—"

"Look!" He held it up with the face toward us. The hands stood at thirteen minutes past seven. "The hour and the moment when it struck the floor," he declared. "And consequently the hour and the moment when Mrs. Jeffrey fell," finished Durbin.

Miss Tuttle said nothing, only gasped.

"Valuable evidence," quoth the captain, putting the watch in his pocket. Then, with a kind look at her, called forth by the sight of her misery:

"Does this hour agree with the time of her leaving the house?"

"I can not say. I think so. It was some time before or after seven. I don't remember the exact minute."

"It would take fifteen for her to walk here. Did she walk?"

"I do not know. I didn't see her leave. My room is at the back of the house."

"You can say if she left alone or in the company of her husband?"

"Mr. Jeffrey was not with her?"

"Was Mr. Jeffrey in the house?"

"He was not."

This last negative was faintly spoken.

The captain noticed this and ventured upon interrogating her further.

"How long had he been gone?"

Her lips parted; she was deeply agitated; but when she spoke it was coldly and with studied precision.

"Mr. Jeffrey was not at home to-night at all. He has not been in all day."

"Not at home? Did his wife know that he was going to dine out?"

"She said nothing about it."

The captain cut short his questions and in another moment I understood why. A gentleman was standing in the doorway, whose face once seen, was enough to stop the words on any man's lips. Miss Tuttle saw this gentleman almost as quickly as we did and sank with an involuntary moan to her knees.

It was Francis Jeffrey come to look upon his dead bride.

I have been present at many tragic scenes and have beheld men under almost every aspect of grief, terror and remorse; but there was something in the face of this man at this dreadful moment that was quite new to me, and, as I judge, equally new to the other hardy officials about me. To be sure he was a gentleman and a very high-bred one at that; and it is but seldom we have to do with any of his ilk.

Breathlessly we awaited his first words.

Not that he showed frenzy or made any display of the grief or surprise natural to the occasion. On the contrary, he was the quietest person present, and among all the emotions his white face mirrored I saw no signs of what might be called sorrow. Yet his appearance was one to wring the heart and rouse the most contradictory conjectures as to just what chord in his evidently highly strung nature throbbed most acutely to the horror and astonishment of this appalling end of so short a married life.

His eye, which was fixed on the prostrate body of his bride, did not yield up its secret. When he moved and came to where she lay and caught his first sight of the ribbon and the pistol attached to it, the most experienced among us were baffled as to the nature of his feelings and thoughts. One thing alone was patent to all. He had no wish to touch this woman whom he had so lately sworn to cherish. His eyes devoured her, he shuddered and strove several times to speak, and though kneeling by her side, he did not reach forth his hand nor did he let a tear fall on the appealing features so pathetically turned upward as if to meet his look.

Suddenly he leaped to his feet.

"Must she stay here?" he demanded, looking about for the person most in authority.

The captain answered by a question:

"How do you account for her being here at all? What explanation have you, as her husband, to give for this strange suicide of your wife?"

For reply, Mr. Jeffrey, who was an exceptionally handsome man, drew forth a small slip of crumpled paper, which he immediately handed over to the speaker.

"Let her own words explain," said he. "I found this scrap of writing in our upstairs room when I returned home to-night. She must have written it just before—before—"

A smothered groan filled up the break, but it did not come from his lips, which were fixed and set, but from those of the woman who crouched amongst us. Did he catch this expression of sorrow from one whose presence he as yet had given no token of recognizing? He did not seem to. His eye was on the captain, who was slowly reading, by the light of a lantern held in a detective's hand, the almost illegible words which Mr. Jeffrey had just said were his wife's last communication.

Will they seem as pathetic to the eye as they did to the ear in that room of awesome memories and present death?

"I find that I do not love you as I thought I did. I can not live, knowing this to be so. I pray God that you may forgive me.

VERONICA"

A gasp from the figure in the corner; then silence. We were glad to hear the captain's voice again.

"A woman's heart is a great mystery," he remarked, with a short glance at Mr. Jeffrey.

It was a sentiment we could all echo; for he, to whom she had alluded in these few lines as one she could not love, was a man whom most women would consider the embodiment of all that was admirable and attractive.

That one woman so regarded him was apparent to all. If ever the heart spoke in a human face, it spoke in that of Miss Tuttle as she watched her sister's husband struggling for composure above the prostrate form of her who but a few hours previous had been the envy of all the fashionable young women in Washington. I found it hard to fix my attention on the next question, interesting and valuable as every small detail was likely to prove in case my theory of this crime should ever come to be looked on as the true one.

"How came you to search here for the wife who had written you this vague and far from satisfactory farewell? I see no hint in these lines of the place where she intended to take her life."

"No! no!" Even this strong man shrank from this idea and showed a very natural recoil as his glances flew about the ill-omened room and finally rested on the fireside over which so repellent a mystery hung in impenetrable shadow. "She said nothing of her intentions; nothing! But the man who came for me told me where she was to be found. He was waiting at the door of my house. He had been on a search for me up and down the town. We met on the stoop."

The captain accepted this explanation without cavil. I was glad he did. But to me the affair showed inconsistencies which I secretly felt it to be my especial duty to unravel.

CHAPTER V

MASTER AND DOG

No further opportunity was afforded me that night for studying the three leading characters in the remarkable drama I saw unfolding before me. A task was assigned me by the captain which took me from the house, and I missed the next scene—the arrival of the coroner. But I repaid myself for this loss in a way I thought justified by the importance of my own theory and the evident necessity there was of collecting each and every point of evidence which could give coloring to the charge, in the event of this crime coming to be looked on at headquarters as one of murder.

Observing that a light was still burning in Uncle David's domicile, I crossed to his door and rang the bell. I was answered by the deep and prolonged howl of a dog, soon cut short by his master's amiable greeting. This latter was a surprise to me. I had heard so often of Mr. Moore's churlishness as a host that I had expected some rebuff. But I encountered no such tokens of hostility. His brow was smooth and his smile cheerfully condescending. Indeed, he appeared anxious to have me enter, and cast an indulgent look at Rudge, whose irrepressible joy at this break in the monotony of his existence was tinged with a very evident dread of offending his master. Interested anew, I followed this man of contradictory impulses into the room toward which he led me.

The time has now come for a more careful description of this peculiar man. Mr. Moore was tall and of that refined spareness of shape which suggests the scholar. Yet he had not the scholar's eye. On the contrary, his regard was quick, if not alert, and while it did not convey actual malice or ill-will, it roused in the spectator an uncomfortable feeling, not altogether easy to analyze. He wore his iron gray locks quite long, and to this distinguishing idiosyncrasy, as well as to his invariable custom of taking his dog with him wherever he went, was due the interest always shown in him by street urchins. On account of his whimsicalities, he had acquired the epithet of Uncle David among them, despite his aristocratic connections and his gentlemanlike bearing. His clothes formed no exception to the general air of individuality which marked him. They were of different cut from those of other men, and in this as in many other ways he was a law to himself; notably so in the following instance: He kept one day of the year religiously, and kept it always in the same way. Long years before, he had been blessed with a wife who both understood and loved him. He had never forgotten this fact, and once a year, presumably on the anniversary of her death, it was his custom to go to the cemetery where she lay and to spend the whole day under the shadow of the stone he had raised to her memory. No matter what the weather, no matter what the condition of his own health, he was always to be seen in this spot, at the hour of seven, leaning against the shaft on which his wife's name was written, eating his supper in the company of his dog. It was a custom he had never omitted. So well known was it to the boys and certain other curious individuals in the neighborhood that he never lacked an audience, though woe betide the daring foot that presumed to invade the precincts of the lot he called his, or the venturesome voice which offered to raise itself in gibe or jeer. He had but to cast a glance at Rudge and an avenging rush scattered the crowd in a twinkling. But he seldom had occasion to resort to this extreme measure for preserving the peace and quiet of his solemn watch. As a rule he was allowed to eat his meal undisturbed, and to pass out unmolested even by ridicule, though his teeth might still be busy over some final tidbit. Often the great tears might be seen hanging undried upon his withered cheeks.

So much for one oddity which may stand as a sample of many others.

One glance at the room into which he ushered me showed why he cherished so marked a dislike for visitors. It was bare to the point of discomfort, and had it not been for a certain quaintness in the shape of the few articles to be seen there, I should have experienced a decided feeling of repulsion, so pronounced was the contrast between this poverty-stricken interior and the polished bearing of its owner. He, I am sure, could have shown no more elevated manners if he had been doing the honors of a palace. The organ, with the marks of home construction upon it, was the only object visible which spoke of luxury or even comfort.

But enough of these possibly uninteresting details. I did not dwell on them myself, except in a vague way and while waiting for him to open the conversation. This he did as soon as he saw that I had no intention of speaking first.

"And did you find any one in the old house?" he asked.

Keeping him well under my eye, I replied with intentional brusqueness:

"She has gone there once too often!"

The stare he gave me was that of an actor who feels that some expression of surprise is expected from him.

"She?" he repeated. "Whom can you possibly mean by she?"

The surprise I expressed at this bold attempt at ingenuousness was better simulated than his, I hope.

"You don't know!" I exclaimed. "Can you live directly opposite a place of such remarkable associations and not interest yourself in who goes in and out of its deserted doors?"

"I don't sit in my front window," he peevishly returned.

I let my eye roam toward a chair standing suspiciously near the very window he had designated.

"But you saw the light?" I suggested.

"I saw that from the door-step when I went out to give Rudge his usual five minutes' breathing spell on the stoop. But you have not answered my question; whom do you mean by she?"

"Veronica Jeffrey," I replied. "She who was Veronica Moore. She has visited this haunted house of hers for the last time."

"Last time!" Either he could not or would not understand me.

"What has happened to my niece?" he cried, rising with an energy that displaced the great dog and sent him, with hanging head and trailing tail, to his own special sleeping-place under the table. "Has she run upon a ghost in those dismal apartments? You interest me greatly. I did not think she would ever have the pluck to visit this house again after what happened at her wedding."

"She has had the pluck," I assured him; "and what is more, she has had enough of it not only to reenter the house, but to reenter it alone. At least, such is the present inference. Had you been blessed with more curiosity and made more frequent use of the chair so conveniently placed for viewing the opposite house, you might have been in a position to correct this inference. It would help the police materially to know positively that she had no companion in her fatal visit."

"Fatal?" he repeated, running his finger inside his neckband, which suddenly seemed to have grown too tight for comfort. "Can it be that my niece has been frightened to death in that old place? You alarm me."

He did not look alarmed, but then he was not of an impressible nature. Yet he was of the same human clay as the rest of us, and, if he knew no more of this occurrence than he tried to make out, could not be altogether impervious to what I had to say next.

"You have a right to be alarmed," I assented. "She was not frightened to death, yet is she lying dead on the library floor." Then, with a glance at the windows about me, I added lightly: "I take it that a pistol-shot delivered over there could not be heard in this room."

He sank rather melodramatically into his seat, yet his face and form did not lose that sudden assumption of dignity which I had observed in him ever since my entrance into the house.

"I am overwhelmed by this news," he remarked. "She has shot herself? Why?"

"I did not say that she had shot herself," I carefully repeated. "Yet the facts point that way and Mr. Jeffrey accepts the suicide theory without question."

"Ah, Mr. Jeffrey is there!"

"Most certainly; he was sent for at once."

"And Miss Tuttle? She came with him of course?"

"She came, but not with him. She is very fond of her sister."

"I must go over at once," he cried, leaping again to his feet and looking about for his hat. "It is my duty to make them feel at home; in short, to—to put the house at their disposal." Here he found his hat and placed it on his head. "The property is mine now, you know," he politely explained, turning, with a keen light in his gray eye, full upon me and overwhelming me with the grand air of a man who has come unexpectedly into his own. "Mrs. Jeffrey's father was my younger brother—the story is an old and long one—and the property, which in all justice should have been divided between us, went entirely to him. But he was a good fellow in the main and saw the injustice of his father's will as clearly as I did, and years ago made one on his own account bequeathing me the whole estate in case he left no issue, or that issue died. Veronica was his only child; Veronica has died; therefore the old house is mine and all that goes with it, all that goes with it."

There was the miser's gloating in this repetition of a phrase sufficiently expressive in itself, or rather the gloating of a man who sees himself suddenly rich after a life of poverty. There was likewise a callousness as regarded his niece's surprising death which I considered myself to have some excuse for noticing.

"You accept her death very calmly," I remarked. "Probably you knew her to be possessed of an erratic mind."

He was about to bestow an admonitory kick on his dog, who had been indiscreet enough to rise at his master's first move, but his foot stopped in mid air, in his anxiety to concentrate all his attention on his answer.

"I am a man of few sentimentalities," he coldly averred. "I have loved but one person in my whole life. Why then should I be expected to mourn over a niece who did not care enough for me to invite me to her wedding? It would be an affectation unworthy the man who has at last come to fill his rightful position in this community as the owner of the great Moore estate. For great it shall be," he emphatically continued. "In three years you will not know the house over yonder. Despite its fancied ghosts and death-dealing fireplace, it will stand A Number One in Washington. I, David Moore, promise you this; and I am not a man to utter fatuous prophecies. But I must be missed over there." Here he gave the mastiff the long delayed kick. "Rudge, stay here! The vestibule opposite is icy. Besides, your howls are not wanted in those old walls tonight even if you would go with me, which I doubt. He has never been willing to cross to that side of the street," the old gentleman went on to complain, with his first show of irritation. "But he'll have to overcome that prejudice soon, even if I have to tear up the old hearthstone and reconstruct the walls. I can't live without Rudge, and I will not live in any other place than in the old home of my ancestors."

I was by this time following him out.

"You have failed to answer the suggestion I made you a minute since," I hazarded. "Will you pardon me if I put it now as a question? Your niece, Mrs. Jeffrey, seemed to have everything in the world to make her happy, yet she took her life. Was there a taint of insanity in her blood, or was her nature so impulsive that her astonishing death in so revolting a place should awaken in you so little wonder?"

A gleam of what had made him more or less feared by the very urchins who dogged his steps and made sport of him at a respectful distance shot from his eye as he glowered back at me from the open door. But he hastily suppressed this sign of displeasure and replied with the faintest tinge of sarcasm:

"There! you are expecting from me feelings which belong to youth or to men of much more heart than understanding. I tell you that I have no feelings. My niece may have developed insanity or she may simply have drunk her cup of pleasure dry at twenty-two and come to its dregs prematurely. I do not know and I do not care. What concerns me is that the responsibility of a large fortune has fallen upon me most unexpectedly and that I have pride enough to wish to show myself capable of sustaining the burden. Besides, they may be tempted to do some mischief to the walls or floors over there. The police respect no man's property. But I am determined they shall respect mine. No rippings up or tearings down will I allow unless I stand by to supervise the job. I am master of the old homestead now and I mean to show it." And with a last glance at the dog, who uttered the most mournful of protests in reply, he shut the front door and betook himself to the other side of the street.

As I noticed his assured bearing as he disappeared within the forbidding portal which, according to his own story, had for so long a time been shut against him, I asked myself if the candle which I had noticed lying on his mantel-shelf was of the same make and size as those I had found in my late investigations in the house he was then entering.

CHAPTER VI

GOSSIP

Next morning the city was in a blaze of excitement. All the burning questions of the hour—the rapid mobilization of the army and the prospect of a speedy advance on Cuba—were forgotten in the one engrossing topic of young Mrs. Jeffrey's death and the awful circumstances surrounding it. Nothing else was in any one's mouth and but little else in any one's heart. Her youth, her prominence, her union with a man of such marked attractions as Mr. Jeffrey, the tragedy connected with her marriage, thrown now into shadow by the still more poignant tragedy which had so suddenly terminated her own life, gave to the affair an interest which for those first twenty-four hours did not call for any further heightening by a premature suggestion of murder.

Though I was the hero of the hour and, as such, subjected to an infinite number of questions, I followed the lead of my superiors in this regard and carefully refrained from advancing any theories beyond the obvious one of suicide. The moment for self-exploitation was not ripe; I did not stand high enough in the confidence of the major, or, I may say, of the lieutenant of my own precinct, to risk the triumph I anticipated ultimately by a premature expression of opinion.

I had an enemy at headquarters; or, rather, one of the men there had always appeared peculiarly interested in showing me up in the worst light. The name of this man was Durbin, and it was he who had uttered something like a slighting remark when on that first night I endeavored to call the captain's attention to some of the small matters which had offered themselves to me in the light of clues. Perhaps it was the prospect of surprising him some day which made me so wary now as well as so alert to fill my mind with all known facts concerning the Jeffreys. One of my first acts was to turn over the files of the Star and reread the following account of the great wedding. As it is a sensational description of a sensational event, I shall make no apology for the headlines which startled all Washington the night they appeared.

"STARTLING TERMINATION OF THE JEFFREY-MOORE WEDDING.

THE TRADITIONAL DOOM FOLLOWS THE OPENING OF THE OLD HOUSE ON WAVERLEY AVENUE.

ONE OF THE GUESTS FOUND LYING DEAD ON THE LIBRARY HEARTHSTONE.

LETTERS IN HIS POCKET SHOW HIM TO HAVE BEEN ONE W. PFEIFFER OF DENVER.

NO INTERRUPTION TO THE CEREMONY FOLLOWS THIS GHASTLY DISCOVERY, BUT THE GUESTS FLY IN ALL DIRECTIONS AS SOON AS THE NUPTIAL KNOT IS TIED.

"The festivities attendant upon the wedding of Miss Veronica Moore to Mr. Francis Jeffrey of this city met with a startling check to-day. As most of our readers know, the long-closed house on Waverley Avenue, which for nearly a century has been in possession of the bride's family, was opened for the occasion at the express wish of the bride. For a week the preparations for this great function have been going on. When at an early hour this morning a line of carriages drew up in front of the historic mansion and the bridal party entered under its once gloomy but now seemingly triumphant portal, the crowds, which blocked the street from curb to curb, testified to the interest felt by the citizens of Washington in this daring attempt to brave the traditions which have marked this house out as solitary, and by a scene of joyous festivity make the past forgotten and restore again to usefulness the decayed grandeurs of an earlier time. As Miss Moore is one of Washington's most charming women, and as this romantic effort naturally lent an extraordinary interest to the ceremony of her marriage, a large number of our representative people assembled to witness it, and by high noon the scene was one of unusual brilliancy.

"Halls which had moldered away in an unbroken silence for years echoed again with laughter and palpitated to the choicest strains of the Marine Band. All doors were open save those of the library—an exception which added a pleasing excitement to the occasion—and when by chance some of the more youthful guests were caught peering behind the two Corinthian pillars guarding these forbidden precincts the memories thus evoked were momentary and the shadow soon passed.

"The wedding had been set for high noon, and as the clock in the drawing-room struck the hour every head was craned to catch the first glimpse of the bride coming down the old-fashioned staircase. But five minutes, ten minutes, a half-hour, passed without this expectation being gratified. The crowd above and below was growing restless, when suddenly a cry was heard from beyond the gilded pillars framing the library door, and a young lady was seen rushing from the forbidden quarter, trembling with dismay and white with horror. It was Miss Abbott of Stratford Circle, who in the interim of waiting had allowed her curiosity to master her dread, and by one peep into the room, which seemed to exercise over her the fascination of a Bluebeard's chamber, discovered the outstretched form of a man lying senseless and apparently dead on the edge of the hearthstone. The terror which instantly spread amongst the guests shows the hold which superstition has upon all classes of humanity. Happily, however, an unseemly panic was averted, by the necessity which all felt of preserving some sort of composure till the ceremony for which they had assembled had been performed. For simultaneously with this discovery of death in the library there had come from above the sound of the approaching bridal procession, and cries were hushed, and beating hearts restrained, as Miss Moore's charming face and exquisite figure appeared between the rows of flowering plants with which the staircase was lined. No need for the murmur to go about, 'Spare the bride! Let nothing but cheer surround her till she is Jeffrey's wife!' The look of joy which irradiated her countenance, and gave a fairy-like aspect to her whole exquisite person would have deterred the most careless and self-centered person there from casting a shadow across her pathway one minute sooner than necessity demanded. The richness of the ancestral veil which covered her features and the natural timidity which prevents a bride from lifting her eyes from the floor she traverses saved her from observing the strange looks by which her presence was hailed. She was consequently enabled to go through the ceremony in happy unconsciousness of the forced restraint which held that surging mass together.

"But the bridesmaids were not so happy. Miss Tuttle especially held herself upright simply by the exercise of her will; and though resplendent in `beauty, suffered so much in her anxiety for the bride that it was a matter of small surprise when she fainted at the conclusion of the ceremony.

"Mr. Jeffrey showed more composure, but the inward excitement under which he was laboring made him trip more than once in his responses, as many there noted whose minds were not fixed too strongly on flight.

"Only Doctor Auchincloss was quite himself, and by means of the solemnity with which he invested his words kept the hubbub down, which was already making itself heard on the outskirts of the crowd. But even his influence did not prevail beyond the moment devoted to the benediction. Once the sacred words were said, such a stampede followed that the bride showed much alarm, and it was left for Mr. Jeffrey to explain to her the cause of this astonishing conduct on the part of her guests. She bore the disclosure well, all things considered, and once she was fully assured that the unhappy man whose sudden death had thus interrupted the festivities was an intruder upon the scene, and quite unknown, not only to herself but to her newly-made husband, she brightened perceptibly, though, like every one around her, she seemed anxious to leave the house, and, indeed, did so as soon as Miss Tuttle's condition warranted it.

"The fact that the bride went through the ceremony without her bridal bouquet is looked upon by many as an unfavorable omen. In her anxiety not to impose any longer upon the patience of her guests, she had descended without it.

"As to the deceased, but little is known of him. Letters found on his person prove his name to be W. Pfeiffer, and his residence Denver. His presence in Miss Moores house at a time so inopportune is unexplained. No such name is on the list of wedding guests, nor was he recognized as one of Miss Moore's friends either by Mr. Jeffrey or by such of her relatives and acquaintances as had the courage to enter the library to see him.

"With the exception of the discolored mark on his temple, showing where his head had come in contact with the hearthstone, his body presents an appearance of natural robustness, which makes his sudden end seem all the more shocking.

"His name has been found registered at the National Hotel."

Turning over the files, I next came upon the following despatch from Denver:

"The sudden death in Washington of Wallace Pfeiffer, one of our best known and most respected citizens, is deeply deplored by all who knew him and his unfortunate mother. He is the last of her three sons, all of whom have died within the year. The demise of Wallace leaves her entirely unprovided for. It was not known here that Mr. Pfeiffer intended to visit Washington. He was supposed to go in quite the opposite direction, having said to more than one that he had business in San Francisco. His intrusion into the house of Miss Moore during the celebration of a marriage in which he could have taken no personal interest is explained in the following manner by such as knew his mental peculiarities: Though a merchant by trade and latterly a miner in the Klondike, he had great interest in the occult and was a strong believer in all kinds of supernatural manifestations. He may have heard of the unhappy reputation attaching to the Moore house in Washington and, fascinated by the mystery involved, embraced the opportunity afforded by open doors and the general confusion incident to so large a gathering to enter the interesting old place and investigate for himself the fatal library. The fact of his having been found secluded in this very room, at a moment when every other person in the house was pushing forward to see the bride, lends color to this supposition; and his sudden death under circumstances tending to rouse the imagination shows the extreme sensitiveness of his nature.

"He will be buried here."

The next paragraph was short. Fresher events were already crowding this three-days-old wonder to the wall.

"Verdict in the case of Wallace Pfeiffer, found lying dead on the hearthstone of the old Moore house library.

"Concussion of the brain, preceded by mental shock or heart failure.

"The body went on to Denver to=day."

And below, separated by the narrowest of spaces:

"Mr. and Mrs. Francis Jeffrey have decided to give up their wedding tour and spend their honeymoon in Washington. They will occupy the Ransome house on K Street."

The last paragraph brought me back to the question then troubling my mind. Was it in the household of this newly married pair and in the possible secret passions underlying their union that one should look for the cause of the murderous crime I secretly imagined to be hidden behind this seeming suicide? Or were these parties innocent and old David Moore the one motive power in precipitating a tragedy, the result of which had been to enrich him and impoverish them? Certainly, a most serious and important question, and one which any man might be pardoned for attempting to answer, especially if that man was a young detective lamenting his obscurity and dreaming of a recognition which would yield him fame and the wherewithal to marry a certain clever but mischievous little minx of whom you are destined to hear more.

But how was that same young detective, hampered as he was, and held in thrall by a fear of ridicule and a total lack of record, to get the chance to push an inquiry requiring opportunities which could only come by special favor? This was what I continually asked myself, and always without result.

True, I might approach the captain or the major with my story of the tell-tale marks I had discovered in the dust covering the southwest chamber mantel-shelf, and, if fortunate enough to find that these had been passed over by the other detectives, seek to gain a hearing thereby and secure for myself the privileges I so earnestly desired. But my egotism was such that I wished to be sure of the hand which had made these marks before I parted with a secret which, once told, would make or mar me. Yet to obtain the slight concession of an interview with any of the principals connected with this crime would be difficult without the aid of one or both of my superiors. Even to enter the house again where but a few hours before I had made myself so thoroughly at home would require a certain amount of pluck; for Durbin had been installed there, and Durbin was a watch-dog whose bite as well as his bark I regarded with considerable respect. Yet into that house I must sooner or later go, if only to determine whether or not I had been alone in my recognition of certain clues pointing plainly toward murder. Should I trust my lucky star and remain for the nonce quiescent? This seemed a wise suggestion and I decided to adopt it, comforting myself with the thought that if after a day or two of modest waiting I failed in obtaining what I wished, I could then appeal to the lieutenant of my own precinct. He, I had sometimes felt assured, did not regard me with an altogether unfavorable eye.

Meantime I spent all my available time in loitering around newspaper offices and picking up such stray bits of gossip as were offered. As no question had yet been raised of any more serious crime than suicide, these mostly related to the idiosyncrasies of the Moore family and the solitary position into which Miss Tuttle had been plunged by this sudden death of her only relative. As this beautiful and distinguished young woman had been and still was a great belle in her special circle, her present homeless, if not penniless, position led to many surmises. Would she marry, and, if so, to which of the many wealthy or prominent men who had openly courted her would she accord her hand? In the present egotistic state of my mind I secretly flattered myself that I was right in concluding that she would say yes to no man's entreaty till a certain newly-made widower's year of mourning had expired.

But this opinion received something of a check when in a quiet talk with a reporter I learned that it was openly stated by those who had courage to speak that the tie which had certainly existed at one time between Mr. Jeffrey and the handsome Miss Tuttle had been entirely of her own weaving, and that the person of Veronica Moore, rather than the large income she commanded, had been the attractive power which had led him away from the older sister. This seemed improbable; for the charms of the poor little bride were not to be compared with those of her maturer sister. Yet, as we all know, there are other attractions than those offered by beauty. I have since heard it broadly stated that the peculiar twitch of the lip observable in all the Moores had proved an irresistible charm in the unfortunate Veronica, making her a radiant image when she laughed. This was by no means a rare occurrence, so they said, before the fancy took her to be married in the ill-starred home of her ancestors.

The few lines of attempted explanation which she had left behind for her husband seemed to impose on no one. To those who knew the young couple well it was an open proof of her insanity; to those who knew them slightly, as well as to the public at large, it was a woman's way of expressing the disappointment she felt in her husband.

That I might the more readily determine which of these two theories had the firmest basis in fact, I took advantage of an afternoon off and slipped away to Alexandria, where, I had been told, Mr. Jeffrey had courted his bride. I wanted a taste of local gossip, you see, and I got it. The air was fully charged with it, and being careful not to rouse antagonism by announcing myself a detective, I readily picked up many small facts. Brought into shape and arranged in the form of a narrative, the result was as follows:

John Judson Moore, the father of Veronica, had fewer oddities than the other members of this eccentric family. It was thought, however, that he had shown some strain of the peculiar independence of his race when, in selecting a wife, he let his choice fall on a widow who was not only encumbered with a child, but who was generally regarded as the plainest woman in Virginia—he who might have had the pick of Southern beauty. But when in the course of time this despised woman proved to be the possessor of those virtues and social graces which eminently fitted her to conduct the large establishment of which she had been made mistress, he was forgiven his lack of taste. Little more was said of his peculiarities until, his wife having died and his child proved weakly, he made the will in his brother's favor which has since given that gentleman such deep satisfaction.

Why this proceeding should have been so displeasing to their friends report says not; but that it was so, is evident from the fact that great rejoicing took place on all sides when Veronica suddenly developed into a healthy child and the probability of David Moore's inheriting the coveted estate decreased to a minimum. It was not a long rejoicing, however, for John Judson followed his wife to the grave before Veronica had reached her tenth year, leaving her and her half-sister, Cora, to the guardianship of a crabbed old bachelor who had been his father's lawyer. This lawyer was morose and peevish, but he was never positively unkind. For two years the sisters seemed happy enough when, suddenly and somewhat peremptorily, they were separated, Veronica being sent to a western school, where she remained, seemingly without a single visit east, till she was seventeen. During this long absence Miss Tuttle resided in Washington, developing under masters into an accomplished woman. Veronica's guardian, severe in his treatment of the youthful owner of the large fortune of which he had been made sole executor, was unexpectedly generous to the penniless sister, hoping, perhaps, in his close, peevish old heart, that the charms and acquired graces of this lovely woman would soon win for her a husband in the brilliant set in which she naturally found herself.

But Cora Tuttle was not easy to please, and the first men of Washington came and went before her eyes without awakening in her any special interest till she met Francis Jeffrey, who stole her heart with a look.

Those who remember her that winter say that under his influence she developed from a handsome woman into a lovely one. Yet no engagement was announced, and society was wondering what held Francis Jeffrey back from so great a prize, when Veronica Moore came home, and the question was forever answered.

Veronica was now nearly eighteen, and during her absence had blossomed into womanhood. She was not as beautiful as her sister, but she had a bright and pleasing expression with enough spice in her temperament to rob her girlish features of insipidity and make her conversation witty, if not brilliant. Yet when Francis Jeffrey turned his attentions from Miss Tuttle and fixed them without reserve, or seeming shame, upon this pretty butterfly, but one term could be found to characterize the proceeding, and that was, fortune hunting. Of small but settled income, he had hitherto shown a certain contentment with his condition calculated to inspire respect and make his attentions to Miss Tuttle seem both consistent and appropriate. But no sooner did Veronica's bright eyes appear than he fell at the young heiress' feet and pressed his suit so close and fast that in two months they were engaged and at the end of the half-year, married—with the disastrous consequences just made known.

So much for the general gossip of the town. Now for the special.

A certain gentleman, whom it is unnecessary to name, had been present at one critical instant in the lives of these three persons. He was not a scandalmonger, and if everything had gone on happily, if Veronica had lived and Cora settled down into matrimony, he would never have mentioned what he heard and saw one night in the great drawing-room of a hotel in Atlantic City.

It was at the time when the engagement was first announced between Jeffrey and the young heiress. This and his previous attentions to Cora had made much talk, both in Washington and elsewhere, and there were not lacking those who had openly twitted him for his seeming inconstancy. This had been over the cups of course, and Jeffrey had borne it well enough from his so-called friends and intimates. But when, on a certain evening in the parlor of one of the large hotels in Atlantic City, a fellow whom nobody knew and nobody liked accused him of knowing on which side his bread was buttered, and that certainly it was not on the side of beauty and superior attainments, Jeffrey got angry. Heedless of who might be within hearing, he spoke up very plainly in these words: "You are all of a kind, rank money-worshipers and self-seeker, or you would not be so ready to see greed in my admiration for Miss Moore. Disagreeable as I find it to air my sentiments in this public manner, yet since you provoke me to it, I will say once and for all, that I am deeply in love with Miss Moore, and that it is for this reason only I am going to marry her. Were she the penniless girl her sister is, and Miss Tuttle the proud possessor of the wealth which, in your eyes, confers such distinction upon Miss Moore, you would still see me at the latter's feet, and at hers only. Miss Tuttle's charms are not potent enough to hold the heart which has once been fixed by her sister's smile."

This was pointed enough, certainly, but when at the conclusion of his words a tall figure rose from a year corner and Cora Tuttle passed the amazed group with a bow, I dare warrant that not one of the men composing it but wished himself a hundred miles away.

Jeffrey himself was chagrined, and made a move to follow the woman he had so publicly scorned, but the look she cast back at him was one to remember, and he hesitated. What was there left for him to say, or even to do? The avowal had been made in all its bald frankness and nothing could alter it. As for her, she behaved beautifully, and by no word or look, so far as the world knew, ever showed that her woman's pride, if not her heart, had been cut to the quick, by the one man she adored.

With this incident filling my mind, I returned to Washington. I had acquainted myself with the open facts of this family's history; but what of its inner life? Who knew it? Did any one? Even the man who confided to me the contretemps in the hotel parlor could not be sure what underlay Mr. Jeffrey's warm advocacy of the woman he had elected to marry. He could not even be certain that he had really understood the feeling shown by Cora Tuttle when she heard the man, who had once lavished attentions on her, express in this public manner a preference for her sister. A woman has great aptness in concealing a mortal hurt, and, from what I had seen of this one, I thought it highly improbable that all was quiet in her passionate breast because she had turned an impassive front to the world.

I was becoming confused in the maze of my own imaginings. To escape the results of this confusion, I determined to drop theory and confine myself to facts.

And thus passed the first few days succeeding the tragic discovery in the Moore house.

CHAPTER VII

SLY WORK

The next morning my duty led me directly in the way of that little friend of mine whom I have already mentioned. It is strange how often my duty did lead me in her way.

She is a demure little creature, with wits as bright as her eyes, which is saying a great deal; and while, in the course of our long friendship, I had admired without making use of the special abilities I saw in her, I felt that the time had now come when they might prove of inestimable value to me.

Greeting her with pardonable abruptness, I expressed my wishes in these possibly alarming words:

"Jinny, you can do something for me. Find out—I know you can, and that, too, without arousing suspicion or compromising either of us—where Mr. Moore, of Waverley Avenue, buys his groceries, and when you have done that, whether or not he has lately resupplied himself with candles."

The surprise which she showed had a touch of naivete in it which was very encouraging.

"Mr. Moore?" she cried, "the uncle of her who—who—"

"The very same," I responded, and waited for her questions without adding a single word in way of explanation.

She gave me a look—oh, what a look! It was as encouraging to the detective as it was welcome to the lover; after which she nodded, once in doubt, once in question and once in frank and laughing consent, and darted off.

I thanked Providence for such a self-contained little aide-decamp and proceeded on my way, in a state of great self-satisfaction.

An hour later I came upon her again. It is really extraordinary how frequently the paths of some people cross.

"Well?" I asked.

"Mr. Moore deals with Simpkins, just two blocks away from his house; and only a week ago he bought some candles there."

I rewarded her with a smile which summoned into view the most exasperating of dimples.

"You had better patronize Simpkins yourself for a little while," I suggested; and by the arch glance with which my words were received, I perceived that my meaning was fully understood.

Experiencing from this moment an increased confidence, not only in the powers of my little friend, but in the line of investigation thus happily established, I cast about for means of settling the one great question which was a necessary preliminary to all future action: Whether the marks detected by me in the dust of the mantel in the southwest chamber had been made by the hand of him who had lately felt the need of candles, albeit his house appeared to be fully lighted by gas?

The subterfuge by which, notwithstanding my many disadvantages, I was finally enabled to obtain unmistakable answer to this query was the fruit of much hard thought. Perhaps I was too proud of it. Perhaps I should have mistrusted myself more from the start. But I was a great egotist in those days, and reckoned quite above their inherent worth any bright ideas which I could safely call my own.

The point aimed at was this: to obtain without Moore's knowledge an accurate impression of his finger-tips.

The task presented difficulties, but these served duly to increase my ardor.

Confiding to the lieutenant of the precinct my great interest in the mysterious house with whose suggestive interior I had made myself acquainted under such tragic circumstances, I asked him as a personal favor to obtain for me an opportunity of spending another night there.

He was evidently surprised by the request, not cherishing, as I suppose, any great longings himself in this direction; but recognizing that for some reason I set great store on this questionable privilege,—I do not think that he suspected in the least what that reason was,—and being, as I have intimated, favorably disposed to me, he exerted himself to such good effect that I was formally detailed to assist in keeping watch over the premises that very night.

I think that it was at this point I began to reckon on the success which, after many failures and some mischances, was yet to reward my efforts.

As I prepared to enter the old house at nightfall, I allowed myself one short glance across the way to see if my approach had been observed by the man whose secret, if secret he had, I was laying plans to surprise. I was met by a sight I had not expected. Pausing on the pavement in front of me stood a handsome elderly gentleman whose appearance was so fashionable and thoroughly up to date, that I should have failed to recognize him if my glance had not taken in at the same instant the figure of Rudge crouching obstinately on the edge of the curb where he had evidently posted himself in distinct refusal to come any farther. In vain his master,—for the well-dressed man before me was no less a personage than the whilom butt of all the boys between the Capitol and the Treasury building,—signaled and commanded him to cross to his side; nothing could induce the mastiff to budge from that quarter of the street where he felt himself safe.

Mr. Moore, glorying in the prospect of unlimited wealth, presented a startling contrast in more ways than one to the poverty-stricken old man whose curious garb and lonely habits had made him an object of ridicule to half the town. I own that I was half amused and half awed by the condescending bow with which he greeted my offhand nod and the affable way in which he remarked:

"You are making use of your prerogatives as a member of the police, I see."

The words came as easily from his lips as if his practice in affability had been of the very longest.

"I wonder how the old place enjoys its present distinction," he went on, running his eye over the dilapidated walls under which we stood, with very evident pride in their vast proportions and the air of gloomy grandeur which signalized them. "If it partakes in the slightest degree of the feelings of its owner, I can vouch for its impatience at the free use which is made of its time-worn rooms and halls. Are these intrusions necessary? Now that Mrs. Jeffrey's body has been removed, do you feel that the scene of her demise need hold the attention of the police any longer?"

"That is a question to put to the superintendent and not to me," was my deprecatory reply. "The major has issued no orders for the watch to be taken off, so we men have no choice. I am sorry if it offends you. Doubtless a few days will end the matter and the keys will be given into your hand. I suppose you are anxious to move in?"

He cast a glance behind him at his dog, gave a whistle which passed unheeded, and replied with dignity, if but little heart:

"When a man has passed his seventh decade he is not apt to be so patient with delay as when he has a prospect of many years before him. I am anxious to enter my own house, yes; I have much to do there."

I came very near asking him what, but feared to seem too familiar, in case he was the cold but upright man he would fain appear, and too interested and inquiring if he were the whited sepulcher I secretly considered him. So with a nod a trifle more pronounced than if I had been unaffected by either hypothesis, I remounted the steps, carelessly remarking:

"I'll see you again after taking a turn through the house. If I discover anything—ghost marks or human marks which might be of interest to you—I'll let you know."

Something like a growl answered me. But whether it came from master or dog, I did not stop to inquire. I had serious work before me; very serious, considering that it was to be done on my own responsibility and without the knowledge of my superiors. But I was sustained by the thought that no whisper of murder had as yet been heard abroad or at headquarters, and that consequently I was interfering in no great case; merely trying to formulate one.

It was necessary, for the success of my plan, that some time should elapse before I reapproached Mr. Moore. I therefore kept my word to him and satisfied my own curiosity by taking a fresh tour through the house. Naturally, in doing this, I visited the library. Here all was dark. The faint twilight still illuminating the streets failed to penetrate here. I was obliged to light my lantern.

My first glance was toward the fireplace. Venturesome hands had been there. Not only had, the fender been drawn out and the grate set aside, but the huge settle had been wrenched free from the mantel and dragged into the center of the room. Rather pleased at this change, for with all my apparent bravado I did not enjoy too close a proximity to the cruel hearthstone, I stopped to give this settle a thorough investigation. The result was disappointing. To all appearance and I did not spare it the experiment of many a thump and knock—it was a perfectly innocuous piece of furniture, clumsy of build, but solid and absolutely devoid of anything that could explain the tragedies which had occurred so near it. I even sat down on its musty old cushion and shut my eyes, but was unrewarded by alarming visions, or disturbance of any sort. Nor did the floor where it had stood yield any better results to the inquiring eye. Nothing was to be seen there but the marks left by the removal of its base from the blackened boards.

Disgusted with myself, if not with this object of my present disappointment, I left that portion of the room in which it stood and crossed to where I had found the little table on the night of Mrs. Jeffrey's death. It was no longer there. It had been set back against the wall where it properly belonged, and the candelabrum removed. Nor was the kitchen chair any longer to be seen near the book shelves. This fact, small as it was, caused me an instant of chagrin. I had intended to look again at the book which I had examined with such unsatisfactory results the time before. A glance showed me that this book had been pushed back level with the others; but I remembered its title, and, had the means of reaching it been at hand, I should certainly have stolen another peep at it.

Upstairs I found the same signs of police interference. The shutter had been fastened in the southwest room, and the bouquet and wrap taken away from the bed. The handkerchief, also, was missing from the mantel where I had left it, and when I opened the closet door, it was to find the floor bare and the second candelabrum and candle removed.

"All gone," thought I; "each and every clue."

But I was mistaken. In another moment I came upon the minute filings I had before observed scattered over a small stand. Concluding from this that they had been passed over by Durbin and his associates as valueless, I swept them, together with the dust in which they lay, into an old envelope I happily found in my pocket. Then I crossed to the mantel and made a close inspection of its now empty shelf. The scratches which I had made there were visible enough, but the impressions for which they stood had vanished in the handling which everything in the house had undergone. Regarding with great thankfulness the result of my own foresight, I made haste to leave the room. I then proceeded to take my first steps in the ticklish experiment by which I hoped to determine whether Uncle David had had any share in the fatal business which had rendered the two rooms I had just visited so memorable.

First, satisfying myself by a peep through the front drawing-room window that he was positively at watch behind the vines, I went directly to the kitchen, procured a chair and carried it into the library, where I put it to a use that, to an onlooker's eye, would have appeared very peculiar. Planting it squarely on the hearthstone,—not without some secret perturbation as to what the results might be to myself,— I mounted it and took down the engraving which I have already described as hanging over this mantelpiece.

Setting it on end against one of the jambs of the fireplace, I mounted the chair once more and carefully sifted over the high shelf the contents of a little package which I had brought with me for this purpose.

Then, leaving the chair where it was, I betook myself out of the front door, ostentatiously stopping to lock it and to put the key in my pocket.

Crossing immediately to Mr. Moore's side of the street, I encountered him as I had expected to do, at his own gateway.

"Well, what now?" he inquired, with the same exaggerated courtesy I had noticed in him on a previous occasion. "You have the air of a man bringing news. Has anything fresh happened in the old house?"

I assumed a frankness which seemed to impose on him.

"Do you know," I sententiously informed him, "I have a wonderful interest in that old hearthstone; or rather in the seemingly innocent engraving hanging over it, of Benjamin Franklin at the Court of France. I tell you frankly that I had no idea of what would be found behind the picture."

I saw, by his quick look, that I had stirred up a hornets' nest. This was just what I had calculated to do.

"Behind it!" he repeated. "There is nothing behind it."

I laughed, shrugged my shoulders, and backed slowly toward the door.

"Of course, you should know," I retorted, with some condescension. Then, as if struck by a sudden remembrance: "Oh, by the way, have you been told that there is a window on that lower floor which does not stay fastened? I speak of it that you may have it repaired as soon as the police vacate. It's the last one in the hall leading to the negro quarters. If you shake it hard enough, the catch falls back and any one can raise it even from the outside."

"I will see to it," he replied, dropping his eyes, possibly to hide their curious twinkle. "But what do you mean about finding something in the wall behind that old picture? I've never heard—"

But though he spoke quickly and shouted the last words after me at the top of his voice, I was by this time too far away to respond save by a dubious smile and a semi-patronizing wave of the hand. Not until I was nearly out of earshot did I venture to shout back the following words:

"I'll be back in an hour. If anything happens—if the boys annoy you, or any one attempts to enter the old house, telephone to the station or summon the officer at the corner. I don't believe any harm will come from leaving the place to itself for a while." Then I walked around the block.

When I arrived in front again it was quite dark. So was the house; but there was light in the library. I felt assured that I should find Uncle David there, and I did. When, after a noiseless entrance and a careful advance through the hall, I threw open the door beyond the gilded pillars, it was to see the tall figure of this old man mounted upon the chair I had left there, peering up at the nail from which I had so lately lifted the picture. He started as I presented myself and almost fell from the chair. But the careless laugh I uttered assured him of the little importance I placed upon this evidence of his daring and unappeasable curiosity, and he confronted me with an enviable air of dignity; whereupon I managed to say:

"Really, Mr. Moore, I'm glad to see you here. It is quite natural for you to wish to learn by any means in your power what that picture concealed. I came back, because I suddenly remembered that I had forgotten to rehang it."

Involuntarily he glanced again at the wall overhead, which was as bare as his hand, save for the nail he had already examined.

"It has concealed nothing," he retorted. "You can see yourself that the wall is bare and that it rings as sound as any chimneypiece ever made." Here he struck it heavily with his fist. "What did you imagine that you had found?"

I smiled, shrugged my shoulders in tantalizing repetition of my former action upon a like occasion and then answered brusquely:

"I did not come back to betray police secrets, but to restore this picture to its place. Or perhaps you prefer to have it down rather than up? It isn't much of an ornament."

He scrutinized me darkly from over his shoulder, a wary gleam showing itself in his shrewd old eyes; and the idea crossed me that the moment might possess more significance than appeared. But I did not step backward, nor give evidence in any way that I had even thought of danger. I simply laid my hand on the picture and looked up at him for orders.

He promptly signified that he wished it hung, adding as I hesitated these words: "The pictures in this house are supposed to stay on the walls where they belong. There is a traditional superstition against removing them."

I immediately lifted the print from the floor. No doubt he had me at a disadvantage, if evil was in his heart, and my position on the hearth was as dangerous as previous events had proved it to be. But it would not do to show the white feather at a moment when his fate, if not my own, hung in the balance; so motioning him to step down, I put foot on the chair and raised the picture aloft to hang it. As I did so, he moved over to the huge settle of his ancestors, and, crossing his arms over its back, surveyed me with a smile I rather imagined than saw.

Suddenly, as I strained to put the cord over the nail he called out:

"Look out! you'll fall."

If he had intended to give me a start in payment for my previous rebuff he did not succeed; for my nerves had grown steady and my arm firm at the glimpse I had caught of the shelf below me. The fine brown powder I had scattered there had been displaced in five distinct spots, and not by my fingers. I had preferred to risk the loss of my balance, rather than rest my hand on the shelf, but he had taken no such precaution. The clue I so anxiously desired and for which I had so recklessly worked, was obtained.

But when half an hour later I found an opportunity of measuring these marks and comparing them with those upstairs, I did not enjoy the full triumph I had promised myself. For the two impressions utterly failed to coincide, thus proving that whoever the person was who had been in this house with Mrs. Jeffrey on the evening she died, it was not her uncle David.

CHAPTER VIII

SLYER WOES

Let me repeat. The person who had left the marks of his presence in the upper chamber of the Moore house was not the man popularly known as Uncle David. Who, then, had it been? But one name suggested itself to me,—Mr. Jeffrey.

It was not so easy for me to reach this man as it had been for me to reach his singular and unimaginative uncle. In the first place, his door had been closed to every one since his wife's death. Neither friends nor strangers could gain admittance there unless they came vested with authority from the coroner. And this, even if I could manage to obtain it, would not answer in my case. What I had to say and do would better follow a chance encounter. But no chance encounter with this gentleman seemed likely to fall to my lot, and finally I swallowed my pride and asked another favor of the lieutenant. Would he see that I was given an opportunity for carrying some message, or of doing some errand which would lead to my having an interview with Mr. Jeffrey? If he would, I stood ready to promise that my curiosity should stop at this point and that I would cease to make a nuisance of myself.

I think he suspected me by this time; but he made no remark, and in a day or so I was summoned to carry a note to the house in K Street.

Mrs. Jeffrey's funeral had taken place the day before and the house looked deserted. But my summons speedily brought a neat-looking, but very nervous maid to the door, whose eyes took on an unmistakable expression of resistance when I announced my errand and asked to see Mr. Jeffrey. The expression would not have struck me as peculiar if she had raised any objection to the interview I had solicited. But she did not. Her fear and antipathy, consequently, sprang from some other source than her interest in the man most threatened by my visit. Was it-could it be, on her own account? Recalling what I had heard whispered about the station concerning a maid of the Jeffreys who always seemed on the point of saying something which never really left her lips, I stopped her as she was about to slip upstairs and quietly asked:

"Are you Loretta?"

The way she turned, the way she looked at me as she gave me a short affirmative, and then quickly proceeded on her way, convinced me that my colleagues were right as to her being a woman who had some cause for dreading police interference. I instantly made up my mind that here was a mine to be worked and that I knew just the demure little soul best equipped to act the part of miner.

In a moment she came back, and I had a chance to note again her pretty but expressionless features, among which the restless eyes alone bespoke character or decision.

"Mr. Jeffrey is in the back room upstairs," she announced. "He says for you to come up."

"Is it the room Mrs. Jeffrey used to occupy?" I asked with open curiosity, as I passed her.

An involuntary shudder proved that she was not without feeling. So did the quick disclaimer:

"No, no! Those rooms are closed. He occupies the one Miss Tuttle had before she went away."

"Oh, then, Miss Tuttle is gone?"

Loretta disdained to answer. She had already said enough to cause her to bite her lip as she disappeared down the basement stair. Decidedly the boys were right. An uneasy feeling followed any conversation with this girl. Yet, while there was slyness in her manner, there was a certain frank honesty visible in it too, which caused me to think that if she could ever be made to speak, her evidence could be relied on.

Mr. Jeffrey was sitting with his back to the door when I entered, but turned as I spoke his name and held out his hand for the note I carried. I had no expectation of his remembering me as one of the men who had stood about that night in the Moore house, and I was not disappointed. To him I was merely a messenger, or common policeman; and he consequently paid me no attention, while I bestowed upon him the most concentrated scrutiny of my whole life. Till now I had seen him only in half lights, or under circumstances precluding my getting a very accurate idea of him as a man and a gentleman. Now he sat with the broad daylight on his face, and I had every opportunity for noting both his features and expression. He was of a distinguished type; but the cloud enshrouding him was as heavy as any I had ever seen darkening about a man of his position and character. His manner, fettered though it was by gloomy thoughts, was not just the manner I had expected to encounter.

He had a large, clear eye, but the veil which hid the brightness of his regard was misty with suspicion, not with tears. He appeared to shrink from observation, and shifted uneasily as long as I stood in front of him, though he said nothing and did not lift his eyes from the letter he was perusing till he heard me step back to the door I had purposely left open and softly close it. Then he glanced up, with a keen, if not an alarmed look, which seemed an exaggerated one for the occasion,—that is, if he had no secret to keep.

"Do you suffer so from drafts?" he asked, rising in a way which in itself was a dismissal.

I smiled an amused denial, then with the simple directness I thought most likely to win me his confidence, entered straight upon my business in these plain words:

"Pardon me, Mr. Jeffrey, I have something to say which is not exactly fitted for the ears of servants." Then, as he pushed his chair suddenly back, I added reassuringly: "It is not a police matter, sir, but an entirely personal one. It may strike you as important, and it may not. Mr. Jeffrey, I was the man who made the unhappy discovery in the Moore mansion, which has plunged this house into mourning."

This announcement startled him and produced a visible change in his manner. His eyes flew first to one door and then to another, as if it were he who feared intrusion now.

"I beg your pardon for speaking on so painful a topic," I went on, as soon as I saw he was ready to listen to me. "My excuse is that I came upon a little thing that same night which I have not thought of sufficient importance to mention to any one else, but which it may interest you to hear about."

Here I took from a book I held, a piece of blotting-paper. It was white on one side and blue on the other. The white side I had thickly chalked, though this was not apparent. Laying down this piece of blotting-paper, chalked side up, on the end of a large table near which we were standing, I took out an envelope from my pocket, and, shaking it gently to and fro, remarked:

"In an upper room of the Moore house—you remember the southwest chamber, sir?"

Ali! didn't he! There was no misdoubting the quick emotion—the shrinking and the alarm with which he heard this room mentioned.

"It was in that room that I found these."

Tipping up the envelope, I scattered over the face of the blotter a few of the glistening particles I had collected from the place mentioned.

He bent over them, astonished. Then, as was natural, brushed them together in a heap with the tips of his fingers, and leaned to look again, just as I breathed a heavy sigh which scattered them far and wide.

Instinctively, he withdrew his hand; whereupon I embraced the opportunity of turning the blotter over, uttering meanwhile the most profuse apologies. Then, as if anxious not to repeat my misadventure, I let the blotter lie where it was, and pouring out the few remaining particles into my palm, I held them toward the light in such a way that he was compelled to lean across the table in order to see them. Naturally, for I had planned the distance well, his finger-tips, white with the chalk he had unconsciously handled, touched the blue surface of the blotter now lying uppermost and left their marks there.

I could have shouted in my elation at the success of this risky maneuver, but managed to suppress my emotion, and to stand quite still while he took a good look at the filings. They seemed to have great and unusual interest for him and it was with no ordinary emotion that he finally asked:

"What do you make out of these, and why do you bring them here?"

My answer was written under his hand; but this it was far from my policy to impart. So putting on my friendliest air, I returned, with suitable respect:

"I don't know what to make of them. They look like gold; but that is for you to decide. Do you want them, sir?"

"No," he replied, starting erect and withdrawing his hand from the blotter. "It's but a trifle, not worth our attention. But I thank you just the same for bringing it to my notice."

And again his manner became a plain dismissal.

This time I accepted it as such without question. Carelessly restoring the piece of blotting-paper to the book from which I had taken it, I made a bow and withdrew toward the door. He seemed to be thinking, and the deep furrows which I am sure had been lacking from his brow a week previous, became startlingly visible. Finally he observed:

"Mrs. Jeffrey was not in her right mind when she so unhappily took her life. I see now that the change in her dates back to her wedding day, consequently any little peculiarity she may have shown at that time is not to be wondered at."

"Certainly not," I boldly ventured; "if such peculiarities were shown after the fright given her by the catastrophe which took place in the library."

His eyes, which were fixed on mine, flashed, and his hands closed convulsively.

"We will not consider the subject," he muttered, reseating himself in the chair from which he had risen.

I bowed again and went out. I did not dwell on the interview in my own mind nor did I allow myself to draw any conclusions from it, till I had carried the blotter into the southwest chamber of the Moore house and carefully compared the impressions made on it with the marks I had scratched on the surface of the mantel-shelf. This I did by laying the one over the other, after having made holes where his finger-tips had touched the blotter.

The holes in the blotter and the marks outlined upon the shelf coincided exactly.

CHAPTER IX

JINNY

I have already mentioned the man whom I secretly looked upon as standing between me and all preferment. He was a good-looking fellow, but he wore a natural sneer which for some reason I felt to be always directed toward myself. This sneer grew pronounced about this time, and that was the reason, no doubt, why I continued to work as long as I did in secret. I dreaded the open laugh of this man, a laugh which always seemed hovering on his lips and which was only held in restraint by the awe we all felt of the major.

Notwithstanding, I made one slight move. Encountering the deputy-coroner, I ventured to ask if he was quite satisfied with the evidence collected in the Jeffrey case.

His surprise did not prevent him from asking my reasons for this question.

I replied to this effect:

"Because I have a little friend, winsome enough and subtle enough to worm the truth out of the devil. I hear that the girl Loretta is suspected of knowing more about this unfortunate tragedy than she is willing to impart. If you wish this little friend of mine to talk to her, I will see that she does so and does so with effect."

The deputy-coroner looked interested.

"Whom do you mean by 'little friend' and what is her name?"

"I will send her to you."

And I did.

The next day I was standing on the corner of Vermont Avenue when I saw Jinny advancing from the house in K Street. She was chipper, and she was smiling in a way which made me say to myself:

"It is fortunate that Durbin is not here."

For Jinny's one weakness is her lack of power to hide the satisfaction she takes in any detective work that comes her way. I had told her of this and had more than once tried to impress upon her that her smile was a complete give-away, but I noticed that if she kept it from her lips, it forced its way out of her eyes, and if she kept it out of her eyes, it beamed like an inner radiance from her whole face. So I gave up the task of making her perfect and let her go on smiling, glad that she had such frequent cause for it.

This morning her smile had a touch of pride in it as well as of delight, and noting this, I remarked:

"You have made Loretta talk."

Her head went up and a demure dimple appeared in her cheek.

"What did she say?" I urged. "What has she been keeping back?"

"You will have to ask the coroner. My orders were strict to bring the results of my interview immediately to him."

"Does that include Durbin?"

"Does it include you?"

"I am afraid not."

"You are right; but why shouldn't it include you?"

"What do you mean, Jinny?"

"Why do you keep your own counsel so long? You have ideas about this crime, I know. Why not mention them?"

"Jinny!"

"A word to the wise is sufficient;" she laughed and turned her pretty face toward the coroner's once. But she was a woman and could not help glancing back, and, meeting my dubious look, she broke into an arch smile and naively added this remark: "Loretta is a busybody ashamed of her own curiosity. So much there can be no harm in telling you. When one's knowledge has been gained by lingering behind doors and peeping through cracks, one is not so ready to say what one has seen and heard. Loretta is in that box, and being more than a little scared of the police, was glad to let her anxiety and her fears overflow into a sympathizing ear. Won't she be surprised when she is called up some fine day by the coroner! I wonder if she will blame me for it?"

"She will never think of doing so," I basely assured my little friend, with an appreciative glance at her sparkling eye and dimpled cheek.

The arch little creature started to move off again. As she did so, she cried: "Be good, and don't let Durbin cut in on you;" but stopped for the second time when half across the street, and when, obedient to her look, I hastily rejoined her, she whispered demurely: "Oh, I forgot to tell you something that I heard this morning, and which nobody but yourself has any right to know. I was following your commands and buying groceries at Simpkins', when just as I was coming out with my arms full, I heard old Mr. Simpkins mention Mr. Jeffrey's name and with such interest that I naturally wanted to hear what he had to say. Having no real excuse for staying, I poked my finger into a bag of sugar I was carrying, till the sugar ran out and I had to wait till it was put up again. This did not take long, but it took long enough for me to hear the old grocer say that he knew Mr. Jeffrey, and that that gentleman had come into his shop only a day or two before his wife's death, to buy—candles!"

The archness with which this was said, together with the fact itself, made me her slave forever. As her small figure faded from sight down the avenue, I decided to take her advice and follow up whatever communication she had to make to the coroner by a confession of my own suspicions and what they had led me into. If he laughed—well, I could stand it. It was not the coroner's laugh, nor even the major's, that I feared; it was Durbin's.

CHAPTER X

FRANCIS JEFFREY

Jinny had not been gone an hour from the coroner's office when an opportunity was afforded for me to approach that gentleman myself.

With few apologies and no preamble, I immediately entered upon my story which I made as concise and as much to the point as possible. I did not expect praise from him, but I did look for some slight show of astonishment at the nature of my news. I was therefore greatly disappointed, when, after a moment's quiet consideration, he carelessly remarked:

"Very good! very good! The one point you make is excellent and may prove of use to us. We had reached the same conclusion, but by another road. You ask, 'Who blew out the candle?' We, 'Who tied the pistol to Mrs. Jeffrey's arm?' It could not have been tied by herself. Who was her accessory then? Ah, you didn't think of that."

I flushed as if a pail of hot water had been dashed suddenly over me. He was right. The conclusion he spoke of had failed to strike me. Why? It was a perfectly obvious one, as obvious as that the candle had been blown out by another breath than hers; yet, absorbed in my own train of thought, I had completely overlooked it. The coroner observing my embarrassment, smiled, and my humiliation was complete or would have been had Durbin been there, but fortunately he was not.

"I am a fool," I cried. "I thought I had discovered something. I might have known that there were keener minds than mine in this office—"

"Easy! easy!" was the good-natured interruption. "You have done well. If I did not think so, I would not keep you here a minute. As it is, I am disposed to let you see that in a case like this, one man must not expect to monopolize all the honors. This matter of the bow of ribbon would strike any old and experienced official. I only wonder that we have not seen it openly discussed in the papers."

Taking a box from his desk, he opened it and held it out toward me. A coil of white ribbon surmounted by a crisp and dainty bow met my eyes.

"You recognize it?" he asked.

Indeed I did.

"It was cut from her wrist by my deputy. Miss Tuttle wished him to untie it, but he preferred to leave the bow intact. Now lift it out. Careful, man, don't soil it; you will see why in a minute."

As I held the ribbon up, he pointed to some spots on its fresh white surface. "Do you see those?" he asked. "Those are dust-marks, and they were made as truly by some one's fingers, as the impressions you noted on the mantel-shelf in the upper chamber. This pistol was tied to her wrist after the deed; possibly by that same hand."

It was my own conclusion but it did not sound as welcome to me from his lips as I had expected. Either my nature is narrow, or my inordinate jealousy lays me open to the most astonishing inconsistencies; for no sooner had he spoken these words than I experienced a sudden revulsion against my own theory and the suspicions which it threw upon the man whom an hour before I was eager to proclaim a criminal.

But Coroner Z. gave me no chance for making such a fool of myself. Rescuing the ribbon from my hands, which no doubt were running a little too freely over its snowy surface, he smiled with the indulgence proper from such a man to a novice like myself, and observed quite frankly:

"You will consider these observations as confidential. You know how to hold your tongue; that you have proved. Hold it then a little longer. The case is not yet ripe. Mr. Jeffrey is a man of high standing, with a hitherto unblemished reputation. It won't do, my boy, to throw the doubt of so hideous a crime upon so fine a gentleman without ample reason. That no such mistake may be made and that he may have every opportunity for clearing himself, I am going to have a confidential talk with him. Do you want to be present?"

I flushed again; but this time from extreme satisfaction.

"I am obliged for your confidence," said I; then, with a burst of courage born of his good nature, I inquired with due respect if my little friend had answered his expectations. "Was she as clever as I said?" I asked.

"Your little friend is a trump," was his blunt reply. "With what we have learned through her and now through you, we can approach Mr. Jeffrey to some purpose. It appears that, before leaving the house on that Tuesday morning, he had an interview with his wife which ought in some way to account for this tragedy. Perhaps he will tell us about it, and perhaps he will explain how he came to wander through the Moore house while his wife lay dying below. At all events we will give him the opportunity to do so and, if possible, to clear up mysteries which provoke the worst kind of conjecture. It is time. The ideas advanced by the papers foster superstition; and superstition is the devil. Go and tell my man out there that I am going to K Street. You may say 'we' if you like," he added with a humor more welcome to me than any serious concession.

Did I feel set up by this? Rather.

Mr. Jeffrey was expecting us. This was evident from his first look, though the attempt he made at surprise was instantaneous and very well feigned. Indeed, I think he was in a constant state of apprehension during these days and that no inroad of the police would have astonished him. But expectation does not preclude dread; indeed it tends to foster it, and dread was in his heart. This he had no power to conceal.

"To what am I indebted for this second visit from you?" he asked of Coroner Z., with an admirable presence of mind. "Are you not yet satisfied with what we have been able to tell you of my poor wife's unhappy end?"

"We are not," was the plain response. "There are some things you have not attempted to explain, Mr. Jeffrey. For instance, why you went to the Moore house previous to your being called there by the death of your wife."

It was a shot that told; an arrow which found its mark. Mr. Jeffrey flushed, then turned pale, rallied and again lost himself in a maze of conflicting emotions from which he only emerged to say:

"How do you know that I was there? Have I said so; or do those old walls babble in their sleep?"

"Old walls have been known to do this," was the grave reply. "Whether they had anything to say in this case is at present quite immaterial. That you were where I charge you with being is evident from your own manner. May I then ask if you have anything to say about this visit. When a person has died under such peculiar circumstances as Mrs. Jeffrey, everything bearing upon the case is of interest to the coroner."

I was sorry he added that last sentence; sorry that he felt obliged to qualify his action by anything savoring of apology; for the time spent in its utterance afforded his agitated hearer an opportunity not only of collecting himself but of preparing an answer for which he would not have been ready an instant before.

"Mrs. Jeffrey's death was a strange one," her husband admitted with tardy self-control. "I find myself as much at a loss to understand it as you do, and am therefore quite ready to answer the question you have so openly broached. Not that my answer has any bearing upon the point you wish to make, but because it is your due and my pleasure. I did visit the Moore house, as I certainly had every right to do. The property was my wife's, and it was for my interest to learn, if I could, the secret of its many crimes."

"Ah!"

Mr. Jeffrey looked quickly up. "You think that an odd thing for me to do?"

"At night. Yes."

"Night is the time for such work. I did not care to be seen pottering around there in daylight."

"No? Yet it would have been so much easier. You would not have had to buy candles or carry a pistol or—"

"I did not carry a pistol. The only pistol carried there was the one with which my demented wife chose to take her life. I do not understand this allusion."

"It grew out of a misunderstanding of the situation, Mr. Jeffrey; excuse me if I supposed you would be likely to provide yourself with some means of defense in venturing alone upon the scene of so many mysterious deaths."

"I took no precaution."

"And needed none, I suppose."

"And needed none."

"When was this visit paid, Mr. Jeffrey? Before or after your wife pulled the trigger which ended her life? You need not hesitate to answer."

"I do not." The elegant gentleman before us had acquired a certain fierceness. "Why should I? Certainly, you don't think that I was there at the same time she was. It was not on the same night, even. So much the walls should have told you and probably did, or my wife's uncle, Mr. David Moore. Was he not your informant?"

"No; Mr. Moore has failed to call our attention to this fact. Did you meet Mr. Moore during the course of your visit to a neighborhood over which he seems to hold absolute sway?"

"Not to my knowledge. But his house is directly opposite, and as he has little to do but amuse himself with what he can see from his front window, I concluded that he might have observed me going in."

"You entered by the front door, then?"

"How else?"

"And on what night?"

Mr. Jeffrey made an effort. These questions were visibly harassing him.

"The night before the one—the one which ended all my earthly happiness," he added in a low voice.

Coroner Z. cast a glance at me. I remembered the lack of dust on the nest of little tables from which the upper one had been drawn forward to hold the candelabrum, and gently shook my head. The coroner's eyebrows went up, but none of his disbelief crept into his voice as he made this additional statement.

"The night on which you failed to return to your own house."

Instantly Mr. Jeffrey betrayed by a nervous action, which was quite involuntary, that his outward calm was slowly giving way under a fire of questions for which he had no ready reply.

"It was odd, your not going home that night," the coroner coldly pursued. "The misunderstanding you had with your wife immediately after breakfast must have been a very serious one; more serious than you have hitherto acknowledged."

"I had rather not discuss the subject," protested Mr. Jeffrey. Then as if he suddenly recognized the official character of his interlocutor, he hastily added: "Unless you positively request me to do so; in which case I must."

"I am afraid that I must insist upon it," returned the other. "You will find that it will be insisted upon at the inquest, and if you do not wish to subject yourself to much unnecessary unpleasantness, you had better make clear to us to-day the cause of that special quarrel which to all intents and purposes led to your wife's death."

"I will try to do so," returned Mr. Jeffrey, rising and pacing the room in his intense restlessness. "We did have some words; her conduct the night before had not pleased me. I am naturally jealous, vilely jealous, and I thought she was a little frivolous at the German ambassador's ball. But I had no idea she would take my sharp speeches so much to heart. I had no idea that she would care so much or that I should care so much. A little jealousy is certainly pardonable in a bridegroom, and if her mind had not already been upset, she would have remembered how I loved her and hopefully waited for a reconciliation."

"You did love your wife, then? It was you and not she who had a right to be jealous? I have heard the contrary stated. It is a matter of public gossip that you loved another woman previous to your acquaintance with Miss Moore; a woman whom your wife regarded with sisterly affection and subsequently took into her new home."

"Miss Tuttle?" Mr. Jeffrey stopped in his walk to fling out this ejaculation. "I admire and respect Miss Tuttle," he went on to declare, "but I never loved her. Not as I did my wife," he finished, but with a certain hard accent, apparent enough to a sensitive ear.

"Pardon me; it is as difficult for me to put these questions as it is for you to hear them. Were you and Miss Tuttle ever engaged?"

I started. This was a question which half of Washington had been asking itself for the last three months.

Would Mr. Jeffrey answer it? or, remembering that these questions were rather friendly than official, refuse to satisfy a curiosity which he might well consider intrusive? The set aspect of his features promised little in the way of information, and we were both surprised when a moment later he responded with a grim emphasis hardly to be expected from one of his impulsive temperament:

"Unhappily, no. My attentions never went so far."

Instantly the coroner pounced on the one weak word which Mr. Jeffrey had let fall.

"Unhappily?" he repeated. "Why do you say, unhappily?"

Mr. Jeffrey flushed and seemed to come out of some dream.

"Did I say unhappily?" he inquired. "Well, I repeat it; Miss Tuttle would never have given me any cause for jealousy."

The coroner bowed and for the present dropped her name out of the conversation.

"You speak again of the jealousy aroused in you by your wife's impetuosities. Was this increased or diminished by the tone of the few lines she left behind her?"

The response was long in coming. It was hard for this man to lie. The struggle he made at it was pitiful. As I noted what it cost him, I began to have new and curious thoughts concerning him and the whole matter under discussion.

"I shall never overcome the remorse roused in me by those few lines," he finally rejoined. "She showed a consideration for me—"

"What!"

The coroner's exclamation showed all the surprise he felt. Mr. Jeffrey tottered under it, then grew slowly pale as if only through our amazed looks he had come to realize the charge of inconsistency to which he had laid himself open.

"I mean—" he endeavored to explain, "that Mrs. Jeffrey showed an unexpected tenderness toward me by taking all the blame of our misunderstanding upon herself. It was generous of her and will do much toward making my memory of her a gentle one."

He was forgetting himself again. Indeed, his manner and attempted explanations were full of contradictions. To emphasize this fact Coroner Z. exclaimed,

"I should think so! She paid a heavy penalty for her professed lack of love. You believe that her mind was unseated?"

"Does not her action show it?"

"Unseated by the mishap occurring at her marriage?"

"Yes."

"You really think that?"

"Yes."

"By anything that passed between you?"

"Yes."

"May I ask you to tell us what passed between you on this point?"

"Yes."

He had uttered the monosyllable so often it seemed to come unconsciously from his lips. But he recognized almost as soon as we did that it was not a natural reply to the last question, and, making a gesture of apology, he added, with the same monotony of tone which had characterized these replies:

"She spoke of her strange guest's unaccountable death more than once, and whenever she did so, it was with an unnatural excitement and in an unbalanced way. This was so noticeable to us all that the subject presently was tabooed amongst us; but though she henceforth spared us all allusion to it, she continued to talk about the house itself and of the previous deaths which had occurred there till we were forced to forbid that topic also. She was never really herself after crossing the threshold of this desolate house to be married. The shadow which lurks within its walls fell at that instant upon her life. May God have mercy—"

The prayer remained unfinished. His head which had fallen on his breast sank lower.

He presented the aspect of one who is quite done with life, even its sorrows.

But men in the position of Coroner Z. can not afford to be compassionate. Everything the bereaved man said deepened the impression that he was acting a part. To make sure that this was really so, the coroner, with just the slightest touch of sarcasm, quietly observed:

"And to ease your wife's mind—the wife you were so deeply angered with—you visited this house, and, at an hour which you should have spent in reconciliation with her, went through its ancient rooms in the hope—of what?"

Mr. Jeffrey could not answer. The words which came from his lips were mere ejaculations.

"I was restless—mad—I found this adventure diverting. I had no real purpose in mind."

"Not when you looked at the old picture?"

"The old picture? What old picture?"

"The old picture in the southwest chamber. You took a look at that, didn't you? Got up on a chair on purpose to do so?"

Mr. Jeffrey winced. But he made a direct reply.

"Yes, I gave a look at that old picture; got up, as you say, on a chair to do so. Wasn't that the freak of an idle man, wandering, he hardly knows why, from room to room in an old and deserted house?"

His tormentor did not answer. Probably his mind was on his next line of inquiry. But Mr. Jeffrey did not take his silence with the calmness he had shown prior to the last attack. As no word came from his unwelcome guest, he paused in his rapid pacing and, casting aside with one impulsive gesture his hitherto imperfectly held restraint, he cried out sharply:

"Why do you ask me these questions in tones of such suspicion? Is it not plain enough that my wife took her own life under a misapprehension of my state of mind toward her, that you should feel it necessary to rake up these personal matters, which, however interesting to the world at large, are of a painful nature to me?"

"Mr. Jeffrey," retorted the other, with a sudden grave assumption of dignity not without its effect in a case of such serious import, "we do nothing without purpose. We ask these questions and show this interest because the charge of suicide which has hitherto been made against your wife is not entirely sustained by the facts. At least she was not alone when she took her life. Some one was in the house with her."

It was startling to observe the effect of this declaration upon him.

"Impossible!" he cried out in a protest as forcible as it was agonized. "You are playing with my misery. She could have had no one there; she would not. There is not a man living before whom she would have fired that deadly shot; unless it was myself,—unless it was my own wretched, miserable self."

The remorseful whisper in which those final words were uttered carried them to my heart, which for some strange and unaccountable reason had been gradually turning toward this man. But my less easily affected companion, seeing his opportunity and possibly considering that it was this gentleman's right to know in what a doubtful light he stood before the law, remarked with as light a touch of irony as was possible:

"You should know better than we in whose presence she would choose to die—if she did so choose. Also who would be likely to tie the pistol to her wrist and blow out the candle when the dreadful deed was over."

The laugh which seemed to be the only means of violent expression remaining to this miserable man was kept down by some amazing thought which seemed to paralyze him. Without making any attempt to refute a suggestion that fell just short of a personal accusation, he sank down in the first chair he came to and became, as it were, lost in the vision of that ghastly ribbon-tying and the solitary blowing out of the candle upon this scene of mournful death. Then with a struggling sense of having heard something which called for answer, he rose blindly to his feet and managed to let fall these words:

"You are mistaken—no one was there, or if any one was—it was not I. There is a man in this city who can prove it."

But when Mr. Jeffrey was asked to give the name of this man, he showed confusion and presently was obliged to admit that he could neither recall his name nor remember anything about him, but that he was some one whom he knew well, and who knew him well. He affirmed that the two had met and spoken near Soldiers' Home shortly after the sun went down, and that the man would be sure to remember this meeting if we could only find him.

As Soldiers' Home was several miles from the Moore house and quite out of the way of all his accustomed haunts, Coroner Z. asked him how he came to be there. He replied that he had just come from Rock Creek Cemetery. That he had been in a wretched state of mind all day, and possibly being influenced by what he had heard of the yearly vigils Mr. Moore was in the habit of keeping there, had taken a notion to stroll among the graves, in search of the rest and peace of mind he had failed to find in his aimless walks about the city. At least, that was the way he chose to account for the meeting he mentioned. Falling into reverie again, he seemed to be trying to recall the name which at this moment was of such importance to him. But it was without avail, as he presently acknowledged.

"I can not remember who it was. My brain is whirling, and I can recollect nothing but that this man and myself left the cemetery together on the night mentioned, just as the gate was being closed. As it closes at sundown, the hour can be fixed to a minute. It was somewhere near seven, I believe; near enough, I am sure, for it to have been impossible for me to be at the Moore house at the time my unhappy wife is supposed to have taken her life. There is no doubt about your believing this?" he demanded with sudden haughtiness, as, rising to his feet, he confronted us in all the pride of his exceptionally handsome person.

"We wish to believe it," assented the coroner, rising in his turn. "That our belief may become certainty, will you let us know, the instant you recall the name of the man you talked with at the cemetery gate? His testimony, far more than any word of yours, will settle this question which otherwise may prove a vexed one."

Mr. Jeffrey's hand went up to his head. Was he acting a part or did he really forget just what it was for his own best welfare to remember? If he had forgotten, it argued that he was in a state of greater disturbance on that night than would naturally be occasioned by a mere lover's quarrel with his wife.

Did the same thought strike my companion? I can not say; I can only give you his next words.

"You have said that your wife would not be likely to end her life in presence of any one but yourself. Yet you must see that some one was with her. How do you propose to reconcile your assertions with a fact so undeniable?"

"I can not reconcile them. It would madden me to try. If I thought any one was with her at that moment—"

"Well?"

Mr. Jeffrey's eyes fell; and a startling change passed over him. But before either of us could make out just what this change betokened he recovered his aspect of fixed melancholy and quietly remarked:

"It is dreadful to think of her standing there alone, aiming a pistol at her young, passionate heart; but it is worse to picture her doing this under the gaze of unsympathizing eyes. I can not and will not so picture her. You have been misled by appearances or what in police parlance is called a clue."

Evidently he did not mean to admit the possibility of the pistol having been fired by any other hand than her own. This the coroner noted. Bowing with the respect he showed every man before a jury had decided upon his guilt, he turned toward the door out of which I had already hurried.

"We hope to hear from you in the morning," he called back significantly, as he stepped down the stairs.

Mr. Jeffrey did not answer; he was having his first struggle with the new and terrible prospect awaiting him at the approaching inquest.

BOOK II

THE LAW AND ITS VICTIM

CHAPTER XI

DETAILS

The days of my obscurity were over. Henceforth, I was regarded as a decided factor in this case—a case which from this time on, assumed another aspect both at headquarters and in the minds of people at large. The reporters, whom we had hitherto managed to hold in check, now overflowed both the coroner's office and police headquarters, and articles appeared in all the daily papers with just enough suggestion in them to fire the public mind and make me, for one, anticipate an immediate word from Mr. Jeffrey calculated to establish the alibi he had failed to make out on the day we talked with him. But no such word came. His memory still played him false, and no alternative was left but to pursue the official inquiry in the line suggested by the interview just recounted.

No proceeding in which I had ever been engaged interested me as did this inquest. In the first place, the spectators were of a very different character from the ordinary. As I wormed myself along to the seat accorded to such witnesses as myself, I brushed by men of the very highest station and a few of the lowest; and bent my head more than once in response to the inquiring gaze of some fashionable lady who never before, I warrant, had found herself in such a scene. By the time I reached my place all the others were seated and the coroner rapped for order.

I was first to take the stand. What I said has already been fully amplified in the foregoing pages. Of course, my evidence was confined to facts, but some of these facts were new to most of the persons there. It was evident that a considerable effect was produced by them, not only on the spectators, but upon the witnesses themselves. For instance, it was the first time that the marks on the mantel-shelf had been heard of outside the major's office, or the story so told as to make it evident that Mrs. Jeffrey could not have been alone in the house at the time of her death.

A photograph had been taken of those marks, and my identification of this photograph closed my testimony.

As I returned to my seat I stole a look toward a certain corner where, with face bent down upon his hand, Francis Jeffrey sat between Uncle David and the heavily-veiled figure of Miss Tuttle. Had there dawned upon him as my testimony was given any suspicion of the trick by which he had been proved responsible for those marks? It was impossible to tell. From the way Miss Tuttle's head was turned toward him, one might judge him to be laboring under an emotion of no ordinary character, though he sat like a statue and hardly seemed to realize how many eyes were at that moment riveted upon his face.

I was followed by other detectives who had been present at the time and who corroborated my statement as to the appearance of this unhappy woman and the way the pistol had been tied to her arm. Then the doctor who had acted under the coroner was called. After a long and no doubt learned description of the bullet wound which had ended the life of this unhappy lady,—a wound which he insisted, with a marked display of learning, must have made that end instantaneous or at least too immediate for her to move foot or hand after it,—he was asked if the body showed any other mark of violence.

To this he replied

"There was a minute wound at the base of one of her fingers, the one which is popularly called the wedding finger."

This statement made all the women present start with renewed interest; nor was it altogether without point for the men, especially when the doctor went on to say:

"The hands were entirely without rings. As Mrs. Jeffrey had been married with a ring, I noticed their absence."

"Was this wound which you characterize as minute a recent one?"

"It had bled a little. It was an abrasion such as would be made if the ring she usually wore there had been drawn off with a jerk. That was the impression I received from its appearance. I do not state that it was so made."

A little thrill which went over the audience at the picture this evoked communicated itself to Miss Tuttle, who trembled violently. It even produced a slight display of emotion in Mr. Jeffrey, whose hand shook where he pressed it against his forehead. But neither uttered a sound, nor looked up when the next witness was summoned.

This witness proved to be Loretta, who, on hearing her name called, evinced great reluctance to come forward. But after two or three words uttered in her ear by the friendly Jinny, who had been given a seat next her, she stepped into the place assigned her with a suddenly assumed air of great boldness, which sat upon her with scant grace. She had need of all the boldness at her command, for the eyes of all in the room were fixed on her, with the exception of the two persons most interested in her testimony. Scrutiny of any kind did not appear to be acceptable to her, if one could read the trepidation visible in the short, quick upheavals of the broad collar which covered her uneasy breast. Was this shrinking on her part due to natural timidity, or had she failings to avow which, while not vitiating her testimony, would certainly cause her shame in the presence of so many men and women? I was not able to decide this question immediately; for after the coroner had elicited her name and the position she held in Mr. Jeffrey's household he asked whether her duties took her into Mrs. Jeffrey's room; upon her replying that they did, he further inquired if she knew Mrs. Jeffrey's rings, and could say whether they were all to be found on that lady's toilet-table after the police came in with news of her death. The answer was decisive. They were all there, her rings and all the other ornaments she was in the daily habit of wearing, with the exception of her watch. That was not there.

"Did you take up those rings?"

"No, sir."

"Did you see any one else take them up?"

"No, sir; not till the officer did so."

"Very well, Loretta, sit down again till we hear what Durbin has to say about these rings."

And then the man I hated came forward, and though I shrank from acknowledging it even to myself, I could but observe how strong and quiet and self-possessed he seemed and how decisive was his testimony. But it was equally brief. He had taken up the rings and he had looked at them; and on one, the wedding-ring, he had detected a slight stain of blood. He had called Mr. Jeffrey's attention to it, but that gentleman had made no comment. This remark had the effect of concentrating general attention upon Mr. Jeffrey. But he seemed quite oblivious of it; his attitude remained unchanged, and only from the quick stretching out and withdrawal of Miss Tuttle's hand could it be seen that anything had been said calculated to touch or arouse this man. The coroner cast an uneasy glance in his direction; then he motioned Durbin aside and recalled Loretta.

And now I began to be sorry for the girl. It is hard to have one's weaknesses exposed, especially if one is more foolish than wicked. But there was no way of letting this girl off without sacrificing certain necessary points, and the coroner went relentlessly to work.

"How long have you been in this house?"

"Three weeks. Ever since Mrs. Jeffrey's wedding day, sir."

"Were you there when she first came as a bride from the Moore house?"

"I was, sir."

"And saw her then for the first time?"

"Yes, sir."

"How did she look and act that first day?"

"I thought her the gayest bride I had ever seen, then I thought her the saddest, and then I did not know what to think. She was so merry one minute and so frightened the next, so full of talk when she came running up the steps and so struck with silence the minute she got into the parlor, that I set her down as a queer one till some one whispered in my ear that she was suffering from a dreadful shock; that ill-luck had attended her marriage and much more about what had happened from time to time at the Moore house."

"And you believed what was told you?"

"Believed?"

"Believed it well enough to keep a watch on your young mistress to see if she were happy or not?"

"Oh, sir!"

"It was but natural," the coroner suavely observed. "Every one felt interested in this marriage. You watched her of course. Now what was the result? Did you consider her well and happy?"

The girl's voice sank and she cast a glance at her master which he did not lift his head to meet.

"I did not think her happy. She laughed and sang and was always in and out of the rooms like a butterfly, but she did not wear a happy look, except now and then when she was seated with Mr. Jeffrey alone. Then I have seen her flush in a way to make the heart ache; it was such a contrast, sir, to other times when she was by herself or—"

"Or what?"

"Or just with her sister, sir."

The defiance with which this was said added point to what otherwise might have been an unimportant admission. Those who had already scrutinized Miss Tuttle with the curiosity of an ill-defined suspicion now scrutinized her with a more palpable one, and those who had hitherto seen nothing in this heavily-veiled woman but the bereaved sister of an irresponsible suicide allowed their looks to dwell piercingly on that concealing veil, as if they would be glad to penetrate its folds and read in those beautiful features the meaning of an allusion uttered with such a sting in the tone.

"You refer to Miss Tuttle?" observed the coroner.

"Mrs. Jeffrey's sister? Yes, sir." The menace was gone from the voice now, but no one could forget that it had been there.

"Miss Tuttle lived in the house with her sister, did she not?"

"Yes, sir; till that sister died and was buried; then she went away."

The coroner did not pursue this topic, preferring to return to the former one.

"So you say that Mrs. Jeffrey showed uneasiness ever since her wedding day. Can you give me any instance of this; mention, I mean, any conversations overheard by you which would show us just what you mean?"

"I don't like to repeat things I hear. But if you say that I must, I can remember once passing Mr. and Mrs. Jeffrey in the hall, just as he was saying: 'You take it too much to heart! I expected a happy honeymoon. Somehow, we have failed—' That was all I heard, sir. But what made me remember his words was that she was dressed for some afternoon reception and looked so charming and so—and so, as if she ought to be happier."

"Just so. Now, when was this? How long before her death?"

"Oh, a week or so. It was very soon after the wedding day."

"And did matters seem to improve after that? Did she appear any better satisfied or more composed?"

"I think she endeavored to. But there was something on her mind, something which she tried to laugh off; something that annoyed Mr. Jeffrey and worried Miss Tuttle; something which caused a cloud in the house, for all the dances and dinners and goings and comings. I am sorry to speak of it, but it was so."

"Something that showed an unsettled mind?"

"Almost. The glitter in her eye was not natural; neither was the way she looked at her sister and sometimes at her husband."

"Did she talk much about the catastrophe which attended her wedding? Did her mind seem to run on that?"

"Incessantly at first; but afterward not so much. I think Mr. Jeffrey frowned on that subject."

"Did he ever frown on her?"

"No, sir—not—not when they were alone or with no one by but me. He seemed to love her then very much."

"What do you mean by that, Loretta; that he lost patience with her when other people were present—Miss Tuttle, for instance?"

"Yes, sir. He used to change very much when—when—when Miss Tuttle came into the room."

"Change toward his wife?"

"Yes, sir."

"How?"

"He grew more distant, much more distant; got up quite fretfully from his seat, if he were sitting beside her, and took up some book or paper."

"And Miss Tuttle?"

"She never seemed to notice but"

"But—?"

"She did not come in very often after this had happened once or twice; I mean into the room upstairs where they used to sit."

"Loretta, I regret to put this question, but after your replies I owe it to the jury, if not to the parties themselves, to make Miss Tuttle's position in this household thoroughly understood. Do you think she was a welcome visitor in this house?"

The girl pursed up her lips, glanced at the lady and gentleman whose feelings she was supposed to pass comment on, and seemed to lose heart. Then, as they failed to respond to her look of appeal, she strove to get the better of her sense of shame and, with a somewhat injured air, replied:

"I can only repeat what I once heard said about this by Mr. Jeffrey himself. Miss Tuttle had just left the diningroom and Mrs. Jeffrey was standing in one of her black moods, with her hand on the top of her chair, ready to go but forgetting to do so. I was there, but neither of them noticed me; he was staring at her, and she was looking down. Neither seemed at ease. Suddenly he spoke and asked, 'Why must Cora remain with us?' She started and her look grew strange and frightened. 'Because I want her to,' she cried. 'I can not live without Cora.'"

These words, so different from what we were expecting, caused a sensation in the room and consequently a stir. As the noise of shifting feet and moving heads began to be heard in all directions, Miss Tuttle's head drooped a little, but Francis Jeffrey did not betray any sign of feeling or even of attention. The coroner, embarrassed, perhaps, by this exhibition of silent misery so near him, hesitated a little before he put his next question. Loretta, on the contrary, had gathered courage with every word she spoke and now looked ready for anything.

"It was Mrs. Jeffrey, then, who clung most determinedly to her sister?" the coroner finally suggested.

"I have told you what she said."

"Yet these sisters spent but little time together?"

"Very little; as little as two persons could who lived together in one house."

This statement, which seemed such a contradiction to her former one, increased the interest; and much disappointment was covertly shown when the coroner veered off from this topic and brusquely inquired "Did you ever know Mr. and Mrs. Jeffrey to have any open rupture?"

The answer was a decided one.

"Yes. On Tuesday morning preceding her death they had a long and angry talk in their own room, after which Mrs. Jeffrey made no further effort to conceal her wretchedness. Indeed, one may say she began to die from that hour."

Mrs. Jeffrey's death had occurred on Wednesday evening.

"Let us hear what you have to say about this quarrel and what happened after it."

The girl, with a renewed flush, cast a deprecatory look at the mass of faces before her, and, meeting on all sides but one look of intense and growing interest, drew up her neat figure with a relieved air and began a story which I will proceed to transcribe for you in the fewest possible words.

Tuesday morning's breakfast had been a silent one. There had been a ball the night before at some great place on Massachusetts Avenue; but no one spoke of it. Miss Tuttle made some remark about a friend she had met there, but as no one listened to her, she soon stopped and in a little while left the table. Mr. and Mrs. Jeffrey sat on, but neither said anything. Finally Mr. Jeffrey rose and, speaking in a voice hardly recognizable, remarked that he had something to say to her, and led the way to their room. Mrs. Jeffrey looked frightened as she followed him; so frightened that it was evident that something very serious had occurred or was about to occur between them. As nothing of this kind had ever happened before, Loretta could not help waiting about till Mr. Jeffrey reappeared; and when he did so and she saw no signs of relief in his face or manner, she watched, with the silly interest of a girl who had nothing else to occupy her mind, to see if he would leave the house in such a mood, and without making peace with his young bride. To her surprise, he did not go out at the usual time, but went to Miss Tuttle's room, where for a full half-hour he remained closeted with his sister-in-law, talking in excited and unnatural tones. Then he went back for a few minutes to where he had left his wife, in her own boudoir. But he could not have had much to say to her this time, for he presently came out again and ran hastily downstairs and out, almost without stopping to catch up his hat.

As it was Mary's business, and not the witness', to make Mrs. Jeffrey's bed in the morning, Loretta could think of no excuse for approaching her mistress' room at this moment; but later, when letters came, followed by various messages and some visitors, she went more than a dozen times to Mrs. Jeffrey's door. She was not admitted, nor were her appeals answered, except by a sharp "Go away!"

Nor was Miss Tuttle received any better, though she tried more than once to see her sister, especially as night came on and the hour approached for Mr. Jeffrey's return. Mrs. Jeffrey was simply determined to remain alone; and when dinner time arrived, and no Mr. Jeffrey, she could be induced to open her door only wide enough to take in the cup of tea which Miss Tuttle insisted upon sending her.

The witness here confessed that she had been very much excited by these unusual proceedings and by the effect which they seemed to have on the lady just mentioned; so she was ready to notice that Mrs. Jeffrey's hand shook like that of an old and palsied woman when she reached out for the tray.

Gladly would Loretta have caught one glimpse of her face, but it was hidden by the door; nor did Mrs. Jeffrey answer a single one of her questions. She simply closed her door and kept it so till toward midnight, when Miss Tuttle, coming into the hall, ordered the house to be closed for the night. Then the long-shut door softly swung open, but before any one could reach it, it was again pulled to and locked.

The next day brought no relief. Miss Tuttle, who had changed greatly during this unhappy day and night, succeeded no better than before in getting access to her sister, nor could Loretta gain the least word from her mistress till toward the latter part of the afternoon, when that lady, ringing her bell, gave her first order.

"A substantial dinner," she cried; and when Loretta, greatly relieved, brought up the required meal she was astonished to find the door open and herself bidden to enter. The sight which met her eyes staggered her. From one end of the room to the other were signs of great nervous unrest and of terrible suffering. The chairs were pushed into corners as if the wretched bride had tramped the floor in an agony of excitement. Curtains were torn and the piano-cover was hanging half on and half off the open upright, as if she had clutched at it to keep herself from falling. On the floor beneath lay several pieces of broken china,—vases of whose value Mrs. Jeffrey had often spoken, but which, jerked off with the cover, had been left where they fell; while immediately in front of the fireplace lay one of the rugs tossed into a heap, as if she had rolled in it on the floor or used it to smother her cries of pain or anger.

So much for the state in which the witness found the boudoir. The adjoining bed-room was not in much better case, though it was evident that the bed itself had not been lain in since it was made up the day before at breakfast time. By this token Mrs. Jeffrey had not slept the night before, or if she had laid her head anywhere it had been on the rug already spoken of.

These signs of extreme mental suffering, so much more extreme than any Loretta had ever before witnessed, frightened her so that the tray shook in her hand as she set it down on the table among the countless objects Mrs. Jeffrey always had about her. The noise seemed to startle her mistress, who had walked to the window after opening the door, for she wheeled impetuously about and Loretta saw her face. It was as if a blight had passed over it. Once gay and animated beyond the power of any one to describe, it had become in twenty-four hours a ghost's face, with the glare of some awful resolve on it. Or so it would appear from the way Loretta described it. But such girls do not always see correctly, and perhaps all that can be safely stated is that Mrs. Jeffrey was unnaturally pale and had lost her butterfly-like way of incessant movement.

Loretta, who was evidently accustomed to seeing her mistress arrayed in brilliant colors and much begemmed, laid great stress on the fact that, though it was on the verge of evening and she was evidently going out, she was dressed in black cloth and without even a diamond or a flower to relieve its severe simplicity. Her hair, too, which was always her pride, was piled in a careless mass upon her head as if she had tried to arrange it herself and had forgotten what she was doing while her fingers were but half through their work. There was a cloak lying on a chair near which she was standing, and she held a hat in her band; but Loretta saw no gloves. As the maid's glance and that of her mistress crossed, Mrs. Jeffrey spoke, and the effort she made in doing so naturally frightened the girl still more. "I am going out," were her words. "I may not be home till late—What are you looking at?"

Loretta declared that the words took her by surprise and that she did not know what to say, but managed to cover up her embarrassment by intimating that if her mistress would let her touch up her hair a bit she would make her look more natural.

At this suggestion, Mrs. Jeffrey cast a glance in the glass and impetuously declared, "It doesn't matter." But she seemed to think better of it the next minute; for, throwing herself in a chair, she bade the girl to bring a comb, and sat quiet enough, though evidently in a great tremor of haste and impatience, while Loretta combed her hair and put it up in the old way.

But the old way was not as becoming as usual, and Loretta was wondering if she ought to call in Miss Tuttle, when Mrs. Jeffrey jumped to her feet and went over to the table and began to eat with the feverish haste of one who forces himself to take food in spite of hurry and distaste.

This was the moment for Loretta to leave the room; but she did not know how to do so. She felt herself fixed to the spot and stood watching Mrs. Jeffrey till that lady, suddenly becoming conscious of the girl's presence, turned, and in the midst of the moans which broke unconsciously from her lips, said with a pitiable effort at her old manner:

"Go away, Loretta; I am ill; have been ill for two days. I don't like people to look at me like that!" Then, as the girl shrank back, added in a breaking voice: "When Mr. Jeffrey comes home—" and said no more for several minutes, during which she clutched her throat with both hands and struggled with herself till she got her voice back and found herself able to repeat: "When Mr. Jeffrey comes,—if he does come,— tell him that I was right about the way that novel ended. Remember that you are to say to him the moment you see him that I was right about the novel, and that he is to look and see if it did not end as I said it would. And Loretta—" here she rose and approached the speaker with a sweet, appealing look which brought tears to the impressionable girl's eyes, "don't go gossiping about me downstairs. I sha'n't be sick long. I am going to be better soon, very soon. By the time you see me here again I shall be quite like my old self. Forget how—how"—and Loretta said she seemed to have difficulty in finding the right word here—"how childish I have been."

Of course Loretta promised, but she is not sure that she would have had the courage to keep all this to herself if she had not heard Mrs. Jeffrey stop in Miss Tuttle's room on her way out. That relieved her, and enabled her to go downstairs to her own supper with more appetite than she had thought ever to have again. Alas! it was the last good meal she was able to eat for days. In three hours afterward a man came from the station house with the news of Mrs. Jeffrey's suicide in the horrible old house in which she had been married only two weeks before.

As this had been a continuous narrative and concisely told, the coroner had not interrupted her. When at this point a little gasp escaped Miss Tuttle and a groan broke from Francis Jeffrey's hitherto sealed lips, the feelings of the whole assemblage seemed to find utterance. A young wife's misery culminating in death on the very spot where she had been so lately married! What could be more thrilling, or appeal more closely to the general heart of humanity? But the cause of that misery! This was what every one present was eager to have explained. This is what we now expected the coroner to bring out. But instead of continuing on the line he had opened up, he proceeded to ask:

"Where were you when this officer brought the news you mention?"

"In the hall, sir. I opened the door for him."

"And to whom did he first mention his errand?"

"To Miss Tuttle. She had come in just before him and was standing at the foot of the stairs."

"What! Was Miss Tuttle out that evening?"

"Yes; she went out very soon after Mrs. Jeffrey left. When she came in she said that she had been around the block, but she must have gone around it more than once, for she was absent two hours."

"Did you let her in?"

"Yes, sir."

"And she said she had been around the block?"

"Yes, sir"

"Did she say anything else?"

"She asked if Mr. Jeffrey had come in"

"Anything else?"

"Then if Mrs. Jeffrey had returned."

"To both of which questions you answered—"

"A plain 'No.'"

"Now tell us about the officer."

"He rang the bell almost immediately after she did. Thinking she would want to slip upstairs before I admitted any one, I waited a minute for her to go, but she did not do so, and when the officer stepped in she—"

"Well!"

"She shrieked."

"What! before he spoke?"

"Yes, sir."

"Just at sight of him?"

"Yes, sir."

"Did he wear his badge in plain view?"

"Yes, on his breast."

"So that you knew him to be a police officer?"

"Yes."

"And Miss Tuttle shrieked at seeing a police officer?"

"Yes, and sprang forward."

"Did she say anything?"

"Not then."

"What did she do?"

"Waited for him to speak."

"Which he did?"

"At once, and very brutally. He asked if she was Mrs. Jeffrey's sister, and when she nodded and gasped 'Yes,' he blurted out that Mrs. Jeffrey was dead; that he had just come from the old house in Waverley Avenue, where she had just been found."

"And Miss Tuttle?"

"Didn't know what to say; just hid her face. She was leaning against the newel-post, so it was easy for her to do so. I remember that the man stared at her for taking it so quietly and asking no questions."

"And did she speak at all?"

"Oh, yes, afterwards. Her face was wrapped in the folds of her cloak, but I heard her whisper, as if to herself: 'No! no! That old hearth is not a lodestone. She can not have fallen there.' And then she looked up quite wildly and cried: 'There is something more! Something which you have not told me.' 'She shot herself, if that's what you mean.' Miss Tuttle's arms went straight up over her head. It was awful to see her. 'Shot herself?' she gasped. 'Oh, Veronica, Veronica!' 'With a pistol,' he went on—I suppose he was going to say, 'tied to her wrist,' but he never got it out, for Miss Tuttle, at the word 'pistol' clapped her hands to her ears and for a moment looked quite distracted, so that he thought better of worrying her any more and only demanded to know if Mr. Jeffrey kept any such weapon. Miss Tuttle's face grew very strange at this. 'Mr. Jeffrey! was he there?' she asked. The man looked surprised. 'They are searching for Mr. Jeffrey,' he replied. 'Isn't he here?' 'No,' came both from her lips and mine. The man acted very impertinently. 'You haven't told me whether a pistol was kept here or not,' said he. Miss Tuttle tried to compose herself, but I saw that I should have to speak if any one did, so I told him that Mr. Jeffrey did have a pistol, which he kept in one of his bureau drawers. But when the officer wanted Miss Tuttle to go up and see if it was there, she shook her head and made for the front door, saying that she must be taken directly to her sister."

"And did no one go up? Was no attempt made to see if the pistol was or was not in the drawer?"

"Yes; the officer went up with me. I pointed out the place where it was kept, and he rummaged all through it, but found no pistol. I didn't expect him to—" Here the witness paused and bit her lip, adding confusedly: "Mrs. Jeffrey had taken it, you see."

The jurors, who sat very much in the shadow, had up to this point attracted but little attention. But now they began to make their presence felt, perhaps because the break in the witness' words had been accompanied by a sly look at Jinny. Possibly warned by this that something lay back of this hitherto timid witness' sudden volubility, one of them now spoke up.

"In what room did you say this pistol was kept?"

"In Mr. and Mrs. Jeffrey's bed-room, sir; the room opening out of the sitting-room where Mrs. Jeffrey had kept herself shut up all day."

"Does this bed-room of which you speak communicate with the hall as well as with the sitting room?"

"No, sir; it is the defect of the house. Mr. and Mrs. Jeffrey often spoke of it as a great annoyance. You had to pass through the little boudoir in order to reach it."

The juryman sank back, evidently satisfied with her replies, but we who marked the visible excitement with which the witness had answered this seemingly unimportant question, wondered what special interest surrounded that room and the pistol to warrant the heightened color with which the girl answered this new interlocutor. We were not destined to know at this time, for the coroner, when he spoke again, pursued a different subject.

"How long was this before Mr. Jeffrey came in."

"Only a few minutes. I was terribly frightened at being left there alone and was on my way to ask one of the other girls to come up and stay with me, when I heard his key in the lock and came back. He had entered the house and was standing near the door talking to an officer, who had evidently come in with him. It was a different officer from the one who had gone away with Miss Tuttle. Mr. Jeffrey was saying, 'What's that? My wife hurt!' 'Dead, sir!' blurted out the man. I had expected to see Mr. Jeffrey terribly shocked, but not in so awful a way. It really frightened me to see him and I turned to run, but found that I couldn't and that I had to stand still and look whether I wanted to or not. Yet he didn't say a word or ask a question."

"What did he do, Loretta?"

"I can not say; he was on his knees and was white—Oh, how white! Yet he looked up when the man described how and where Mrs. Jeffrey, had been found and even turned toward me when I said something about his wife having left a message for him when she went out. This message, which I almost hesitated to give after the awful news of her death, was about the ending of some story, as you remember, and it seemed heartless to speak of it at a moment like this, but as she had told me to, I didn't dare to disobey her. So, with the man listening to my every word, and Mr. Jeffrey looking as if he would fall to the ground before I could finish, I repeated her words to him and was surprised enough when he suddenly started upright and went flying upstairs. But I was more surprised yet when, at the top of the first flight, he stopped and, looking over the balustrade, asked in a very strange voice where Miss Tuttle was. For he seemed just then to want her more than anything else in the world and looked beaten and wild when I told him that she was already gone to Waverley Avenue. But he recovered himself before the man could draw near enough to see his face, and rushed into the sitting-room above and shut the door behind him, leaving the officer and me standing down by the front door. As I didn't know what to say to a man like him, and he didn't know what to say to me, the time seemed long, but it couldn't have been very many minutes before Mr. Jeffrey came back with a slip of paper in his hand and a very much relieved look on his face. 'The deed was premeditated,' he cried. 'My unfortunate wife has misunderstood my affection for her.' And from being a very much broken-down man, he stood up straight and tall and prepared himself very quietly to go to the Moore house. That is all I can tell about the way the news was received by him."

Were these details necessary? Many appeared to regard them as futile and uncalled for. But Coroner Z. was never known to waste time on trivialities, and if he called for these facts, those who knew him best felt certain that they were meant as a preparation for Mr. Jeffrey's testimony, which was now called for.

CHAPTER XII

THRUST AND PARRY

When Francis Jeffrey's hand fell from his forehead and he turned to face the assembled people, an instinctive compassion arose in every breast at sight of his face, which, if not open in its expression, was at least surcharged with the deepest misery. In a flash the scene took on new meaning. Many remembered that less than a month before his eye had been joyous and his figure a conspicuous one among the favored sons of fortune. And now he stood in sight of a crowd, drawn together mainly by curiosity, to explain as best he might why this great happiness and hope had come to a sudden termination, and his bride of a fortnight had sought death rather than continue to live under the same roof with him.

So much for what I saw on the faces about me. What my own face revealed I can not say. I only know that I strove to preserve an impassive exterior. If I secretly held this man's misery to be a mask hiding untold passions and the darkness of an unimaginable deed, it was not for me to disclose in this presence either my suspicions or my fears. To me, as to those about me, he apparently was a man who at some sacrifice to his pride, would, yet be able to explain whatever seemed dubious in the mysterious case in which he had become involved.

His wife's uncle, who to all appearance shared the general curiosity as to the effect which this woeful tragedy had had upon his niece's most interested survivor, eyed with a certain cold interest, eminently in keeping with his general character, the pallid forehead, sunken eyes and nervously trembling lip of the once "handsome Jeffrey" till that gentleman, rousing from his depression, manifested a realization of what was required of hire and turned with a bow toward the coroner.

Miss Tuttle settled into a greater rigidity. I pass over the preliminary examination of this important witness and proceed at once to the point when the coroner, holding out the two or three lines of writing which Mr. Jeffrey had declared to have been left him by his wife, asked:

"Are these words in your wife's handwriting?"

Mr. Jeffrey replied hastily, and, with just a glance at the paper offered him:

"They are."

The coroner pressed the slip upon him.

"Look at them carefully," he urged. "The handwriting shows hurry and in places is scarcely legible. Are you ready to swear that these words were written by your wife and by no other?"

Mr. Jeffrey, with just a slight contraction of his brow expressive of annoyance, did as he was bid. He scanned, or appeared to scan, the small scrap of paper which he now took into his own hand.

"It is my wife's writing," he impatiently declared. "Written, as all can see, under great agitation of mind, but hers without any doubt."

"Will you read aloud these words for our benefit?" asked the coroner:

It was a cruel request, causing an instinctive protest from the spectators. But no protest disturbed Coroner Z. He had his reasons, no doubt, for thus trying this witness, and when Coroner Z. had reason for anything it took more than the displeasure of the crowd to deter him.

Mr. Jeffrey, who had subdued whatever indignation he may have felt at this unmistakable proof of the coroner's intention to have his own way with him whatever the cost to his sensitiveness or pride, obeyed the latter's command in firmer tones than I expected.

The lines he was thus called upon to read may bear repetition:

"I find that I do not love you as I thought. I can not live knowing this to be so. Pray God you may forgive me!

VERONICA."

As the last word fell with a little tremble from Mr. Jeffrey's lips, the coroner repeated:

"You still think these words were addressed to you by your wife; that in short they contain an explanation of her death?"

"I do."

There was sharpness in the tone. Mr. Jeffrey was feeling the prick. There was agitation in it, too; an agitation he was trying hard to keep down.

"You have reason, then," persisted the coroner, "for accepting this peculiar explanation of your wife's death; a death which, in the judgment of most people, was of a nature to call for the strongest provocation possible."

"My wife was not herself. My wife was in an over strained and suffering condition. For one so nervously overwrought many allowances must be made. She may have been conscious of not responding fully to my affection. That this feeling was strong enough to induce her to take her life is a source of unspeakable grief to me, but one for which you must find explanation, as I have so often said, in the terrors caused by the dread event at the Moore house, which recalled old tragedies and emphasized a most unhappy family tradition."

The coroner paused a moment to let these words sink into the ears of the jury, then plunged immediately into what might be called the offensive part of his examination.

"Why, if your wife's death caused you such intense grief, did you appear so relieved at receiving this by no means consoling explanation?"

At an implication so unmistakably suggestive of suspicion Mr. Jeffrey showed fire for the first time.

"Whose word have you for that? A servant's, so newly come into my house that her very features are still strange to me. You must acknowledge that a person of such marked inexperience can hardly be thought to know me or to interpret rightly the feelings of my heart by any passing look she may have surprised upon my face."

This attitude of defiance so suddenly assumed had an effect he little realized. Miss Tuttle stirred for the first time behind her veil, and Uncle David, from looking bored, became suddenly quite attentive. These two but mirrored the feelings of the general crowd, and mine especially.

"We do not depend on her judgment alone," the coroner now remarked. "The change in you was apparent to many others. This we can prove to the jury if they require it."

But no man lifting a voice from that gravely attentive body, the coroner proceeded to inquire if Mr. Jeffrey felt like volunteering any explanations on this head. Receiving no answer from him either, he dropped the suggestive line of inquiry and took up the consideration of facts. The first question he now put was:

"Where did you find the slip of paper containing these last words from your wife?"

"In a book I picked out of the book-shelf in our room upstairs. When Loretta gave me my wife's message I knew that I should find some word from her in the novel we had just been reading. As we had been interested in but one book since our marriage, there was no possibility of my making an' mistake as to which one she referred."

"Will you give us the name of this novel?"

"COMPENSATION."

"And you found this book called COMPENSATION in your room upstairs?"

"Yes."

"On the book-shelf?"

"Yes."

"Where does this book-shelf stand?"

Mr. Jeffrey looked up as much as to say, "Why so many small questions about so simple a matter?" but answered frankly enough:

"At the right of the door leading into the bedroom."

"And at right angles to the door leading into the hall?"

"Yes."

"Very good. Now may I ask you to describe the cover of this book?"

"The cover? I never noticed the cover. Why do you—. Excuse me, I suppose you have your reasons for asking even these puerile and seemingly unnecessary questions. The cover is a queer one I believe; partly red and partly green; and that is all I know about it."

"Is this the book?"

Mr. Jeffrey glanced at the volume the coroner held up before him.

"I believe so; it looks like it."

The book had a flaming cover, quite unmistakable in its character.

"The title shows it to be the same," remarked the coroner. "Is this the only book with a cover of this kind in the house?"

"The only one, I should say."

The coroner laid down the book.

"Enough of this, then, for the present; only let the jury remember that the cover of this book is peculiar and that it was kept on a shelf at the right of the opening leading into the adjoining bed-room. And now, Mr. Jeffrey, we must ask you to look at these rings; or, rather, at this one. You have seen it before; it is the one you placed on Mrs. Jeffrey's hand when you were married to her a little over a fortnight ago. You recognize it?"

"I do."

"Do you also recognize this small mark of blood on it as having been here when it was shown to you by the detective on your return from seeing her dead body at the Moore house?"

"I do; yes."

"How do you account for that spot and the slight injury made to her finger? Should you not say that the ring had been dragged from her hand?"

"I should."

"By whom was it dragged? By you?"

"No, sir."

"By herself, then?"

"It would seem so."

"Much passion must have been in that act. Do you think that any ordinary quarrel between husband and wife would account for the display of such fury? Are we not right in supposing a deeper cause for the disturbance between you than the slight one you offer in way of explanation?"

An inaudible answer; then a sudden straightening of Francis Jeffrey's fine figure. And that was all.

"Mr. Jeffrey, in the talk you had with your wife on Tuesday morning was Miss Tuttle's name introduced?"

"It was mentioned; yes, sir."

"With recrimination or any display of passion on the part of your wife?"

"You would not believe me if I said no," was the unexpected rejoinder.

The coroner, taken aback by this direct attack from one who had hitherto borne all his innuendoes with apparent patience, lost countenance for a moment, but, remembering that in his official capacity he was more than a match for the elegant gentleman, who under other circumstances would have found it only too easy to put him to the blush, he observed with dignity:

"Mr. Jeffrey, you are on oath. We certainly have no reason for not believing you."

Mr. Jeffrey bowed. He was probably sorry for his momentary loss of self-control, and gravely, but with eyes bent downward, answered with the abrupt phrase:

"Well, then, I will say no."

The coroner shifted his ground.

"Will you make the same reply when I ask if the like forbearance was shown toward your wife's name in the conversation you had with Miss Tuttle immediately afterward?"

A halt in the eagerly looked-for reply; a hesitation, momentary indeed, but pregnant with nameless suggestions, caused his answer, when it did come, to lose some of the emphasis he manifestly wished to put into it.

"Miss Tuttle was Mrs. Jeffrey's half-sister. The bond between them was strong. Would she would I—be apt to speak of my young wife with bitterness?"

"That is not an answer to my question, Mr. Jeffrey. I must request a more positive reply."

Miss Tuttle made a move. The strain on all present was so great we could but notice it. He noticed it too, for his brows came together with a quick frown, as he emphatically replied:

"There were no recriminations uttered. Mrs. Jeffrey had displeased me and I said so, but I did not forget that I was speaking of my wife and to her sister."

As this was in the highest degree non-committal, the coroner could be excused for persisting.

"The conversation, then, was about your wife?"

"It was."

"In criticism of her conduct?"

"Yes."

"At the ambassador's ball?"

"Yes."

Mr. Jeffrey was a poor hand at lying. That last "yes" came with great effort.

The coroner waited, possibly for the echo of this last "yes" to cease; then he remarked with a coldness which lifted at once the veil from his hitherto well disguised antagonism to this witness.

"If you will recount to us anything which your wife said or did on that evening which, in your mind, was worthy of all this coil, it might help us to understand the situation."

But the witness made no attempt to do so, and while many of us were ready to pardon him this show of delicacy, others felt that under the circumstances it would have been better had he been more open.

Among the latter was the coroner himself, who, from this moment, threw aside all hesitation and urged forward his inquiries in a way to press the witness closer and closer toward the net he was secretly holding out for him. First, he obliged him to say that his conversation with Miss Tuttle had not tended to smooth matters; that no reconciliation with his wife had followed it, and that in the thirty-six hours which elapsed before he returned home again he had made no attempt to soothe the feelings of one, who, according to his own story, he considered hardly responsible for any extravagances in which she might have indulged. Then when this inconsistency had been given time to sink into the minds of the jury, Coroner Z. increased the effect produced by confronting Jeffrey with witnesses who testified to the friendly, if not lover-like relations which had existed between himself and Miss Tuttle prior to the appearance of his wife upon the scene; closing with a question which brought out the denial, by no means new, that an engagement had ever taken place between him and Miss Tuttle and hence that a bond had been canceled by his marriage with Miss Moore.

But his manner and careful choice of words in making this denial did not satisfy those present of his entire candor; especially as Miss Tuttle, for all her apparent immobility, showed, by the violent locking of her hands, both her anxiety and the suffering she was undergoing during this painful examination. Was the suffering merely one of outraged delicacy? We felt justified in doubting it, and looked forward, with cruel curiosity I admit, to the moment when this renowned and universally admired beauty would be called on to throw aside her veil axed reveal the highly praised features which had been so openly scorned for the sake of one whose chief claims to regard lay in her great wealth.

But this moment was as yet far distant. The coroner was a man of method, and his plan was now to prove, as had been apparent to most of us from the first, that the assumption of suicide on the part of Mrs. Jeffrey was open to doubt. The communication suggesting such an end to her troubles was the strongest proof Mr. Jeffrey could bring forward that her death had been the result of her own act. Consequently it was now the coroner's business to show that this communication was either a forgery, or a substitution, and that if she left some word in the book to which she had in so peculiar a manner directed his attention, it was not necessarily the one bewailing her absence of love for him and her consequent intention of seeking relief from her disappointment in death.

Some hint of what the coroner contemplated had already escaped him in the persistent and seemingly inconsequent questions to which he had subjected this witness in reference to these very matters. But the time had now come for a more direct attack, and the interest rose correspondingly high, when the coroner, lifting again to sight the scrap of paper containing the few piteous lines so often quoted, asked of the now anxious and agitated witness, if he had ever noticed any similarity between the handwriting of his wife and that of Miss Tuttle.

An indignant "No!" was about to pass his lips, when he suddenly checked himself and said more mildly: "There may have been a similarity; I hardly know, I have seen too little of Miss Tuttle's hand to judge."

This occasioned a diversion. Specimens of Miss Tuttle's handwriting were produced, which, after having been duly proved, were passed down to the jury along with the communication professedly signed by Mrs. Jeffrey. The grunts of astonishment which ensued as the knowing heads drew near over these several papers caused Mr. Jeffrey to flush and finally to cry out with startling emphasis:

"I know that those words were written by my wife."

But when the coroner asked him his reasons for this conviction, he could, or would not state them.

"I have said," he stolidly repeated; and that was all.

The coroner made no comment, but when, after some further inquiry, which added little to the general knowledge, he dismissed Mr. Jeffrey and recalled Loretta, there was that in his tone which warned us that the really serious portion of the day's examination was about to begin.

CHAPTER XIII

CHIEFLY THRUST

The appearance of this witness had undergone a change since she last stood before us. She was shame-faced still, but her manner showed resolve and a feverish determination to face the situation which could but awaken in the breasts of those who had Mr. Jeffrey's honor and personal welfare at heart a nameless dread; as if they already foresaw the dark shadow which minute by minute was slowly sinking over a household which, up to a week ago, had been the envy and admiration of all Washington society.

The first answer she made revealed both the cause of her shame and the reason of her firmness. It was in response to the question whether she, Loretta, had seen Miss Tuttle before she went out on the walk she was said to have taken immediately after Mrs. Jeffrey's final departure from the house.

Her words were these

"I did sir. I do not think Miss Tuttle knows it, but I saw her in Mrs. Jeffrey's room."

The emphatic tone, offering such a contrast to her former manner of speech, might have drawn all eyes to the speaker had not the person she mentioned offered a still more interesting subject to the general curiosity. As it was, all glances flew to that silent and seemingly impassive figure upon which all open suggestions and covert innuendo had hitherto fallen without creating more than a pressure of her interlaced fingers. This direct attack, possibly the most threatening she had received, appeared to produce no more effect upon her than the others; less, perhaps, for no stir was visible in her now, and to some eyes she hardly seemed to breathe.

Curiosity, thus baffled, led the gaze on to Mr. Jeffrey, and even to Uncle David; but the former had dropped his head again upon his hand, and the other—well, there was little to observe in Mr. Moore at any time, save the immense satisfaction he seemed to take in himself; so attention returned to the witness, who, by this time, had entered upon a consecutive tale.

As near as I can remember, these are the words with which she prefaced it:

"I am not especially proud of what I did that night, but I was led into it by degrees, and I am sure I beg the lady's pardon." And then she went on to relate how, after she had seen Mrs. Jeffrey leave the house, she went into her room with the intention of putting it to rights. As this was no more than her duty, no fault could be found with her; but she owned that when she had finished this task and removed all evidence of Mrs. Jeffrey's frenzied condition, she had no business to linger at the table turning over the letters she found lying there.

Here the coroner stopped her and made some inquiries in regard to these letters, but as they seemed to be ordinary epistles from friends and quite foreign to the investigation, he allowed her to proceed.

Her cheeks were burning now, for she had found herself obliged to admit that she had read enough of these letters to be sure that they had no reference to the quarrel then pending between her mistress and Mr. Jeffrey. Her eyes fell and she looked seriously distressed as she went on to say that she was as conscious then as now of having no business with these papers; so conscious, indeed, that when she heard Miss Tuttle's step at the door, her one idea was to hide herself.

That she could stand and face that lady never so much as occurred to her. Her own guilty consciousness made her cheeks too hot for her to wish to meet an eye which had never rested on her any too kindly;

so noticing how straight the curtains fell over one of the windows on the opposite side of the room, she dashed toward it and slipped in out of sight just as Miss Tuttle came in. This window was one seldom used, owing to the fact that it overlooked an adjoining wall, so she had no fear of Miss Tuttle's approaching it. Consequently, she could stand there quite at her ease, and, as the curtains in falling behind her had not come quite together, she really could not help seeing just what that lady did.

Here the witness paused with every appearance of looking for some token of disapprobation from the crowd.

But she encountered nothing there but eager anxiety for her to proceed, so without waiting for the coroner's question, she added in so many words:

"She went first to the book-shelves"

We had expected it; but yet a general movement took place, and a few suppressed exclamations could be heard.

"And what did she do there?"

"Took down a book, after looking carefully up and down the shelves."

"What color of book?"

"A green one with red figures on it. I could see the cover plainly as she took it down."

"Like this one?"

"Exactly like that one."

"And what did she do with this book?"

"Opened it, but not to read it. She was too quick in closing it for that."

"Did she take the book away?"

"No; she put it back on the shelf."

"After opening and closing it?"

"Yes, sir."

"Did you see whether she put anything into the book?"

"I can not swear that she did; but then her back was to me, and I could not have seen it if she had."

The implied suggestion caused some excitement, but the coroner, frowning on this, pressed the girl to continue, asking if Miss Tuttle left the room immediately after turning from the book-shelves. Loretta replied no; that, on the contrary, she stood for some minutes near them, gazing, in what seemed like a great distress of mind, straight upon the floor; after which she moved in an agitated way and with more than one anxious look behind her into the adjoining room where she paused before a large bureau. As this bureau was devoted entirely to Mr. Jeffrey's use, Loretta experienced some surprise at seeing his wife's sister approach it in so stealthy a manner. Consequently she was watching with all her might, when this young lady opened the upper drawer and, with very evident emotion, thrust her hand into it.

What she took out, or whether she took out anything, this spy upon her movements could not say, for when Loretta heard the drawer being pushed back into place she drew the curtains close, perceiving that Miss Tuttle would have to face this window in coming back. However, she ventured upon one other peep through them just as that lady was leaving the room, and remembered as if it were yesterday how clay-white her face looked, and how she held her left hand pressed close against the folds of her dress. It was but a few minutes after this that Miss Tuttle left the house.

As we all knew what was kept in that drawer, the conclusion was obvious. Whatever excuse Miss Tuttle might give for going into her sister's room at this time, but one thought, one fear, or possibly one hope, could have taken her to Mr. Jeffrey's private drawer. She wished to see if his pistol was still there, or if it had been taken away by her sister,—a revelation of the extreme point to which her thoughts had flown at this crisis, and one which effectually contradicted her former statement that she had been conscious of no alarm in behalf of her sister and had seen her leave the house without dread or suspicion of evil.

The temerity which had made it possible to associate the name of such a man as Francis Jeffrey with an outrageous crime having been thus in a measure explained, the coroner recalled that gentleman and again thoroughly surprised the gaping public.

Had the witness accompanied his wife to the Moore house?

"No"

Had he met her there by any appointment he had made with her or which had been made for them both by some third person?

"No"

Had he been at the Moore house on the night of the eleventh at any time previous to the hour when he was brought there by the officials?

"No."

Would he glance at this impression of certain finger-tips which had been left in the dust of the southwest chamber mantel?

He had already noted them.

Now would he place his left hand on the paper and see—

"It is not necessary," he burst forth, in great heat. "I own to those marks. That is, I have no doubt they were made by my hand" Here, unconsciously, his eyes flew to the member thus referred to, as if conscious that in some way it had proved a traitor to him; after which his gaze traveled slowly my way, with an indescribable question in it which roused my conscience and made the trick by which I had got the impression of his hand seem less of a triumph than I had heretofore considered it. The next minute he was answering the coroner under oath, very much as he had answered him in the unofficial interview at which I had been present.

"I acknowledge having been in the Moore house and even having been in its southwest chamber, but not at the time supposed. It was on the previous night." He went on to relate how, being in a nervous condition and having the key to this old dwelling in his pocket, he had amused himself by going through its dilapidated interior. All of this made a doubtful impression which was greatly emphasized when, in reply to the inquiry as to where he got the light to see by, he admitted that he had come upon a candle in an upstairs room and made use of that; though he could not remember what he had done with this candle afterward, and looked dazed and quite at sea, till the coroner suggested that he might have carried it into the closet of the room where his fingers had left their impression in the dust of the mantel-shelf. Then he broke down like a man from whom some prop is suddenly snatched and looked around for a seat. This was given him, while a silence, the most dreadful I ever experienced, held every one there in check. But he speedily rallied and, with the remark that he was a little confused in regard to the incidents of that night, waited with a wild look in his averted eye for the coroner's next question.

Unhappily for him it was in continuation of the same subject. Had he bought candles or not at the grocer's around the corner? Yes, he had. Before visiting the house? Yes. Had he also bought matches? Yes. What kind? Common safety matches. Had he noticed when he got home that the box he had just bought was half empty? No. Nevertheless he had used many matches in going through this old house, had he not? Possibly. To light his way upstairs, perhaps? It might be. Had he not so used them? Yes. Why had he done so, if he had candles in his pocket, which were so much easier to hold and so much more lasting than a lighted match? Ah, he could not say; he did not know; his mind was confused. He was awake when he should have been asleep. It was all a dream to him.

The coroner became still more persistent.

"Did you enter the library on your solitary visit to this old house?"

"I believe so."

"What did you do there?"

"Pottered around. I don't remember."

"What light did you use?"

"A candle, I think."

"You must know."

"Well, I had a candle; it was in a candelabrum."

"What candle and what candelabrum?"

"The same I used upstairs, of course"

"And you can not remember where you left this candle and candelabrum when you finally quitted the house?"

"No. I wasn't thinking about candles."

"What were you thinking about?"

"The rupture with my wife and the bad name of the house I was in."

"Oh! and this was on Tuesday night?"

"Yes, sir."

"How can you prove this to us?"

"I can not."

"But you swear—"

"I swear that it was Tuesday night, the night immediately preceding the one when—when my wife's death robbed me of all earthly happiness."

It was feelingly uttered, and several faces lightened; but the coroner repeating: "Is there no way you can prove this to our satisfaction?" the shadow settled again, and on no head more perceptibly than on that of the unfortunate witness.

It was now late in the day and the atmosphere of the room had become stifling; but no one seemed to be conscious of any discomfort, and a general gasp of excitement passed through the room when the coroner, taking out a box from under a pile of papers, disclosed to the general gaze the famous white ribbon with its dainty bow, lying on top of the fatal pistol.

That this special feature, the most interesting one of all connected with this tragedy, should have been kept so long in reserve and brought out just at this time, struck many of Mr. Jeffrey's closest friends as unnecessarily dramatic; but when the coroner, lifting out the ribbon, remarked tentatively, "You know this ribbon?" we were more struck by the involuntary cry of surprise which rose from some one in the crowd about the door, than by the look with which Mr. Jeffrey eyed it and made the necessary reply. That cry had something more than nervous excitement in it. Identifying the person who had uttered it as a certain busy little woman well known in town, I sent an officer to watch her; then recalled my attention to the point the coroner was attempting to make. He had forced Mr. Jeffrey to recognize the ribbon as the one which had fastened the pistol to his wife's arm; now he asked whether, in his opinion, a woman could tie such a bow to her own wrist, and when in common justice Mr. Jeffrey was obliged to say no, waited a third time before he put the general suspicion again into words:

"Can not you, by some means or some witness, prove to us that it was on Tuesday night and not on Wednesday you spent the hours you speak of on this scene of your marriage and your wife's death?"

The hopelessness which more than once had marked Mr. Jeffrey's features since the beginning of this inquiry, reappeared with renewed force as this suggestive question fell again upon his ears; and he was about to repeat his plea of forgetfulness when the coroner's attention was diverted by a request made in his ear by one of the detectives. In another moment Mr. Jeffrey had been waved aside and a new witness sworn in.

You can imagine every one's surprise, mine most of all, when this witness proved to be Uncle David.

CHAPTER XIV

"TALLMAN! LET US HAVE TALLMAN!"

I do not know why the coroner had so long delayed to call this witness. In the ordinary course of events his testimony should have preceded mine, but the ordinary course of events had not been followed, and it was only at the request of Mr. Moore himself that he was now allowed the privilege of appearing before this coroner and jury.

I speak of it as a privilege because he himself evidently regarded it as such. Indeed, his whole attitude and bearing as he addressed himself to the coroner showed that he was there to be looked at and that he secretly thought he was very well worth this attention. Possibly some remembrance of the old days, in which he had gone in and out before these people in a garb suggestive of penury, made the moment when he could appear before them in a guise more befitting his station one of incalculable importance to him.

At all events, he confronted us all with an aspect which openly challenged admiration. When, in answer to the coroner's inquiries, it became his duty to speak, he did so with a condescension which would have called up smiles if the occasion had been one of less seriousness, and his connection with it as unimportant as he would have it appear.

What he said was in the way of confirming the last witness' testimony as to his having been at the Moore house on Tuesday evening. Mr. Moore, who was very particular as to dates and days, admitted that the light which he had seen in a certain window of his ancestral home on the evening when he summoned the police was but the repetition of one he had detected there the evening before. It was this repetition which alarmed him and caused him to break through all his usual habits and leave his home at night to notify the police.

"The old sneak!" thought I. "Why didn't he tell us this before?" And I allowed myself afresh doubt of his candor which had always seemed to me somewhat open to question. It is possible that the coroner shared my opinion, or that he felt it incumbent upon him to get what evidence he could from the sole person living within view of the house in which such ghastly events had taken place. For, without betraying the least suspicion, and yet with the quiet persistence for which men in his responsible position are noted, he subjected this suave old man to such a rigid examination as to what he had seen, or had not seen, from his windows, that no possibility seemed to remain of his concealing a single fact which could help to the elucidation of this or any other mystery connected with the old mansion.

He asked him if he had seen Mr. Jeffrey go in on the night in question; if he had ever seen any one go in there since the wedding; or even if he had seen any one loitering about the steps, or sneaking into the rear yard. But the answer was always no; these same noes growing more and more emphatic, and the gentleman more and more impenetrable and dignified as the examination went on. In fact, he was as unassailable a witness as I have ever heard testify before any jury. Beyond the fact already mentioned of his having observed a light in the opposite house on the two evenings in question, he admitted nothing. His life in the little cottage was so engrossing—he had his organ—his dog—why should he look out of the window? Had it not been for his usual habit of letting his dog run the pavements for a quarter of an hour before finally locking up for the night, he would not have seen as much as he did.

"Have you any stated hour for doing this?" the coroner now asked.

"Yes; half-past nine"

"And was this the hour when you caw that light?"

"Yes, both times."

As he had appeared at the station-house at a few minutes before ten he was probably correct in this statement. But, notwithstanding this, I did not feel implicit confidence in him. He was too insistent in his regret at not being able to give greater assistance in the disentanglement of a mystery so affecting the honor of the family of which he was now the recognized head. His voice, nicely attuned to the occasion, was admirable; so was his manner; but I mentally wrote him down as one I should enjoy outwitting if the opportunity ever came my way.

He wound up with such a distinct repetition of his former emphatic assertion as to the presence of light in the old house on Tuesday as well as Wednesday evening that Mr. Jeffrey's testimony in this regard received a decided confirmation. I looked to see some open recognition of this, when suddenly, and with a persistence understood only by the police, the coroner recalled Mr. Jeffrey and asked him what proof he had to offer that his visit of Tuesday had not been repeated the next night and that he was not in the building when that fatal trigger was pulled.

At this leading question, a lawyer sitting near me, edged himself forward as if he hoped for some sign from Mr. Jeffrey which would warrant him in interfering. But Mr. Jeffrey gave no such sign. I doubt if he even noticed this man's proximity, though he knew him well and had often employed him as his legal adviser in times gone by. He was evidently exerting himself to recall the name which so persistently eluded his memory, putting his hand to his head and showing the utmost confusion.

"I can not give you one," he finally stammered. "There is a man who could tell—if only I could remember his name." Suddenly with a loud cry which escaped him involuntarily, he gave a gurgling laugh and we heard the name "Tallman!" leap from his lips.

The witness had at last remembered whom he had met at the cemetery gate at the hour, or near the hour, his wife lay dying in the lower part of the city.

The effect was electrical. One of the spectators—some country boor, no doubt—so far forgot himself as to cry out loud enough for all to hear:

"Tallman! Let us have Tallman!"

Of course he met with an instant rebuke, but I did not wait to hear it, or to see order restored, for a glance from the coroner had already sent me to the door in search of this new witness.

My destination was the Cosmos Club, for Phil Tallman and his habits and haunts were as well known in Washington as the figure of Liberty on the summit of the Capitol dome. When I saw him I did not wonder. Never have I seen a more amiable looking man, or one with a more absentminded expression. To my query as to whether he had ever met Mr. Jeffrey at or near the entrance of Rock Creek Cemetery, he replied with an amazed look and the quick response:

"Of course I did. It was the very night that his wife— But what's up? You look excited for a detective."

"Come to the morgue and see. This testimony of yours will prove invaluable to Mr. Jeffrey."

I shall never forget the murmur of suppressed excitement which greeted us as I reappeared before coroner and jury accompanied by the gentleman who had been called for in such peremptory tones a short time before.

Mr. Jeffrey, who had attempted to rise at our entrance, but seemed to lack the ability, gave a faint smile as Tallman's good-natured face appeared; and the coroner, feeling, perhaps, that some cords are liable to break if stretched too strongly, administered the oath and made the necessary inquiries with as little delay as was compatible with the solemnity of the occasion.

The result was an absolute proof that Mr. Jeffrey had been near Soldiers' Home as late as seven, which was barely fifteen minutes previous to the hour Mrs. Jeffrey's watch was stopped by her fall in the old house on Waverley Avenue. As the distance between the two places could not be compassed in that time, Mr. Jeffrey's alibi could be regarded as established.

When we were all rising, glad of an adjournment which restored free movement and an open interchange of speech, a sudden check in the general rush called our attention back to Mr. Jeffrey. He was standing facing Miss Tuttle, who was still sitting in a strangely immovable attitude in her old place. He had just touched her on the arm, and now, with a look of alarm, he threw up the veil which had kept her face hidden from all beholders.

A vision of loveliness greeted us, but that was not all. It was an unconscious loveliness. Miss Tuttle had fainted away, sitting upright in her chair.

CHAPTER XV

WHITE BOW AND PINK

Mr. Jeffrey's examination and its triumphant conclusion created a great furor in town. Topics which had hitherto absorbed all minds were forgotten in the discussion of the daring attempt which had been made by the police to fix crime upon one of Washington's most esteemed citizens, and the check which they had rightly suffered for this outrage. What might be expected next? Something equally bold and reprehensible, of course, but what? It was a question which at the next sitting completely filled the inquest room.

To my great surprise, Mr. Jeffrey was recalled to the stand. He had changed since the night before. He looked older, and while still handsome, for nothing could rob him of his regularity of feature and extreme elegance of proportion, showed little of the spirit which, in spite of the previous day's depression, had upheld him through its most trying ordeal and kept his eye bright, if only from excitement. This was fact number one, and one which I stored away in my already well-furnished memory.

Miss Tuttle sat in a less conspicuous position than on the previous day, and Mr. Moore, her uncle, was not thereat all.

The testimony called for revived an old point which, seemingly, had not been settled to the coroner's satisfaction.

Had Mr. Jeffrey placed the small stand holding the candelabrum on the spot where it had been found? No. Had he carried into the house, at the time of his acknowledged visit, the candles which had been afterward discovered there? No. He had had time to think since his hesitating and unsatisfactory replies of the day before, and he was now in a position to say that while he distinctly remembered buying candles on his way to the Moore house, he had not found them in his pocket on getting there and had been obliged to make use of the matches he always carried on his person in order to find his way to the upstairs room where he felt positive he would find a candle.

This gave the coroner an opportunity to ask:

"And why did you expect to find a candle there?"

The answer astonished me and, I have no doubt, many others.

"It was the room in which my wife had dressed for the ceremony. It had not been disturbed since that time. My wife had little ways of her own; one was to complete her toilet by using a curling iron on a little lock she wore over her temple. When at home she heated this curling iron in the gas jet, but there being no gas in the Moore house, I naturally concluded that she had made use of a candle, as the curl had been noticeable under her veil."

Oh, the weariness in his tone! I could scarcely interpret it. Was he talking by rote, or was he utterly done with life and all its interests? No one besides myself seemed to note this strange passivity. To the masses he was no longer a suffering man, but an individual from whom information was to be got. The next question was a vital one.

He had accounted for one candle in the house; could he account for the one found in the tumbler or for the one lying crushed and battered on the closet floor?

He could not.

And now we all observed a change of direction in the inquiry. Witnesses were summoned to corroborate Mr. Jeffrey's statements, statements which it seemed to be the coroner's present wish to establish. First came the grocer who had sold Mr. Jeffrey the candles. He acknowledged, much to Jinny's discomfort, that an hour after Mr. Jeffrey had left the store, he had found on the counter the package which that gentleman had forgotten to take. Poor Jinny had not stayed long enough to hear his story out. The grocer finished his testimony by saying that immediately upon his discovery he had sent the candles to Mr. Jeffrey's house.

This the coroner caused to be emphasized to such an extent that we were all convinced of its importance. But as yet his purpose was not evident save to those who were more in his confidence than myself.

The other witnesses were men from Rauchers, who had acted as waiters at the time of the marriage. One of them testified that immediately on Miss Moore's arrival he had been sent for a candle and a box of matches. The other, that he had carried up to her room a large candelabrum from the drawing-room mantel. A pair of curling tongs taken from the dressing table of this room was next produced, together with other articles of toilet use which had been allowed to remain there uncared for, though they were of solid silver and of beautiful design.

The next witness was a member of Mr. Jeffrey's own household. Chloe was her name, and her good black face worked dolefully as she admitted that the package of candles which the grocer boy had left on the kitchen table, with the rest of the groceries on the morning of that dreadful day when "Missus" killed herself, was not to be found when she came to put the things away. She had looked and looked for it, but it was not there.

Further inquiry brought out the fact that but one other member of the household was in the kitchen when these groceries were delivered; and that this person gave a great start when the boy shouted out, "The candles there were bought by Mr. Jeffrey," and hurried over to the table and handled the packages, although Chloe did not see her carry any of them away.

"And who was this person?"

"Miss Tuttle."

With the utterance of this name the veil fell from the coroner's intentions and the purpose of this petty but prolonged inquiry stood revealed. It was to all a fearful and impressive moment. To me it was as painful as it was triumphant. I had not anticipated such an outcome when I put my wits to work to prove that murder, and not suicide, was answerable for young Mrs. Jeffrey's death.

When the murmur which had hailed this startling turn in the inquiry had subsided, the coroner drew a deep breath, and, with an uneasy glance at the jury, who, to a man, seemed to wish themselves well out of this job, he dismissed the cook and summoned a fresh witness.

Her name made the people stare.

"Miss Nixon."

Miss Nixon! That was a name well known in Washington; almost as well known as that of Uncle David, or even of Mr. Tallman. What could this quaint and characteristic little body have to do with this case of doubtful suicide? A word will explain. She was the person who, on the day before, had made that loud exclamation when the box containing the ribbon and the pistol had been disclosed to the jury.

As her fussy little figure came forward, some nudged and some laughed, possibly because her bonnet was not of this year's style, possibly because her manner was peculiar and as full of oddities as her attire. But they did not laugh long, for the little lady's look was appealing, if not distressed. The fact that she was generally known to possess one of the largest bank accounts in the District, made any marked show of disrespect toward her a matter of poor judgment, if not of questionable taste.

The box in the coroner's hand prepared us for what was before us. As he opened it and disclosed again the dainty white bow which, as I have before said, was of rather a fantastic make, the whole roomful of eager spectators craned forward and were startled enough when he asked:

"Did you ever see a bow like this before?"

Her answer came in the faintest of tones.

"Yes, I have one like it; very like it; so like it that yesterday I could not suppress an exclamation on seeing this one."

"Where did you get the one you have? Who fashioned it, I mean, or tied it for you, if that is what I ought to say?"

"It was tied for me by—Miss Tuttle. She is a friend of mine, or was—and a very good one; and one day while watching me struggling with a piece of ribbon, which I wanted made into a bow, she took it from my hand and tied a knot for which I was very much obliged to her. It was very pretty."

"And like this?"

"Almost exactly, sir."

"Have you that knot with you?"

She had.

"Will you show it to the jury?"

Heaving a sigh which she had much better have suppressed, she opened a little bag she carried at her side and took out a pink satin bow. It had been tied by a deft hand; and more than one pair of eyes fell significantly at sight of it.

Amid a silence which was intense, two or three other witnesses were called to prove that Miss Tuttle's skill in bow-tying was exceptional, and was often made use of, not only by members of her household, but, as in Miss Nixon's case, by outsiders; the special style shown in the one under consideration being the favorite.

During all this, I kept my eyes on Mr. Jeffrey. It had now become so evident which way the coroner's inquiries tended that I wished to be the first to note their effect on him. It was less marked than I had anticipated. The man seemed benumbed by accumulated torment and stared at the witnesses filing before him as if they were part of some wild phantasmagoria which confused, without enlightening him. When finally several persons of both sexes were brought forward to prove that his attentions to Miss Tuttle had once been sufficiently marked for an announcement of their engagement to be daily looked for, he let his head fall forward on his breast as if the creeping horror which had seized him was too much for his brain if not for his heart. The final blow was struck when the man whom I had myself seen in Alexandria testified to the contretemps which had occurred in Atlantic City; an additional point being given to it by the repetition of some old conversation raked up for the purpose, by which an effort was made to prove that Miss Tuttle found it hard to forgive injuries even from those nearest and dearest to her. This subject might have been prolonged, but some of the jury objected, and the time being now ripe for the great event of the day, the name of the lady herself was called.

After so significant a preamble, the mere utterance of Miss Tuttle's name had almost the force of an accusation; but the dignity with which she rose calmed all minds, and subdued every expression of feeling. I could but marvel at her self-poise and noble equanimity, and asked myself if, in the few days which had passed since first the murmur of something more serious than suicide had gone about, she had so schooled herself for all emergencies that nothing could shake her self-possession, not even the suggestion that a woman of her beauty and distinction could be concerned in a crime. Or had she within herself some great source of strength, which sustained her in this most dreadful ordeal? All were on watch to see. When the veil dropped from before her features and she stepped into the full sight of the expectant crowd, it was not the beauty of her face, notable and conspicuous as that was, which roused the hum of surprise that swept from one end of the room to the other, but the calmness, almost the elevation of her manner, a calmness and elevation so unlooked for in the light of the strange contradictions offered by the evidence to which we had been listening for a day and a half, that all were affected; many inclined even to believe her innocent of any undue connection with her sister's death before she had stretched forth her hand to take the oath.

I was no exception to the rest. Though I had exerted myself from the first to bring matters to a climax— but not to this one—I experienced such a shock under the steady gaze of her sad but gentle eyes, that I found myself recoiling before my own presumption with something like secret shame till I was relieved by the thought that a perfectly innocent woman would show more feeling at so false and cruel a position. I felt that only one with something to conceal would turn so calm a front upon men ready, as she knew, to fix upon her a great crime. This conviction steadied me and made me less susceptible to her grace and to the tone of her quiet voice and the far-away sadness of her look. She faltered only when by chance she glanced at the shrinking figure of Francis Jeffrey.

Her name which she uttered without emphasis and yet in a way to arouse attention sank into all hearts with more or less disturbance. "Alice Cora Tuttle!" How in days gone by, and not so long gone by, either, those three words had aroused the enthusiasm of many a gallant man and inspired the toast at many a gallant feast! They had their charm yet, if the heightened color observable on many a cheek there was a true index to the quickening heart below.

"How are you connected with the deceased Mrs. Jeffrey?"

"I am the child of her mother by a former husband. We were half-sisters."

No bitterness in this statement, only an infinite sadness. The coroner continued to question her. He asked for an account of her childhood, and forced her to lay bare the nature of her relations with her sister. But little was gained by this, for their relations seemed to have been of a sympathetic character up to the time of Veronica's return from school, when they changed somewhat; but how or why, Miss Tuttle was naturally averse to saying. Indeed she almost refused to do so, and the coroner, feeling his point gained more by this refusal than by any admission she might have made, did not press this subject but passed on to what interested us more: the various unexplained actions on her part which pointed toward crime.

His first inquiry was in reference to the conversation held between her and Mr. Jeffrey at the time he visited her room. We had listened to his account of it and now we wished to hear hers. But the cue which had been given her by this very account had been invaluable to her, and her testimony naturally coincided with his. We found ourselves not an inch advanced. They had talked of her sister's follies and she had advised patience, and that was all she could say on the subject—all she would say, as we presently saw.

The coroner introduced a fresh topic.

"What can you tell us about the interview you had with you sister prior to her going out on the night of her death?"

"Very little, except that it differed entirely from what is generally supposed. She did not come to my room for conversation but simply to tell me that she had an engagement. She was in an excited mood but said nothing to alarm me. She even laughed when she left me; perhaps to put me off my guard, perhaps because she was no longer responsible."

"Did she know that Mr. Jeffrey had visited you earlier in the day? Did she make any allusion to it, I mean?"

"None at all. She shrugged her shoulders when I asked if she was well, and anticipated all further questions by running from the room. She was always capricious in her ways and never more so than at that moment. Would to God that it had been different! Would to God that she had shown herself to be a suffering woman! Then I might have reached her heart and this tragedy would have been averted."

The coroner favored the witness with a look of respect, perhaps because his next question must necessarily be cruel.

"Is that all you have to say concerning this important visit, the last you held with your sister before her death?"

"No, sir, there is something else, something which I should like to relate to this jury. When she came into my room, she held in her hand a white ribbon; that is, she held the two ends of a long satin ribbon which seemed to come from her pocket. Handing those two ends to me, she asked me to tie them about her wrist. 'A knot under and a bow on top,' she said, 'so that it can not slip off.' As this was something I had often been called on to do for her, I showed no hesitation in complying with her request. Indeed, I felt none. I thought it was her fan or her bouquet she held concealed in the folds of her dress, but it proved to be—Gentlemen, you know what. I pray that you will not oblige me to mention it."

It was such a stroke as no lawyer would have advised her to make,—I heard afterward that she had refused the offices of a dozen lawyers who had proffered her their services. But uttered as it was with a noble air and a certain dignified serenity, it had a great effect upon those about her and turned in a moment the wavering tide of favor in her direction.

The coroner, who doubtless was perfectly acquainted with the explanation with which she had provided herself, but who perhaps did not look for it to antedate his attack, bowed in quiet acknowledgment of her request and then immediately proceeded to ignore it.

"I should be glad to spare you," said he, "but I do not find it possible. You knew that Mr. Jeffrey had a pistol?"

"I did."

"That it was kept in their apartment?"

"Yes."

"In the upper drawer of a certain bureau?"

"Yes."

"Now, Miss Tuttle, will you tell us why you went to that drawer—if you did go to that drawer—immediately after Mrs. Jeffrey left the house?"

She had probably felt this question coming, not only since the coroner began to speak but ever since the evidence elicited from Loretta proved that her visit to this drawer had been secretly observed. Yet she had no answer ready.

"I did not go for the pistol," she finally declared. But she did not say what she had gone for, and the coroner did not press her.

Again the tide swung back.

She seemed to feel the change but did not show it in the way naturally looked for. Instead of growing perturbed or openly depressed she bloomed into greater beauty and confronted with steadier eye, not us, but the men she instinctively faced as the tide of her fortunes began to lower. Did the coroner perceive this and recognize at last both the measure of her attractions and the power they were likely to carry with them? Perhaps, for his voice took an acrid note as he declared:

"You had another errand in that room?"

She let her head droop just a trifle.

"Alas!" she murmured.

"You went to the book-shelves and took out a book with a peculiar cover, a cover which Mr. Jeffrey has already recognized as that of the book in which he found a certain note."

"You have said it," she faltered.

"Did you take such a book out?"

"I did."

"For what purpose, Miss Tuttle?"

She had meant to answer quickly. But some consideration made her hesitate and the words were long in coming; when she did speak, it was to say:

"My sister asked another favor of me after I had tied the ribbon. Pausing in her passage to the door, she informed me in a tone quite in keeping with her whole manner, that she had left a note for her husband in the book they were reading together. Her reason for doing this, she said, was the very natural one of wishing him to come upon it by chance, but as she had placed it in the front of the book instead of in the back where they were reading, she was afraid that he would fail to find it. Would I be so good as to take it out for her and insert it again somewhere near the end? She was in a hurry or she would return and do it herself. As she and Mr. Jeffrey had parted in anger, I hailed with joy this evidence of her desire for a reconciliation, and it was in obedience to her request, the singularity of which did not strike me as forcibly then as now, that I went to the shelves in her room and took down the book."

"And did you find the note where she said?"

"Yes, and put it in toward the end of the story."

"Nothing more? Did you read the note?"

"It was folded," was Miss Tuttle's quiet answer. Certainly this woman was a thoroughbred or else she was an adept in deception such as few of us had ever encountered. The gentleness of her manner, the easy tone, the quiet eyes, eyes in whose dark depths great passions were visible, but passions that were under the control of an equally forcible will, made her a puzzle to all men's minds; but it was a fascinating puzzle that awoke a species of awe in those who attempted to understand her. To all appearances she was the unlikeliest woman possible to cherish criminal intents, yet her answers were rather clever than convincing, unless you allowed yourself to be swayed by the look of her beautiful face or the music of her rich, sad voice.

"You did not remain before these book-shelves long?" observed the coroner.

"You have a witness who knows more about that than I do," she suggested; and doubtless aware of the temerity of this reply, waited with unmoved countenance, but with a visibly bounding breast, for what would doubtless prove a fresh attack.

It was a violent one and of a character she was least fitted to meet. Taking up the box I have so often mentioned, the coroner drew away the ribbon lying on top and disclosed the pistol. In a moment her hands were over her ears.

"Why do you do that?" he asked. "Did you think I was going to discharge it?"

She smiled pitifully as she let her hands fall again.

"I have a dread of firearms," she explained. "I always have had. Now they are simply terrible to me, and this one—"

"I understand," said the coroner, with a slight glance in the direction of Durbin. They had evidently planned this test together on the strength of an idea suggested to Durbin by her former action when the memory of this shot was recalled to her.

"Your horror seems to lie in the direction of the noise they make," continued her inexorable interlocutor. "One would say you had heard this pistol discharged."

Instantly a complete breaking-up of her hitherto well maintained composure altered her whole aspect and she vehemently cried:

"I did, I did. I was on Waverley Avenue that night, and I heard the shot which in all probability ended my sister's life. I walked farther than I intended; I strolled into the street which had such bitter memories for us and I heard—No, I was not in search of my sister. I had not associated my sister's going out with any intention of visiting this house; I was merely troubled in mind and anxious and—and—"

She had overrated her strength or her cleverness. She found herself unable to finish the sentence, and so did not try. She had been led by the impulse of the moment farther than she had intended, and, aghast at her own imprudence, paused with her first perceptible loss of courage before the yawning gulf opening before her.

I felt myself seized by a very uncomfortable dread lest her concealments and unfinished sentences hid a guiltier knowledge of this crime than I was yet ready to admit.

The coroner, who is an older man than myself, betrayed a certain satisfaction but no dread. Never did the unction which underlies his sharpest speeches show more plainly than when he quietly remarked:

"And so under a similar impulse you, as well as Mr. Jeffrey, chose this uncanny place to ramble in. To all appearance that old hearth acted much more like a lodestone upon members of your family than you were willing at one time to acknowledge."

This reference to words she had herself been heard to use seemed to overwhelm her. Her calmness fled and she cast a fleeting look of anguish at Mr. Jeffrey. But his face was turned from sight, and, meeting with no help there, or anywhere, indeed, save in her own powerful nature, she recovered as best she could the ground she had lost and, with a trembling question of her own, attempted to put the coroner in fault and reestablish herself.

"You say 'ramble through.' Do you for a moment think that I entered that old house?"

"Miss Tuttle," was the grave, almost sad reply, "did you not know that in some earth, dropped from a flower-pot overturned at the time when a hundred guests flew in terror from this house, there is to be seen the mark of a footstep,—a footstep which you are at liberty to measure with your own?"

"Ah!" she murmured, her hands going up to her face.

But in another moment she had dropped them and looked directly at the coroner.

"I walked there—I never said that I did not walk there—when I went later to see my sister and in sight of a number of detectives passed straight through the halls and into the library."

"And that this footstep," inexorably proceeded the coroner, "is not in a line with the main thoroughfare extending from the front to the back of the house, but turned inwards toward the wall as if she who made it had stopped to lean her head against the partition?"

Miss Tuttle's head drooped. Probably she realized at this moment, if not before, that the coroner and jury had ample excuse for mistrusting one who had been so unmistakably caught in a prevarication; possibly her regret carried her far enough to wish she had not disdained all legal advice from those who had so earnestly offered it. But though she showed alike her shame and her disheartenment, she did not give up the struggle.

"If I went into the house," she said, "it was not to enter that room. I had too great a dread of it. If I rested my head against the wall it was in terror of that shot. It came so suddenly and was so frightful, so much more frightful than anything you can conceive."

"Then you did enter the house?"

"I did."

"And it was while you were inside, instead of outside, that you heard the shot?"

"I must admit that, too. I was at the library door."

"You acknowledge that?"

"I do."

"But you did not enter the library?"

"No, not then; not till I was taken back by the officer who told me of my sister's death."

"We are glad to hear this precise statement from you. It encourages me to ask again the nature of the freak which took you into this house. You say that it was not from any dread on your sister's account? What, then, was it? No evasive answer will satisfy us, Miss Tuttle."

She realized this as no one else could.

Mr. Jeffrey's reason for his visit there could not be her reason, yet what other had she to give? Apparently none.

"I can not answer," she said.

And the deep sigh which swept through the room was but an echo of the despair with which she saw herself brought to this point.

"We will not oblige you to," said the coroner with apparent consideration. But to those who knew the law against forcing a witness to incriminate himself, this was far from an encouraging concession.

"However," he now went on, with suddenly assumed severity, "you may answer this. Was the house dark or light when you entered it? And, how did you get in?"

"The house was dark, and I got in through the front door, which I found ajar."

"You are more courageous than most women! I fear there are few of your sex who could be induced to enter it in broad daylight and under every suitable protection."

She raised her figure proudly.

"Miss Tuttle, you have heard Chloe say that you were in the kitchen of Mr. Jeffrey's house when the grocer boy delivered the candles which had been left by your brother-in-law on the counter of the store where he bought them. Is this true?"

"Yes, sir, it is true."

"Did you see those candles?"

"No, sir."

"You did not see them?"

"No, sir."

"Yet you went over to the table?"

"Yes, sir, but I did not meddle with the packages. I had really no business with them."

The coroner, surveying her sadly, went quickly on as if anxious to terminate this painful examination.

"You have not told us what you did when you heard that pistol-shot."

"I ran away as soon as I could move; I ran madly from the house."

"Where?"

"Home."

"But it was half-past ten when you got home."

"Was it?"

"It was half-past ten when the man came to tell you of your sister's death."

"It may have been."

"Your sister is supposed to have died in a few minutes. Where were you in the interim?"

"God knows. I do not."

A wild look was creeping into her face, and her figure was swaying. But she soon steadied it. I have never seen a more admirable presence maintained in the face of a dreadful humiliation.

"Perhaps I can help you," rejoined the coroner, not unkindly. "Were you not in the Congressional Library looking up at the lunettes and gorgeously painted walls?"

"I?" Her eyes opened wide in wondering doubt. "If I was, I did not know it. I have no remembrance of it."

She seemed to lose sight of her present position, the cloud under which she rested, and even the construction which might be put upon such a forgetfulness at a time confessedly prior to her knowledge of the purpose and effect of the shot from which she had so incontinently fled.

"Your condition of mind and that of Mr. Jeffrey seem to have been strangely alike," remarked the coroner.

"No, no!" she protested.

"Arguing a like source."

"No, no," she cried again, this time with positive agony. Then with an effort which awakened respect for her powers of mind, if for nothing else, she desperately added: "I can not say what was in his heart that night, but I know what was in mine—dread of that old house, to which I had been drawn in spite of myself, possibly by the force of the tragedy going on inside it, culminating in a delirium of terror, which sent me flying in an opposite direction from my home and into places I had been accustomed to visit when my heart was light and untroubled."

The coroner glanced at the jury, who unconsciously shook their heads. He shook his, too, as he returned to the charge.

"Another question, Miss Tuttle. When you heard a pistol-shot sounding from the depths of that dark library, what did you think it meant?"

She put her hands over her ears—it seemed as if she could not prevent this instinctive expression of recoil at the mention of the death-dealing weapon—and in very low tones replied:

"Something dreadful; something superstitious. It was night, you remember, and at night one has such horrible thoughts."

"Yet an hour or two later you declared that the hearth was no lodestone. You forgot its horrors and your superstition upon returning to your own house."

"It might be;" she murmured; "but if so, they soon returned. I had reason for my horror, if not for my superstition, as the event showed."

The coroner did not attempt to controvert this. He was about to launch a final inquiry.

"Miss Tuttle; upon the return of yourself and Mr. Jeffrey to your home after your final visit to the Moore house, did you have any interview that was without witnesses?"

"No."

"Did you exchange any words?"

"I think we did exchange some words; it would be only natural."

"Are you willing to state what words?"

She looked dazed and appeared to search her memory.

"I don't think I can," she objected.

"But something was said by you and some answer was made by him?"

"I believe so."

"Can not you say definitely?"

"We did speak."

"In English?"

"No, in French."

"Can not you translate that French for us?"

"Pardon me, sir; it was so long ago my memory fails me."

"Is it any better for the second and longer interview between you the next day?"

"No-sir."

"You can not give us any phrase or word that was uttered there?"

"No."

"Is this your final reply on this subject?"

"It is."

She never had been subjected to an interrogation like this before. It made her proud soul quiver in revolt, notwithstanding the patience with which she had fortified herself. With red cheeks and glistening eyes she surveyed the man who had made her suffer so, and instantly every other man there suffered with her; excepting possibly Durbin, whose heart was never his strong point. But our hearts were moved, our reasons were not convinced, as was presently shown, when, with a bow of dismissal, the coroner released her, and she passed back to her seat.

Simultaneously with her withdrawal the gleam of sensibility left the faces of the jury, and the dark and brooding look which had marked their countenances from the beginning returned, and returned to stay.

What would their verdict be? There were present two persons who affected to believe that it would be one of suicide occasioned by dementia. These were Miss Tuttle and Mr. Jeffrey, who, now that the critical period had come, straightened themselves boldly in their seats and met the glances concentrated upon them with dignity, if not with the assurance of complete innocence. But from the carefulness with which they avoided each other's eyes and the almost identical expression mirrored upon both faces, it was visible to all that they regarded their cause as a common one, and that the link which they denied, as having existed between them prior to Mrs. Jeffrey's death, had in some way been supplied by that very tragedy; so that they now unwittingly looked with the same eyes, breathed with the same breath, and showed themselves responsive to the same fluctuations of hope and fear.

The celerity with which that jury arrived at its verdict was a shock to us all. It had been a quiet body, offering but little assistance to the coroner in his questioning; but when it fell to these men to act, the precision with which they did so was astonishing. In a half-hour they returned from the room into which they had adjourned, and the foreman gave warning that he was prepared to render a verdict.

Mr. Jeffrey and Miss Tuttle both clenched their hands; then Miss Tuttle pulled down her veil.

"We find," said the solemn foreman, "that Veronica Moore Jeffrey, who on the night of May eleventh was discovered lying dead on the floor of her own unoccupied house in Waverley Avenue, came to her death by means of a bullet, shot from a pistol connected to her wrist by a length of white satin ribbon.

"That the first conclusion of suicide is not fully sustained by the facts;

"And that attempt should be made to identify the hand that fired this pistol."

It was as near an accusation of Miss Tuttle as was possible without mentioning her name. A groan passed through the assemblage, and Mr. Jeffrey, bounding to his feet, showed an inclination to shout aloud in his violent indignation. But Miss Tuttle, turning toward him, lifted her hand with a commanding gesture and held it so till he sat down again.

It was both a majestic and an utterly incomprehensible movement on her part, giving to the close of these remarkable proceedings a dramatic climax which set all hearts beating and, I am bound to say, all tongues wagging till the room cleared.

CHAPTER XVI

Had the control of affairs been mine at this moment I am quite positive that I should have found it difficult to deny these two the short interview which they appeared to crave and which would have been to them such an undeniable comfort. But a sterner spirit than mine was in charge, and the district attorney, into whose hands the affair had now fallen, was inexorable. Miss Tuttle was treated with respect, with kindness, even, but she was not allowed any communication with her brother-in-law beyond the formal "Good afternoon" incident upon their separation; while he, scorning to condemn his lips to any such trite commonplace, said nothing at all, only looked a haggard inquiry which called forth from her the most exalted look of patience and encouraging love it has ever been my good fortune to witness. Durbin was standing near and saw this look as plainly as I did, but it did not impose on him, he said. But what in the nature of human woe could impose on him? Durbin is a machine—a very reliable and useful machine, no doubt, yet when all is said, a simple contrivance of cogs and wheels; while I— well, I hope that I am something more than that; or why was I a changed man toward her from the moment I saw the smile which marked this accused woman's good by to Francis Jeffrey. No longer believing in her guilt, I went about my business with tumult in brain and heart, asking in my remorse for an opportunity to show her some small courtesy whereby to relieve the torture I felt at having helped the coroner in the inquiries which had brought about what looked to me now like a cruel and unwarranted result.

That it should be given to Durbin to hold such surveillance over her as her doubtful position demanded added greatly to my discomfort. But I was enabled to keep my lips firmly shut over any expression of secret jealousy or displeasure; and this was fortunate, as otherwise I might have failed to obtain the chance of aiding her later on, in other and deeper matters.

Meanwhile, and before any of us had left this room, one fact had become apparent. Mr. Jeffrey was not going to volunteer any fresh statement in face of the distinct disapproval of his sister-in-law. As his eye fell upon the district attorney, who had lingered near, possibly in the hope of getting something more from this depressed and almost insensible man, he made one remark, but it was an automatic one, calculated to produce but little effect on the discriminating ears of this experienced official.

"I do not believe that my wife was murdered." This was what he said. "It was a wicked verdict. My wife killed herself. Wasn't the pistol found tied to her?"

Either from preoccupation or a dazed condition of mind, he seemed to forget that Miss Tuttle had owned to tying on this pistol; and that nothing but her word went to prove that this was done before and not after the shot had been delivered in the Moore house library. I thought I understood him and was certain that I sympathized with his condition; but in the ears of those less amiably disposed toward him, his statements had lost force and the denial went for little.

Meanwhile a fact which all had noted and commented on had recurred to my mind and caused me to ask a brother officer who was walking out beside me what he thought of Mr. Moore's absence from an inquiry presumably of such importance to all members of this family.

The fellow laughed and said:

"Old Dave has lost none of his peculiarities in walking into his fortune. This is his day at the cemetery. Didn't you know that? He will let nothing on earth get in the way of his pilgrimage to that spot on the twenty-third of May, much less so trivial an occurrence as an inquest over the remains of his nearest relative."

I felt my gorge rise; then a thought struck me and I asked how long the old gentleman kept up his watch.

"From sunrise to sundown, the boys say. I never saw him there myself. My beat lies in an opposite direction."

I left him and started for Rock Creek Cemetery. There were two good hours yet before sundown and I resolved to come upon Uncle David at his post.

It took just one hour and a quarter to get there by the most direct route I could take. Five minutes more to penetrate the grounds to where a superb vehicle stood, drawn by two of the finest horses I had seen in Washington for many a long day. As I was making my way around this equipage I came upon a plot in a condition of upheaval preparatory to new sodding and the planting of several choice shrubs. In the midst of the sand thus exposed a single head-stone rose. On his knees beside this simple monument I saw the figure of Uncle David, dressed in his finest clothes and showing in his oddly contorted face the satisfaction of great prosperity, battling with the dissatisfaction of knowing that one he had so loved had not lived to share his elevation. He was rubbing away the mold from the name which, by his own confession, was the only one to which his memory clung in sympathy or endearment. At his feet lay an open basket, in which I detected the remains of what must have been a rather sumptuous cold repast. To all appearance he had foregone none of his ancient customs; only those customs had taken on elegance with his rise in fortune. The carriage and the horses, and most of all, the imperturbable driver, seemed to awaken some awe in the boys. They were still in evidence, but they hung back sheepishly and eyed the basket of neglected food as if they hoped he would forget to take it away. Meanwhile the clattering of chains against the harness, the pawing of the horses and the low exclamations of the driver caused me the queerest feelings. Advancing quite unceremoniously upon the watcher by the grave, I remarked aloud;

"The setting sun will soon release you, Mr. Moore. Are you going immediately into town?"

He paused in his rubbing, which was being done with a very tender hand, and as if he really loved the name he was endeavoring to bring into plainer view. Scowling a little, he turned and met me point-blank with a look which had a good deal of inquiry in it.

"I am not usually interrupted here," he emphasized; "except by the boys," he added more mildly. "They sometimes approach too closely, but I am used to the imps and scarcely notice them. Ah! there are some of my old friends now! Well, it is time they knew that a change has taken place in my fortunes. Hi, there! Hands up and catch this, and this, and this!" he shouted. "But keep quiet about it or next year you will get pennies again."

And flinging quarters right and left, he smiled in such a pompous, self-satisfied way at the hurrah and scramble which ensued, that it was well worth my journey there just to see this exhibition of combined vanity and good humor.

"Now go!" he vociferated; and the urchins, black and white, flew away, flinging up their heels in delight and shouting: "Bully for you, Uncle David! We'll come again next year, not for twenty-fives but fifties."

"I will make it dollars if I only live so long," he muttered. And deigning now to remember the question I had put to him, he grandly remarked:

"I am going straight into town. Can I do anything for you?"

"Nothing. I thought you might like to know what awaits you there. The city is greatly stirred up. The coroner's jury in the Jeffrey-Moore case has just brought in a verdict to the effect that suicide has not been proved. Naturally, this is equivalent to one of murder."

"Ah!" he ejaculated, slightly taken aback for one so invariably impassive.

"And to whom is the guilt of this crime ascribed?" he presently ventured.

"There was mention of no name; but the opprobrium naturally falls on Miss Tuttle."

"Miss Tuttle? Ah!"

"Since Mr. Jeffrey is proved to have been too far away at the time to have fired that shot, while she—"

"I am following you—"

"Was in the very house—at the door of the library in fact—and heard the pistol discharged, if she did not discharge it herself—which some believe, notably the district attorney. You should have been there, Mr. Moore."

He looked surprised at this suggestion.

"I never am anywhere but here on the twenty-third of May," he declared.

"Miss Tuttle needed some adviser."

"Ah, probably."

"You would have been a good one."

"And a welcome one, eh?"

I hardly thought he would have been a welcome one, but I did not admit the fact. Nevertheless he seized on the advantage he evidently thought he had gained and added, mildly enough, or rather without any display of feeling:

"Miss Tuttle likes me even less than Veronica did. I do not think she would have accepted, certainly she would not have desired, my presence in her counsels. But of one thing I wish her to be assured, her and the world in general. Any money she may need at this—at this unhappy crisis in her life, she will find amply supplied. She has no claims on me, but that makes little difference where the family honor is concerned. Her mother's husband was my brother—the girl shall have all she needs. I will write her so."

He was moving toward his carriage.

"Fine turnout?" he interrogatively remarked.

I assented with all the surprise,—with all the wonder even—which his sublime egotism seemed to invite.

"It is the best that Downey could raise in the time I allotted him. When I really finger the money, we shall see, we shall see."

His foot was on the carriage-step. He looked up at the west. The sun was almost down but not quite. "Have you any special business with me?" he asked, lingering with what I thought a surprising display of conscientiousness till the last ray of direct sunlight had disappeared.

I glanced up at the coachman sitting on his box as rigid as any stone.

"You may speak," said he; "Caesar neither hears nor sees anything but his horses when he drives me."

The black did not wink. He was as completely at home on the box and as quiet and composed in his service as if he had driven this man for years.

"He understands his duty," finished the master, but with no outward appearance of pride. "What have you to say to me?"

I hesitated no longer.

"Miss Tuttle is supposed to have secretly entered the Moore house on the night you summoned us. She even says she did. I know that you have sworn to having seen no one go into that house; but notwithstanding this, haven't you some means at your disposal for proving to the police and to the world at large that she never fired that fatal shot? Public opinion is so cruel. She will be ruined whether innocent or guilty, unless it can be very plainly shown that she did not enter the library prior to going there with the police."

"And how can you suppose me to be in a position to prove that? Say that I had sat in my front window all that evening, and watched with uninterrupted assiduity the door through which so many are said to have passed between sunset and midnight—something which I did not do, as I have plainly stated on oath—how could you have expected me to see what went on in the black interior of a house whose exterior is barely discernible at night across the street?"

"Then you can not aid her?" I asked.

With a light bound he leaped into the carriage. As he took his seat he politely remarked:

"I should be glad to, since, though not a Moore, she is near enough the family to affect its honor. But not having even seen her enter the house I can not testify in any way in regard to her. Home, Caesar, and drive quickly. I do not thrive under these evening damps."

And leaning back, with an inexpressible air of contentment with himself, his equipage and the prospect of an indefinite enjoyment of the same, the last representative of the great Moore family was quietly driven away.

CHAPTER XVII

A FRESH START

I was far from being good company that night. I knew this without being told. My mind was too busy. I was too full of regrets and plans, seasonings and counter reasonings. In my eyes Miss Tuttle had suddenly become innocent, consequently a victim. But a victim to what? To some exaggerated sense of duty? Possibly; but to what duty? That was the question, to answer which offhand I would, in my present excitement, have been ready to sacrifice a month's pay.

For I was moved, not only by the admiration and sympathy which all men must feel for a beautiful woman caught in such a deadly snare of circumstantial evidence, but by the conviction that Durbin, whose present sleek complacency was more offensive to me than the sneering superiority of a week ago, believed her to be a guilty woman, and as such his rightful prey. This alone would have influenced me to take the opposite view; for we never ran along together, and in a case where any division of opinion was possible, always found ourselves, consciously or unconsciously, on different sides. Yet I did not really dislike Durbin, who is a very fine fellow. I only hated his success and the favor which rewarded it.

I know that I have some very nasty failings and I do not shrink from owning them. My desire is to represent myself as I am, and I must admit that it was not entirely owing to disinterested motives that I now took the secret stand I did in Miss Tuttle's favor. To prove her innocent whom once I considered the cause of, if not the guilty accessory to her sister's murder, now became my dream by night and my occupation by day. Though I seemed to have no sympathizer in this effort and though the case against her was being pushed very openly in the district attorney's office, yet I clung to my convictions with an almost insensate persistence, inwardly declaring her the victim of circumstances, and hoping against hope that some clue would offer itself by means of which I might yet prove her so. But where was I to seek for this clue?

Alas, no ready answer to this very important query was forthcoming. All possible evidence in this case seemed to have been exhausted save such as Mr. Jeffrey and Miss Tuttle withheld. And so the monstrous accusation stood, and before it all Washington—my humble self included—stood in a daze of mingled doubt and compassion, hunting for explanations which failed to appear and seeking in vain for some guiltier party, who evermore slipped from under our hand. Had Mr. Jeffrey's alibi been less complete he could not have stood up against the suspicions which now ran riot. But there was no possibility of shifting the actual crime back to him after the testimony of so frank and trustworthy a man as Tallman. If the stopping of Mrs. Jeffrey's watch fixed the moment of her death as accurately as was supposed,—and I never heard the least doubt thrown out in this regard,—he could not by any means of transit then known in Washington have reached Waverley Avenue in time to fire that shot. The gates of the cemetery were closed at sundown; sundown took place that night at one minute past seven, and the distance into town is considerable. His alibi could not be gainsaid. So his name failed to be publicly broached in connection with the shooting, though his influence over Miss Tuttle could not be forgotten, suggesting to some that she had acted as his hand in the deed which robbed him of an undesirable wife. But this I would not believe. I preferred to accept the statement that she had stopped short of the library door in her suspicious visit there, and that the ribbon-tying, which went for so much, had been done at home. That these facts, especially the latter, called for more than common credulity, I was quite ready to acknowledge; and had her feeling for Francis Jeffrey shown less unselfishness, I should certainly have joined my fellows in regarding these assertions as very lame attempts to explain what could only be explained by a confession of guilt.

So here was a tangle without a frayed end to pull at, unless the impervious egotism of Uncle David afforded one, which I doubted. For how could any man with a frightful secret in his breast show that unmixed delight in his new equipage and suddenly acquired position, which had so plainly beamed from that gentleman's calm eye and assured bearing? When he met my scrutiny in the sacred precincts where the one love of his heart lay buried, he did so without a quiver or any sign of inner disturbance. His tone to Caesar as he drove off had been the tone of a man who can afford to speak quietly because he is conscious of being so undeniably the master; and when his foot rose to the carriage step it was with the confidence of one who had been kept out of his rights for most of his natural life, but who feels in his present enjoyment of them no apprehension of a change. His whole bearing and conversation on that day were, as I am quite ready to admit, an exhibition of prodigious selfishness; but it was also an exhibition of mental poise incompatible with a consciousness of having acquired his fortune by any means which laid him open to the possibility of losing it. Or so I judged.

Finding myself, with every new consideration of the tantalizing subject, deeper and deeper in the quagmire of doubt and uncertainty, I sought enlightenment by making a memorandum of the special points which must have influenced the jury in their verdict, as witness:

1. The relief shown by Mr. Jeffrey at finding an apparent communication from his wife hinting at suicide.

2. The possibility, disclosed by the similarity between the sisters' handwriting, of this same communication being a forgery substituted for the one really written by Mrs. Jeffrey.

3. The fact that, previous to Mr. Jeffrey's handling of the book in which this communication was said to have been hidden, it had been seen in Miss Tuttle's hands.

4. That immediately after this she had passed to the drawer where Mr. Jeffrey's pistol was kept.

5. That while this pistol had not been observed in her hand, there was as yet no evidence to prove that it had been previously taken from the drawer, save such as was afforded by her own acknowledgment that she had tied some unknown object, presumably the pistol, to her sister's wrist before that sister left the house.

6. That if this was so, the pistol and the ribbon connecting it with Mrs. Jeffrey's wrist had been handled again before the former was discharged, and by fingers which had first touched dust—of which there was plenty in the old library.

7. That Miss Tuttle had admitted, though not till after much prevarication and apparent subterfuge, that she had extended her walk on that fatal night not only as far as the Moore house, but that she had entered it and penetrated as far as the library door at the very moment the shot was fired within.

8. That in acknowledging this she had emphatically denied having associated the firing of this shot with any idea of harm to her sister; yet was known to have gone from this house in a condition of mind so

serious that she failed to recollect the places she visited or the streets she passed through till she found herself again in her sister's house face to face with an officer.

9. That her first greeting of this officer was a shriek, betraying a knowledge of his errand before he had given utterance to a word.

10. That the candles found in the Moore house were similar to those bought by Mr. Jeffrey and afterward delivered at his kitchen door.

11. That she was the only member of the household besides the cook who was in the kitchen at the time, and that it was immediately after her departure from the room that the package containing the candles had been missed.

12. That opportunities of coming to an understanding with Mr. Jeffrey after his wife's death had not been lacking and it was not until after such opportunities had occurred that any serious inquiry into this matter had been begun by the police. To which must be added, not in way of proof but as an important factor in the case, that her manner, never open, was such throughout her whole public examination as to make it evident to all that only half of what had occurred in the Jeffreys' house since the wedding had been given out by her or by the man for whose release from a disappointing matrimonial entanglement she was supposed to have worked; this, though the suspicion hanging over them both called for the utmost candor.

Verily, a serious list; and opposed to this I had as yet little to offer but my own belief in her innocence and the fact, but little dwelt on and yet not without its value, that the money which had come to Mr. Jeffrey, and the home which had been given her, had both been forfeited by Mrs. Jeffrey's death.

As I mused and mused over this impromptu synopsis, in my vain attempt to reach some fresh clue to a proper understanding of the inconsistencies in Miss Tuttle's conduct by means of my theory of her strong but mistaken devotion to Mr. Jeffrey, a light suddenly broke upon me from an entirely unexpected quarter. It was a faint one, but any glimmer was welcome. Remembering a remark made by Mr. Jeffrey in his examination, that Mrs. Jeffrey had not been the same since crossing the fatal doorstep of the Moore house, I asked myself if we had paid enough attention to the mental condition and conduct of the bride prior to the alarm which threw a pall of horror over her marriage; and caught by the idea, I sought for a fuller account of the events of that day than had hitherto been supplied by newspaper or witness.

Hunting up my friend, the reporter, I begged him to tell me where he had obtained the facts from which he made that leading article in the Star which had so startled all Washington on the evening of the Jeffrey wedding. That they had come from some eye-witness I had no doubt, but who was the eye-witness? Himself? No. Who then? At first he declined to tell me, but after a fuller understanding of my motives he mentioned the name of a young lady, who, while a frequent guest at the most fashionable functions, was not above supplying the papers with such little items of current gossip as came under her own observation.

How I managed to approach this lady and by what means I succeeded in gaining her confidence are details quite unnecessary to this narrative. Enough that I did obtain access to her and that she talked quite frankly to me, and in so doing supplied me with a clue which ultimately opened up to me an entirely new field of inquiry. We had been discussing Mr. Jeffrey and Miss Tuttle, when suddenly, and with no apparent motive beyond the natural love of gossip which was her weakness, she launched out into remarks about the bride. The ceremony had been late; did I know it? A half-hour or three-quarters past the time set for it. And why? Because Miss Moore was not ready. She had chosen to array herself in the house and had come early enough for the purpose; but she would not accept any assistance, not even that of her maid, and of course she kept every one waiting. "Oh, there was no more uneasy soul in the whole party that morning than the bride!" Let other people remark upon the high look in Cora Tuttle's face, or gossip about the anxious manner of the bridegroom; she, the speaker, could tell things about the bride which would go to show that she was not all right even before that ominous death's-head reared itself into view at her marriage festival. Why, the fact that she came downstairs and was married without her bridal bouquet was enough. Had there not been so much else to talk about, people would have talked about that. But the big event had so effectually swallowed up the little that only herself, and possibly two other ladies she might name, seemed to retain any memory of the matter.

"What ladies?" I asked.

"Oh, it doesn't matter what ladies. Two of the very best sort. I know they noticed it, because I heard them talking about it. We were all standing in the upper hall and were all crowded into a passage leading to the room where the bride was dressing. It was before the alarm had gone around of what had been discovered in the library, and we were all impatient enough for the appearance of the bride, who, we had been told, intended to wear the old point in which her great-grandmother was married. I have a weakness for old point and I was determined to stand where I could see her come out, even if I lost sight of the ceremony itself. But it would have been tedious enough waiting in that close hall if the ladies behind me had not kept up a conversation, which I, of course, pretended not to hear. I remember it, every word, for it was my sole amusement for half an hour. What was it? Oh, it was about that same bouquet, which, by the way, I had the privilege of staring at all the time they chatted. For the boy who brought it had not been admitted into Miss Moore's room, and, not knowing what else to do with it, was lingering before her door, with the great streamers falling from his hands, and the lilies making the whole place heavy with a sickening perfume. From what I heard the ladies say, he had been standing there an hour, and the timid knock he gave from time to time produced in me an odd feeling which those ladies behind me seemed to share.

"'It's a shame!' I heard one of them cry. 'Veronica Moore has no excuse for such thoughtlessness. It is an hour now that she has been shut up in her room alone. She won't have even her maid in. She prefers to dress alone, she says. Peculiar in a bride, isn't it? But one thing is certain: she can not put on her veil without help. She will have to call some one in for that.' At which the other volunteered that the Moores were all queer, and that she didn't envy Francis Jeffrey. 'What! not with fifty thousand a year to lighten her oddities?' returned her companion with a shrug which communicated itself to me, so closely were we packed together. 'I have a son who could bear with them under such circumstances.' Indeed she has, and all Washington knows it, but the remark passed without comment, for they had not yet exhausted the main event, and the person they now attacked was Miss Tuttle. 'Why doesn't she come and see that that bouquet is taken in? I declare it's not decent. Mr. Jeffrey would not feel complimented if he knew the fate of those magnificent lilies and roses. I presume he furnished the bouquet.'

"'Miss Tuttle has looked out of her room once,' I heard the other reply. 'She is in splendid beauty to-day, but pale. But she never could control Veronica.' 'Hush! you speak louder than you think' This amused me, and I do believe that in another moment I should have laughed outright if another boy had not appeared in the hall before us, who, shoving aside the first, rapped on the door with a spirit which called for answer. But he was no more successful than the other boy had been; so, being a brisk fellow, with no time for nonsense, he called out, 'Your bouquet, Miss, and a message, which I am to give you before you go downstairs! The gentleman is quite particular about it.' These words were literally shouted at the door, but in the hubbub of voices about us I don't believe any one heard them but ourselves and the bride. I know that she heard them, for she opened the door a very little way,—such a very little way that the boy had to put his lips to the crack when he spoke, and then turn and place his ear where his lips had been in order to catch her reply. This, for some reason, seemed a long time in coming, and the fellow grew so impatient that he amused himself by snatching the bouquet from the other boy and thrusting it in through the crack, to the very great detriment of its roses and lilies. When she took it he bawled for his answer, and when he got it, he stared and muttered doubtfully to himself as he worked his way out again through the crowd, which by this time was beginning to choke up all the halls and stairways.

"But why have I told you all this nonsense?" she asked quite suddenly. "It isn't of the least consequence that Veronica Moore kept a boy waiting at her door while she dressed herself for her wedding; but it shows that she was queer even then, and I for one believe in the theory of suicide, and in that alone, and in the excuse she gave for it, too; for if she had really loved Francis Jeffrey she would not have been so slow to take in the magnificent bouquet he had provided for her."

But comment, even from those who had known these people well, was not what I wanted at this moment, but facts. So, without much attention to these words, I said:

"You will excuse me if I suggest that you are going on too fast. The door of the bride's room has just been shut upon the boy who brought her a message. When was it opened again?"

"Not for a good half-hour; not till every one had grown nervous and Miss Tuttle and one or two of her most intimate friends had gone more than once to her door; not, in fact, till the hour for the ceremony had come and gone and Mr. Jeffrey had crossed the hall twice under the impression that she was ready for him. Then, when weariness was general and people were asking what kept the bride and how much longer they were to be kept waiting, her door suddenly opened and I caught a glimpse of her face and heard her ask at last for her maid. O, I repeat that Veronica Moore was not all right that day, and though I have heard no one comment on the fact, it has been a mystery to me ever since why she gave that sudden recoil when Francis Jeffrey took her hand after the benediction. It was not timidity, nor was it fear, for she did not know till a minute afterward what had happened in the house. Did some sudden realization of what she had done in marrying a man whom she herself declared she did not love come when it was too late? What do you think?"

Miss Freeman had forgotten herself; but the impetuosity which had led her into asking my opinion made her forget in another moment that she had done so. And when in my turn I propounded a question and inquired whether she ever again saw the boy who besieged the bride's door with a message, she graciously replied:

"The boy; let me see. Yes, I saw him twice; once in a back hall talking earnestly to Mr. Jeffrey, and secondly at the carriage door just before the bridal party rode away. It was Mrs. Jeffrey who was talking to him then, and I wondered to see him look so pleased when everybody in and about the house was pale as ashes."

"Do you know the name of that boy?" I carelessly inquired.

"His name? O no. He is one of Raucher's waiters; the curly-haired one. You see him everywhere; but I don't know his name. Do you flatter yourself that he can tell you anything that other people don't know? Why, if he knew the least thing that wasn't in everybody's mouth, you would have heard from him long ago. Those men are the greatest gossips in town"—I wonder what she thought of herself,— "and so proud to be of any importance." This was true enough, though I did not admit it at the time; and when the interview was closed and I went away, I have no doubt she considered me quite the most heavy person she had ever met. But this did not disturb me. The little facts she had stated were new to me and, repeating my former method, I was already busy arranging them in my mind. Witness the result:

1. The ceremony of marriage between Francis Jeffrey and Veronica Moore was fully three-quarters of an hour late.

2. This was owing to the caprice of the bride, who would not have any one in the room with her, not even her maid.

3. The bridal bouquet did not figure in the ceremony. In the flurry of the moment it was forgotten or purposely left behind by the bride. As this bouquet was undoubtedly the gift of Mr. Jeffrey, the fact may be significant.

4. She received a message of a somewhat peremptory character before going below. From whom? Her bridegroom? It would so appear from the character of the message.

5. The messenger showed great astonishment at the reply he was given to carry back. Yet he has not been known to mention the matter. Why? When every one talked he was silent. Through whose influence? This was something to find out.

6. Though at the time the benediction was pronounced every one was in a state of alarm except the bride, it was noticed that she gave an involuntary recoil when her bridegroom stooped for the customary kiss. Why? Were the lines of her last farewell true then, and did she experience at that moment a sudden realization of her lack of love?

7. She did not go again upstairs, but very soon fled from the house with the rest of the bridal party.

Petty facts, all, but possibly more significant than appeared. I made up my mind to find the boy who brought the bouquet and also the one who carried back her message.

But here a surprise, if not a check, awaited me. The florist's boy had left his place and no one could tell where he had gone. Neither could I find the curly-haired waiter at Raucher's. He had left also, but it was to join the volunteers at San Antonio.

Was there meaning in this coincidence? I resolved to know. Visiting the former haunts of both boys, I failed to come upon any evidence of an understanding between them, or of their having shown any special interest in the Jeffrey tragedy. Both seemed to have been strangely reticent in regard to it, the florist's boy showing stupidity and the waiter such satisfaction in his prospective soldiering that no other topic was deemed worthy his attention. The latter had a sister and she could not say enough of the delight her brother had shown at the prospect of riding a horse again and of fighting in such good company. He had had some experience as a cowboy before coming to Washington, and from the moment war was declared had expressed his intention of joining the recruits for Cuba as soon as he could see her so provided for that his death would not rob her of proper support. How this had come about she did not know. Three weeks before he had been in despair over the faint prospect of doing what he wished; then suddenly, and without any explanation of how the change had come about, he had rushed in upon her with the news that he was going to enlist in a company made up of bronco busters and rough riders from the West, that she need not worry about herself or about him, for he had just put five hundred dollars to her account in bank, and that as for himself he possessed a charmed life and was immune, as she well knew, and need fear bullets no more than the fever. By this he meant that he had had yellow fever years before in Louisiana, and that a ball which had once been fired at him had gone clean through his body without taking his life.

"What was the date of the evening on which he told you he had placed money in bank for you?"

"April the twenty-ninth."

Two days after the Jeffrey-Moore wedding!

Convinced now that his departure from town was something more than a coincidence, I pursued my inquiries and found that he had been received, just as she had said, into the First Volunteer Corps under Colonel Wood. This required influence. Whose was the influence? It took me some time to find out, but after many and various attempts, most of which ended in failure, I succeeded in learning that the man who had worked and obtained for him a place in this favored corps was FRANCIS JEFFREY.

CHAPTER XVIII

IN THE GRASS

I did some tall thinking that night. I remembered that this man had held some conversation with the Jeffreys at their carriage door previous to their departure from the Moore house, and found myself compelled to believe that only a matter of importance to themselves as well as to him would have detained them at such a minute. Oh, that Tampa were not so far off or that I had happened on this clue earlier! But Tampa was at that moment a far prospect for me and I could only reason from such facts as I had been able to collect in Washington.

Fixing my mind now on Mrs. Jeffrey, I asked the cause of the many caprices which had marked her conduct on her wedding morning. Why had she persisted in dressing alone, and what occasioned the absorption which led to her ignoring all appeals at her door at a time when a woman is supposed to be more than usually gracious? But one answer suggested itself. Her heart was not in her marriage, and that last hour of her maidenhood had been an hour of anguish and struggle. Perhaps she not only failed to love Francis Jeffrey, but loved some other man. This seemed improbable, but things as strange as this have happened in our complex society and no reckoning can be made with a woman's fancy. If this was so—and what other theory would better or even so well account for her peculiar behavior both then and afterward? The hour usually given by brides to dress and gladsome expectation was with her one of farewell to past hopes and an unfortunate, if not passionate, attachment. No wonder that she wished to be alone. No wonder that interruption angered her. Perhaps it had found her on her knees. Perhaps—
Here I felt myself seized by a strong and sudden excitement. I remembered the filings I had gathered up

from the small stand by the window, filings which had glittered and which must have been of gold. What was the conclusion? In this last hour of her maiden life she had sought to rid herself of some article of jewelry which she found it undesirable to carry into her new life. What article of jewelry? In consideration of the circumstances and the hour, I could think of but one. A ring! the symbol of some old attachment.

The slight abrasion at the base of her third finger, which had been looked upon as the result of too rough and speedy a withdrawing of the wedding-ring on the evening of her death, was much more likely to have been occasioned by the reopening of some little wound made two weeks before by the file. If Durbin and the rest had taken into account these filings, they must have come to very much the same conclusion; but either they had overlooked them in their search about the place, or, having noted them, regarded them as a clue leading nowhere.

But for me they led the way to a very definite inquiry. Asking to see the rings Mrs. Jeffrey had left behind her on the night she went for the last time to the Moore house, I looked them carefully over, and found that none of them showed the least mark of the file. This strengthened my theory, and I proceeded to take my next step with increased confidence. It seemed an easy one, but proved unexpectedly difficult. My desire was to ascertain whether she had worn previous to her marriage any rings which had not been seen on her finger since, and it took me one whole week to establish the fact that she had.

But that fact once learned, the way cleared before me. Allowing my fancy full rein, I pictured to myself her anxious figure standing alone in that ancient and ghostly room filing off this old ring from her dainty finger. Then I asked myself what she would be likely to do with this ring after disengaging it from her hand? Would she keep it? Perhaps; but if so, why could it not be found? None such had been discovered among her effects. Or had she thrown it away, and if so, where? The vision of her which I had just seen in my mind's eye came out with a clearness at this, which struck me as providential. I could discern as plainly as if I had been a part of the scene the white-clad form of the bride bending toward the light which came in sparsely through the half-open shutter she had loosened for this task. This was the shutter which had never again been fastened and whose restless blowing to and fro had first led attention to this house and the crime it might otherwise have concealed indefinitely. Had some glimpse of the rank grass growing underneath this window lured her eye and led her to cast away the ring which she had no longer any right to keep? It would be like a woman to yield to such an impulse; and on the strength of the possibility I decided to search this small plot for what it might very reasonably conceal.

But I did not wish to do this openly. I was not only afraid of attracting Durbin's attention by an attempt which could only awaken his disdain, but I hesitated to arouse the suspicion of Mr. Moore, whose interest in his newly acquired property made him very properly alert to any trespass upon it.

The undertaking, therefore, presented difficulties. But it was my business to overcome these, and before long I conceived a plan by which every blade of grass in the narrow strip running in front of this house might be gone over without rousing anything more serious than Uncle David's ire.

Calling together a posse of street urchins, I organized them into a band, with the promise of a good supper all around if one of them brought me the pieces of a broken ring which I had lost in the grass plot of a house where I had been called upon to stay all night. That they might win the supper in the shortest possible time and before the owner of this house, who lived opposite, could interfere, I advised them to start at the fence in a long line and, proceeding on their knees, to search, each one, the ground before him to the width of his own body. The fortunate one was to have the privilege of saying what the supper should consist of. To give a plausible excuse for this search, a ball was to be tossed up and down the street till it lighted in the Moore house inclosure.

It was a scheme to fire the street boy's soul, and I was only afraid of failure from the over-enthusiasm it aroused. But the injunctions which I gave them to spare the shrubs and not to trample the grass any more than was necessary were so minute and impressive that they moved away to their task in unexpected order and with a subdued cheerfulness highly promising of success.

I did not accompany them. Jinny, who has such an innocent air on the street, took my place and promenaded up and down the block, just to see that Mr. Moore did not make too much trouble. And it was well she did so, for though he was not at home,—I had chosen the hour of his afternoon ride, his new man-servant was; and he no sooner perceived this crowd of urchins making for the opposite house than he rushed at them, and would have scattered them far and wide in a twinkling if the demure dimples of my little ally had not come into play and distracted his attention so completely as to make him forget the throng of unkempt hoodlums who seemed bound to invade his master's property. She was looking for Mr. Moore's house, she told him. Did he know Mr. Moore, and his house which was somewhere near? Not his new, great, big house, where the horrible things took place of which she had read in the papers, but his little old house, which she had heard was soon to be for rent, and which she thought would be just the right size for herself and mother. Was that it? That dear little place all smothered in vines? How lovely! and what would the rent be, did he think? and had it a back-yard with garden-room enough for her to raise pinks and nasturtiums? and so on, and so on, while he stared with delighted eyes, and tried to put in a word edgewise, and the boys—well, they went through that strip of grass in just ten minutes. My brave little Jinny had just declared with her most roguish smile that she would run home and tell her mother all about this sweetest of sweet little places, when a shout rose from the other side of the street, and that collection of fifteen or twenty boys scampered away as if mad, shouting in joyous echo of the boy at their head:

"It's to be chicken, heaping plates of ice cream and sponge cake."

By which token she knew that the ring had been found.

When they brought this ring to me I would not have exchanged places with any man on earth. As Jinny herself was curious enough to stroll along about this time, I held it out where we both could see it and draw our conclusions.

It was a plain gold circlet set with a single small ruby. It was cut through and twisted out of shape, just as I had anticipated; and as I examined it I wondered what part it had played and was yet destined to play in the drama of Veronica Jeffrey's mysterious life and still more mysterious death. That it was a factor of some importance, arguing some early school-girl love, I could but gather from the fact that its removal from her finger was effected in secrecy and under circumstances of such pressing haste. How could I learn the story of that ring and the possible connection between it and Mr. Jeffrey's professed jealousy of his wife and the disappointing honeymoon which had followed their marriage? That this feeling on his part had antedated the ambassador's ball no one could question; but that it had started as far back as the wedding day was a new idea to me and one which suggested many possibilities. Could this idea be established, and, if so, how? But one avenue of inquiry offered itself. The waiter, who had been spirited away so curiously immediately after the wedding; might be able to give us some information on this interesting point. He had been the medium of the messages which had passed between her and Mr. Jeffrey just prior to the ceremony; afterward he had been seen talking earnestly to that gentleman and later with her. Certainly, it would add to our understanding of the situation to know what reply she had sent to the peremptory demand made upon her at so critical a time; an understanding so desirable that the very prospect of it was almost enough to warrant a journey to Tampa. Yet, say that the results were disappointing, how much time lost and what a sum of money! I felt the need of advice in this crisis, yet hesitated to ask it. My cursed pride and my no less cursed jealousy of Durbin stood very much in my way at this time.

A week had now passed since the inquest, and, while Miss Tuttle still remained at liberty, it was a circumscribed liberty which must have been very galling to one of her temperament and habits. She rode and she walked, but she entered no house unattended nor was she allowed any communication with Mr. Jeffrey. Nevertheless she saw him, or at least gave him the opportunity of seeing her. Each day at three o'clock she rode through K Street, and the detective who watched Mr. Jeffrey's house said that she never passed it without turning her face to the second-story window, where he invariably stood. No signs passed between them; indeed, they scarcely nodded; but her face, as she lifted it to meet his eye, showed so marked a serenity and was so altogether beautiful that this same detective had a desire to see if it maintained like characteristics when she was not within reach of her brother-in-law. Accordingly, the next day he delegated his place to another and took his stand farther down the street. Alas! it was not the same woman's face he saw; but a far different and sadder one. She wore that look of courage and brave hope only in passing Mr. Jeffrey's house. Was it simply an expression of her secret devotion to him or the signal of some compact which had been entered into between them?

Whichever it was, it touched my heart, even in his description of it. After advising with Jinny I approached the superintendent, to whom, without further reserve, I opened my heart.

The next day I found myself on the train bound for Tampa, with full authority to follow Curly Jim until I found him.

BOOK III

THE HOUSE OF DOOM

CHAPTER XIX

IN TAMPA

When I started on this desperate search after a witness, war had been declared, but no advance as yet ordered on Cuba. But during my journey south the long expected event happened, and on my arrival in Tampa I found myself in the midst of departure and everything in confusion.

Of course, under such conditions it was difficult to find my man on the instant. Innumerable inquiries yielded no result, and in the absence of any one who would or could give me the desired information I wandered from one end of the camp to the other till I finally encountered a petty officer who gave signs of being a Rough Rider. Him I stopped, and, with some hint of my business, asked where James Calvert could be found.

His answer was a stare and a gesture toward the hospital tents.

Nothing could have astonished me more.

"Sick?" I cried.

"Dying," was his answer.

Dying! Curly Jim! Impossible. I had misled my informant as to the exact man I wanted, or else there were two James Calverts in Tampa. Curly Jim, the former cowboy, was not the fellow to succumb in camp before he had ever smelt powder.

"It is James Calvert of the First Volunteer Corps I am after," said I. "A sturdy fellow—"

"No doubt, no doubt. Many sturdy fellows are down. He's down to stay. Typhoid, you know. Bad case. No hope from the start. Pity, but—"

I heard no more. Dying! Curly Jim. He who was considered to be immune! He who held the secret—

"Let me see him," I demanded. "It is important—a police matter—a word from him may save a life. He is still breathing?"

"Yes, but I do not think there is any chance of his speaking. He did not recognize his nurse five minutes ago."

As bad as that! But I did not despair. I did not dare to. I had staked everything on this interview, and I was not going to lose its promised results from any lack of effort on my own part.

"Let me see him," I repeated.

I was taken in. The few persons I saw clustered about a narrow cot in one corner gave way and I was cut to the heart to see that they did this not so much out of consideration for me or my errand there as from the consciousness that their business at the bedside of this dying man was over. He was on the point of breathing his last. I pressed forward, and after one quick scrutiny of the closed eyes and pale face I knelt at his side and whispered a name into his ear. It was that of Veronica Moore.

He started; they all saw it. On the threshold of death, some emotion—we never knew what one—drew him back for an instant, and the pale cheek showed a suspicion of color. Though the eyes did not open, the lips moved, and I caught these words:

"Kept word—told no one—she was so—"

And that was all. He died the next instant.

Well! I was woefully done up by this sudden extinction of all my hopes. They had been extravagant, no doubt, but they had sustained me through all my haps and mishaps, trials and dangers, till now, here, they ended with the one inexorable fact-death. Was I doomed to defeat, then? Must I go back to the major with my convictions unchanged but with no fresh proof, no real evidence to support them? I certainly must. With the death of this man, all means of reaching the state of Mrs. Jeffrey's mind immediately preceding her marriage were gone. I could never learn now what to know would make a man of me and possibly save Cora Tuttle.

Bending under this stroke of Providence, I passed out. A little boy was sobbing at the tent door. I stared at him curiously, and was hurrying on, when I felt myself caught by the hand.

"Take me with you," cried a choked and frightened voice in my ear. "I have no friend here, now he is gone; take me back to Washington."

Washington! I turned and looked at the lad who, kneeling in the hot sand at the door of the tent, was clutching me with imploring hands.

"Who are you?" I asked; "and how came you here? Do you belong to the army?"

"I helped care for his horse," he whispered. "He found me smuggled on board the train—for I was bound to go to the war—and he was sorry for me and used to give me bits of his own rations, but—but now no one will give me anything. Take me back; she won't care. She's dead, they say. Besides, I wouldn't stay here now if she was alive and breathing. I have had enough of war since he—Oh, he was good to me—I never cared for any one so much."

I looked at the boy with an odd sensation for which I have no name.

"Whom are you talking about?" I asked. "Your mother your sister?"

"Oh, no;" the tone was simplicity itself. "Never had no mother. I mean the lady at the big house; the one that was married. She gave me money to go out of Washington, and, wanting to be a soldier, I followed Curly Jim. I didn't think he'd die—he looked so strong— What's the matter, sir? Have I said anything I shouldn't?"

I had him by the arm. I fear that I was shaking him.

"The lady!" I repeated. "She who was married—who gave you money. Wasn't it Mrs. Jeffrey?"

"Yes, I believe that was the name of the man she married. I didn't know him; but I saw he r-"

"Where? And why did she give you money? I will take you home with me if you tell me the truth about it."

He glanced back at the tent from which I had slightly drawn him and a hungry look crept into his eyes.

"Well, it's no secret now," he muttered. "He used to say I must keep my mouth shut; but he wouldn't say so now if he knew I could get home by telling. He used to be sorry for me, he used. What do you want to know?"

"Why Mrs. Jeffrey gave you money to leave Washington."

The boy trembled, drew a step away, and then came back, and under those hot Florida skies, in the turmoil of departing troops, I heard these words:

"Because I heard what she said to Jim."

I felt my heart go down, then up, up, beyond anything I had ever experienced in my whole life. The way before me was not closed then. A witness yet remained, though Jim was dead. The boy was oblivious of my emotion; he was staring with great mournfulness t the tent.

"And what was that?" said I.

His attention, which had been wandering, came back, and it was with some surprise he said:

"It was not much. She told him to take the gentleman into the library. But it was the library where men died, and he just went and died there, too, you remember, and Jim said he wasn't ever going to speak of it, and so I promised not to, neither, but—but—when do you think you will be starting, sir?"

I did not answer him. I was feeling very queer, as men feel, I suppose, who in some crisis or event recognize an unexpected interposition of Providence.

"Are you the boy who ran away from the florist's in Washington?" I inquired when ready to speak. "The boy who delivered Miss Moore's bridal bouquet?"

"Yes, sir."

I let go of his hand and sat down. Surely there was a power greater than chance governing this matter. Through what devious ways and from what unexpected sources had I come upon this knowledge?

"Mrs. Jeffrey, or Miss Moore, as she was then, told Jim to seat the gentleman in the library," I now said. "Why?"

"I do not know. He told her the gentleman's name and then she whispered him that. I heard her, and that was why I got money, too. But it's all gone now. Oh, sir, when are you going back?"

I started to my feet. Was it in answer to this appeal or because I realized that I had come at last upon a clue calling for immediate action?

"I am going now," said I, "and you are going with me. Run! for the train we take leaves inside of ten minutes. My business here is over."

CHAPTER XX

"THE COLONEL'S OWN"

Words can not express the tediousness of that return journey. The affair which occupied all my thoughts was as yet too much enveloped in mystery for me to contemplate it with anything but an anxious and inquiring mind. While I clung with new and persistent hope to the thread which had been put in my hand, I was too conscious of the maze through which we must yet pass, before the light could be reached, to feel that lightness of spirit which in itself might have lessened the hours, and made bearable those days of forced inaction. To beguile the way a little, I made a complete analysis of the facts as they appeared to me in the light of this latest bit of evidence. The result was not strikingly encouraging, yet I will insert it, if only in proof of my diligence and the extreme interest I experienced in each and every stage of this perplexing affair. It again took the form of a summary and read as follows:

Facts as they now appear:

1. The peremptory demand for an interview which had been delivered to Miss Moore during the half-hour preceding her marriage had come, not from the bridegroom as I had supposed, but from the so-called stranger, Mr. Pfeiffer.

2. Her reply to this demand had been an order for that gentleman to be seated in the library.

3. The messenger carrying this order had been met and earnestly talked with by Mr. Jeffrey either immediately before or immediately after the aforementioned gentleman had been so seated.

4. Death reached Mr. Pfeiffer before the bride did.

5. Miss Moore remained in ignorance of this catastrophe till after her marriage, no intimation of the same having been given her by the few persons allowed to approach her before she descended to her nuptials; yet she was seen to shrink unaccountably when her husband's lips touched hers, and when informed of the dreadful event before which she beheld all her guests fleeing, went from the house a changed woman.

6. For all this proof that Mr. Pfeiffer was well known to her, if not to the rest of the bridal party, no acknowledgment of this was made by any of them then or afterward, nor any contradiction given either by husband or wife to the accepted theory that this seeming stranger from the West had gone into this fatal room of the Moores' to gratify his own morbid curiosity.

7. On the contrary, an extraordinary effort was immediately made by Mr. Jeffrey to rid himself of the only witnesses who could tell the truth concerning those fatal ten minutes; but this brought no peace to the miserable wife, who never again saw a really happy moment.

8. Extraordinary efforts at concealment argue extraordinary causes for fear. Fully too understand the circumstances of Mrs. Jeffrey's death, it would be necessary first to know what had happened in the Moore house when Mr. Jeffrey learned from Curly Jim that the man, whose hold upon his bride had been such that he dared to demand an interview with her just as she was on the point of descending to her nuptials, had been seated, or was about to be seated, in the room where death had once held its court and might easily be persuaded to hold court again.

This was the limit of my conclusions. I could get no further, and awaited my arrival in Washington with the greatest impatience. But once there, and the responsibility of this new inquiry shifted to broader shoulders than my own, I was greatly surprised and as deeply chagrined to observe the whole affair lag unaccountably and to note that, in spite of my so-called important discoveries, the prosecution continued working up the case against Miss Tuttle in manifest intention of presenting it to the grand jury at its fall sitting.

Whether Durbin was to blame for this I could not say. Certainly his look was more or less quizzical when next we met, and this nettled me so that I at once came to the determination that whatever was in his mind, or in the minds of the men whose counsels he undoubtedly shared, I was going to make one more great effort on my own account; not to solve the main mystery, which had passed out of my hands, but to reach the hidden cause of the equally unexplained deaths which had occurred from time to time at the library fireplace.

For nothing could now persuade me that the two mysteries were not indissolubly connected, or that the elucidation of the one would not lead to the elucidation of the other.

To be sure, it was well accepted at headquarters that all possible attempts had been made in this direction and with nothing but failure as a result. The floor, the hearth, the chimney, and, above all, the old settle, had been thoroughly searched. But to no avail. The secret had not been reached and had almost come to be looked upon as insolvable.

But I was not one to be affected by other men's failures. The encouragement afforded me by my late discoveries was such that I felt confident that nothing could hinder my success save the necessity of completely pulling down the house. Besides, all investigation had hitherto started, if it had not ended, in the library. I was resolved to begin work in quite a different spot. I had not forgotten the sensations I had experienced in the southwest chamber.

During my absence this house had been released from surveillance. But the major still held the keys and I had no difficulty in obtaining them. The next thing was to escape its owner's vigilance. This I managed to do through the assistance of Jinny, and when midnight came and all lights went out in the opposite cottage I entered boldly upon the scene.

As before, I went first of all to the library. It was important to know at the outset that this room was in its normal condition. But this was not my only reason for prefacing my new efforts by a visit to this scene of death and mysterious horror. I had another, so seemingly puerile, that I almost hesitate to mention it and would not if the sequel warranted its omission.

I wished to make certain that I had exhausted every suspected, as well as every known clue, to the information I sought. In my long journey home and the hours of thought it had forced upon me, I had more than once been visited by flitting visions of things seen in this old house and afterward nearly forgotten. Among these was the book which on that first night of hurried search had given proofs of being in some one's hand within a very short period. The attention I had given it at a moment of such haste was necessarily cursory, and when later a second opportunity was granted me of looking into it again, I had allowed a very slight obstacle to deter me. This was a mistake I was anxious to rectify. Anything which had been touched with purpose at or near the time of so mysterious a tragedy,—and the position of this book on a shelf so high that a chair was needed to reach it proved that it had been sought and touched with purpose, held out the promise of a clue which one on so blind a trail as myself could not afford to ignore.

But when I had taken the book down and read again its totally uninteresting and unsuggestive title and, by another reference to its dim and faded leaves, found that my memory had not played me false and that it contained nothing but stupid and wholly irrelevant statistics, my confidence in it as a possible aid in the work I had in hand departed just as it had on the previous occasion. I was about to put it back on the shelf, when I bethought me of running my hand in behind the two books between which it had stood. Ah! that was it! Another book lay flat against the wall at the back of the shelf; and when, by the removal of those in front I was enabled to draw this book out, I soon saw why it had been relegated to such a remote place of concealment on the shelves of the Moore library.

It was a collection of obscure memoirs written by an English woman, but an English woman who had been in America during the early part of the century, and who had been brought more or less into contact with the mysteries connected with the Moore house in Washington. Several passages were marked, one particularly, by a heavy pencil-line running the length of the margin. As the name of Moore was freely scattered through these passages as well as through two or three faded newspaper clippings which I discovered pasted on the inside cover, I lost no time in setting about their perusal.

The following extracts are from the book itself, taken in the order in which I found them marked:

"It was about this time that I spent a week in the Moore house; that grand and historic structure concerning which and its occupants so many curious rumors are afloat. I knew nothing then of its discreditable fame; but from the first moment of my entrance into its ample and well lighted halls I experienced a sensation which I will not call dread, but which certainly was far from being the impulse of pure delight which the graciousness of my hostess and the imposing character of the place itself were calculated to produce. This emotion was but transitory, vanishing, as was natural, in the excitement of my welcome and the extraordinary interest I took in Callista Moore, who in those days was a most fascinating little body. Small to the point of appearing diminutive, and lacking all assertion in manner and bearing, she was nevertheless such a lady that she easily dominated all who approached her, and produced, quite against her will I am sure, an impression of aloofness seasoned with kindness, which made her a most surprising and entertaining study to the analytic observer. Her position as nominal mistress of an establishment already accounted one of the finest in Washington,—the real owner, Reuben Moore, preferring to live abroad with his French wife,—gave to her least action an importance which her shy, if not appealing looks, and a certain strained expression most difficult to characterize, vainly attempted to contradict. I could not understand her, and soon gave up the attempt; but my admiration held firm, and by the time the evening was half over I was her obedient slave. I think from what I know of her now that she would have preferred to be mine.

"I was put to sleep in a great chamber which I afterward heard called 'The Colonel's Own.' It was very grand and had a great bed in it almost royal in its size and splendor. I believe that I shrank quite unaccountably from this imposing piece of furniture when I first looked at it; it seemed so big and so out of proportion to my slim little body. But admonished by the look which I surprised on Mistress Callista's high-bred face, I quickly recalled an expression so unsuited to my position as guest, and, with a gush of well-simulated rapture, began to expatiate upon the interesting characteristics of the room, and express myself as delighted at the prospect of sleeping there.

"Instantly the nervous look left her, and, with the quiet remark, 'It was my father's room,' she set down the candles with which both her hands were burdened, and gave me a kiss so warm and surcharged with feeling that it sufficed to keep me happy and comfortable for a half-hour or more after she passed out.

"I had thought myself a very sleepy girl, but when, after a somewhat lengthened brooding over the dying embers in the open fireplace, I lay down behind the curtains of the huge bed, I found myself as far from sleep as I had ever been in my whole life.

"And I did not recover from this condition for the entire night. For hours I tossed from one side of the bed to the other in my efforts to avoid the persistent eyes of a scarcely-to-be-perceived drawing facing me from the opposite wall. It had no merit as a picture, this drawing, but seen as it was under the rays of a gibbous moon looking in through the half-open shutter, it exercised upon me a spell such as I can not describe and hope never again to experience. Finally I rose and pulled the curtains violently together across the foot of the bed. This shut out the picture; but I found it worse to imagine it there with its haunting eyes peering at me through the intervening folds of heavy damask than to confront it openly; so I pushed the curtains back again, only to rise a half-hour later and twitch them desperately together once more.

"I fidgeted and worried so that night that I must have looked quite pale when my attentive hostess met me at the head of the stairs the next morning. For her hand shook quite perceptibly as she grasped mine, and her voice was pitched in no natural key as she inquired how I had slept. I replied, as truth, if not courtesy, demanded, 'Not as well as usual,' whereupon her eyes fell and she remarked quite hurriedly; 'I am so sorry; you shall have another room tonight,' adding, in what appeared to be an unconscious whisper: 'There is no use; all feel it; even the young and the gay;' then aloud and with irrepressible anxiety: 'You didn't see anything, dear?'

"'No!' I protested in suddenly awakened dismay; 'only the strange eyes of that queer drawing peering at me through the curtains of my bed. Is it—is it a haunted room?'

"Her look was a shocked one, her protest quite vehement. 'Oh, no! No one has ever witnessed anything like a ghost there, but every one finds it impossible to sleep in that bed or even in the room. I do not know why, unless it is that my father spent so many weary years of incessant wakefulness inside its walls.'

"'And did he die in that bed?' I asked.

"She gave a startled shiver, and drew me hurriedly downstairs. As we paused at the foot, she pressed my hand and whispered:

"'Yes; at night; with the full of the moon upon him.'

"I answered her look with one she probably understood as little as I did hers. I had heard of this father of hers. He had been a terrible old man and had left a terrible memory behind him.

"The next day my room was changed according to her promise, but in the light of the charges I have since heard uttered against that house and the family who inhabit it, I am glad that I spent one night in what, if it was not a haunted chamber, had certainly a very thrilling effect upon its occupants."

Second passage; the italics showing where it was most heavily marked.

"The house contained another room as interesting as the one I have already mentioned. It went by the name of the library and its walls were heavily lined with books; but the family never sat there, nor was I ever fortunate enough to see it with its doors unclosed except on the occasion of the grand reception Mistress Callista gave in my honor. I have a fancy for big rooms and more than once urged my hostess to tell me why this one stood neglected. But the lady was not communicative on this topic and it was from another member of the household I learned that its precincts had been forever clouded by the unexpected death within them of one of her father's friends, a noted army officer.

"Why this should have occasioned a permanent disuse of the spot I could not understand, and as every one who conversed on this topic invariably gave the impression of saying less than the subject demanded, my curiosity soon became too much for me and I attacked Miss Callista once again in regard to it. She gave me a quick smile, for she was always amiable, but shook her head and introduced another topic. But one night when the wind was howling in the chimneys and the sense of loneliness was even greater than usual in the great house, we drew together on the rug in front of my bedroom fire, and, as the embers burned down to ashes before us, Miss Callista became more communicative.

"Her heart was heavy, she told me; had been heavy for years. Perhaps some ray of comfort would reach her if she took a friend into her confidence. God knew that she needed one, especially on nights like this, when the wind woke echoes all over the house and it was hard to tell which most to fear, the sounds which came from no one knew where, or the silence which settled after.

"She trembled as she said this, and instinctively drew nearer my side so that our heads almost touched over the flickering flame from whose heat and light we sought courage. She seemed to feel grateful for this contact, and the next minute, flinging all her scruples to the wind, she began a relation of events which more or less answered my late unwelcome queries.

"The death in the library, about which her most perplexing memory hung, took place when she was a child and her father held that high governmental position which has reflected so much credit upon the family. Her father and the man who thus perished had been intimate friends. They had fought together in the War of 1812 and received the same distinguishing marks of presidential approval afterward. They were both members of an important commission which brought them into diplomatic relations with England. It was while serving on this commission that the sudden break occurred which ended all intimate relations between them, and created a change in her father that was equally remarked at home and abroad. What occasioned this break no one knew. Whether his great ambition had received some check through the jealousy of this so-called friend—a supposition which did not seem possible, as he rose rapidly after this—or on account of other causes darkly hinted at by his contemporaries, but never breaking into open gossip, he was never the same man afterwards. His children, who used to rush with effusion to greet him, now shrank into corners at his step, or slid behind half open doors, whence they peered with fearful interest at his tall figure, pacing in moody silence the halls of his ancestral home, or sitting with frowning brows over the embers dying away on the great hearthstone of his famous library.

"Their mother, who was an invalid, did not share these terrors. The father was ever tender of her, and the only smile they ever saw on his face came with his entrance into her darkened room.

"Such were Callista Moore's first memories. Those which followed were more definite and much more startling. President Jackson, who had a high opinion of her father's ability, advanced him rapidly. Finally a position was given him which raised him into national prominence. As this had been the goal of his ambition for years, he was much gratified by this appointment, and though his smiles came no more frequently, his frowns lightened, and from being positively threatening, became simply morose.

"Why this moroseness should have sharpened into menace after an unexpected visit from his once dear, but long estranged companion-in-arms, his daughter, even after long years of constant brooding upon this subject, dares not decide. If she could she might be happier.

"The general was a kindly man, sharp of face and of a tall thin figure, but with an eye to draw children and make them happy with a look. But his effect on the father was different. From the moment the two met in the great hall below, the temper of the host betrayed how little he welcomed this guest. He did not fail in courtesy—the Moores are always gentlemen—but it was a hard courtesy, which cut while it flattered. The two children, shrinking from its edge without knowing what it was that hurt them, slunk to covert, and from behind the two pillars which mark the entrance to the library, watched the two men as they walked up and down the halls discussing the merits of this and that detail of the freshly furnished mansion. These two innocent, but eager spies, whom fear rather than curiosity held in hiding, even caught some of the sentences which passed between tire so-called friends; and though these necessarily conveyed but little meaning to their childish minds, the words forming them were never forgotten, as witness these phrases confided to me by Mistress Callista twenty-five years afterward.

"'You have much that most men lack,' remarked the general, as they paused to admire some little specimen of Italian art which had been lately received from Genoa. 'You have money—too much money, Moore, by an amount I might easily name—a home which some might call palatial, a lovely, if not altogether healthy wife, two fine children, and all the honor which a man in a commonwealth like this should ask for. Drop politics.'

"'Politics are my life,' was the cold response. 'To bid me drop them is to bid me commit suicide.' Then, as an afterthought to which a moment of intervening silence added emphasis, 'And for you to drive me from them would be an act little short of murder.'

"'Justice dealt upon a traitor is not murder,' was the stern and unyielding reply. 'By one black deed of treacherous barter and sale, of which none of your countrymen is cognizant but myself, you have forfeited the confidence of this government. Were I, who so unhappily surprised your secret, to allow you to continue in your present place of trust, I myself would be a traitor to the republic for which I have fought and for which I am ready to die. That is why I ask you to resign before—'

"The two children did not catch the threat latent in that last word, but they realized the force of it from their father's look and were surprised when he quietly said:

"'You declare yourself to be the only man on the commission who is acquainted with the facts you are pleased to style traitorous?'

"The general's lips curled. 'Have I not said?' he asked.

"Something in this stern honesty seemed to affect the father. His face turned away and it was the other's voice which was next heard. A change had taken place in it and it sounded almost mellow as it gave form to these words:

"'Alpheus, we have been friends. You shall have two weeks in which to think over my demand and decide. If at the end of that time you have not returned to domestic life you may expect another visit from me which can not fail of consequences. You know my temper when roused. Do not force me into a position which will cause us both endless regret.'

"Perhaps the father answered; perhaps he did not. The children heard nothing further, but they witnessed the gloom with which he rode away to the White House the next day. Remembering the general's threat, they imagined in their childish hearts that their father had gone to give up his post and newly acquired honors. But he returned at night without having done so, and from that day on carried his head higher and showed himself more and more the master, both at home and abroad.

"But he was restless, very restless, and possibly to allay a great mental uneasiness, he began having some changes made in the house; changes which occupied much of his time and with which he never seemed satisfied. Men working one day were dismissed the next and others called in until this work and everything else was interrupted by the return of his late unwelcome guest, who kept his appointment to a day.

"At this point in her narrative Mistress Callista's voice fell and the flame which had thrown a partial light on her countenance died down until I could but faintly discern the secretly inquiring look with which she watched me as she went on to say

"'Reuben and I,'—Reuben was her brother,—'were posted in the dark corner under the stairs when my father met the general at the door. We had expected to hear high words, or some explosion of bitter feeling between them, and hardly knew whether to be glad or sorry when our father welcomed his guest with the same elaborate bow we once saw him make to the president in the grounds of the White House. Nor could we understand what followed. We were summoned in to supper. Our mother was there—a great event in those days—and toasts were drunk and our father proposed one to the general's health. This Reuben thought was an open signal of peace, and turned upon me his great round eyes in surprise; but I, who was old enough to notice that this toast was not responded to and that the general did not even touch his lips to the glass he had lifted in compliment to our mother, who had lifted hers, felt that there was something terrifying rather than reassuring in this attempt at good fellowship.

Though unable to reason over it at the time, I have often done so since, and my father's attitude and look as he faced this strange guest has dwelt so persistently in my memory that scarcely a year passes without the scene coming up in my dreams with its accompanying emotions of fear and perplexity. For—perhaps you know the story—that hour was the general's last. He died before leaving the house; died in that same dark library concerning which you have asked so many questions.

"'I remember the circumstances well, how well down to each and every detail. Our mother had gone back to her room, and the general and my father, who did not linger over their wine—why should they, when the general would not drink?—had withdrawn to the library at the suggestion of the general, whose last words are yet lingering in my ears.

"'The time has come for our little talk,' said he. 'Your reception augurs—'

"'You do not look well,' my father here broke in, in what seemed an unnaturally loud voice. 'Come and sit down—'

"'Here the door closed.

"'We had hung about this door, curious children that we were, in hopes of catching a glimpse of the queer new settle which had been put into place that day. But we scampered away at this, and were playing in and out of the halls when the library door again opened and my father came out.

"'Where's Samba?' he cried. 'Tell him to carry a glass of wine in to the general. I do not like his looks. I am going upstairs for some medicine.' This he whispered in choked tones as he set foot on the stairs. Why I remember it I do not know, for Reuben, who was standing where he could look into the library when our father came out and saw the settle and the general sitting at one end of it, was chattering about it in my ear at the very moment our father was giving his orders.

"'Reuben is a man now, and I have asked him more than once since then how the general looked at that critical instant. It is important to me, very, very important, and to him, too, now that he has come to know a man's passions and temptations. But he will never tell me, never relieve my mind, and I can only hope that there were real signs of illness on the general's brow; for then I could feel that all had been right and that his death was the natural result of the great distress he felt at opposing my father in the one desire of his heart. That glimpse which Reuben had of him before he fell has always struck me with strange pathos. A little child looking in upon a man, who, for all his apparent health, will in another moment be in eternity—I do not wonder he does not like to talk of it, and yet—

"'It was Samba who came upon the general first. Our father had not yet descended. When he did, it was with loud cries and piteous ejaculations. Word had gone upstairs and surprised him in the room with my mother. I recollect wondering in all childish simplicity why he wrung his hands so over the death of a man he so hated and feared. Nor was it till years had passed and our mother had been laid in the grave and the house had settled into a gloom too heavy and somber for Reuben to endure, that I recognized in my father the signs of a settled remorse. These I endeavored to account for by the fact that he had been saved from what he looked upon as political death by the sudden but opportune decease of his best friend. This caused a shock to his feelings which had unnerved him for life. Don't you think this the true explanation of his invariably moody brow and the great distaste he always showed for this same library? Though he would live in no other house, he would not enter that room nor look at the gloomy settle from which the general had fallen to his death. The place was virtually tabooed, and though, as the necessity arose, it was opened from time to time for great festivities, the shadow it had acquired never left it and my father hated its very door until he died. Is it not natural that his daughter should share this feeling?'

"It was, and I said so; but I would say no more, though she cast me little appealing looks which acquired an eery significance from the pressure of her small fingers on my arm and the wailing sound of the wind which at that moment blew down in one gust, scattering the embers and filling the house with banshee calls. I simply kissed her and advised her to go back with me to England and forget this old house and all its miserable memories. For that was the sum of the comfort at my poor command. When, after another restless night, I crept down in the early morning to peer into the dim and unused room whose story I had at last learned, I can not say but that I half expected to behold the meager ghost of the unfortunate general rise from the cushions of the prodigious bench which still kept its mysterious watch over the deserted hearthstone."

So much for the passages culled from the book itself. The newspaper excerpts, to which I next turned, bore a much later date, and read as follows:

"A strange coincidence marks the death of Albert Moore in his brother's house yesterday. He was discovered lying with his head on the identical spot where General Lloyd fell forty years before. It is said that this sudden demise of a man hitherto regarded as a model of physical strength and endurance was preceded by a violent altercation with his elder brother. If this is so, the excitement incident upon such a break in their usually pleasant relations may account for his sudden death. Edward Moore, who, unfortunately, was out of the room when his brother succumbed—some say that he was in his grandfather's room above—was greatly unnerved by this unexpected end to what was probably merely a temporary quarrel, and now lies in a critical condition.

"The relations between him and the deceased Albert have always been of the most amicable character until they unfortunately fell in love with the same woman."

Attached to this was another slip, apparently from a later paper.

"The quarrel between the two brothers Moore, just prior to the younger one's death, turns out to have been of a more serious nature than was first supposed. It has since leaked out that an actual duel was fought at that time between these two on the floor of the old library; and that in this duel the elder one was wounded. Some even go so far as to affirm that the lady's hand was to be the reward of him who drew the first blood; it is no longer denied that the room was in great disorder when the servants first rushed in at the sound he made in falling. Everything movable had been pushed back against the wall and an open space cleared, in the center of which could be seen one drop of blood. What is certain is that Mr. Moore is held to the house by something even more serious than his deep grief, and that the young lady who was the object of this fatal dispute has left the city."

Pasted under this was the following short announcement:

"Married on the twenty-first of January, at the American consulate in Rome, Italy, Edward Moore, of Washington, D. C., United States of America, to Antoinette Sloan, daughter of Joseph Dewitt Sloan, also of that city."

With this notice my interest in the book ceased and I prepared to step down from the chair on which I had remained standing during the reading of the above passages.

As I did so I spied a slip of paper lying on the floor at my feet. As it had not been there ten minutes before there could be little doubt that it had slipped from the book whose leaves I had been turning over so rapidly. Hastening to recover it, I found it to be a sheet of ordinary note paper partly inscribed with words in a neat and distinctive handwriting. This was a great find, for the paper was fresh and the handwriting one which could be readily identified. What I saw written there was still more remarkable. It had the look of some of the memoranda I had myself drawn up during the most perplexing moments of this strange case. I transcribe it just as it read:

"We have here two separate accounts of how death comes to those who breathe their last on the ancestral hearthstone of the Moore house library.

"Certain facts are emphasized in both:

"Each victim was alone when he fell.

"Each death was preceded by a scene of altercation or violent controversy between the victim and the alleged master of these premises.

"In each case the master of the house reaped some benefit, real or fancied, from the other's death."

A curious set of paragraphs. Some one besides myself was searching for the very explanation I was at that moment intent upon. I should have considered it the work of our detectives if the additional lines I now came upon could have been written by any one but a Moore. But no one of any other blood or associations could have indited the amazing words which followed. The only excuse I could find for them was the difficulty which some men feel in formulating their thoughts otherwise than with pen and paper, they were so evidently intended for the writer's eye and understanding only, as witness:

"Let me recall the words my father was uttering when my brother rushed in upon us with that account of my misdeeds which changed all my prospects in life. It was my twenty-first birthday and the old man had just informed me that as the eldest son I might expect the house in which we stood to be mine one day and with it a secret which has been handed down from father to son ever since the Moores rose to eminence in the person of Colonel Alpheus. Then he noted that I was now of age and immediately went on to say: 'This means that you must be told certain facts, without the knowledge of which you would be no true Moore. These facts you must hereafter relate to your son or whoever may be fortunate enough to inherit from you. It is the legacy which goes with this house and one which no inheritor as yet has refused either to receive or to transmit. Listen. You have often noted the gold filigree ball which I wear on my watch-guard. This ball is the talisman of our house, of this house. If, in the course of your life you find yourself in an extremity from which no issue seems possible mind the strictness of the injunction— an extremity from which no issue seems possible (I have never been in such a case; the gold filigree ball has never been opened by me) you will take this trinket from its chain, press upon this portion of it so, and use what you will find inside, in connection with—' Alas! it was at this point John Judson came rushing in and those disclosures were made which lost me my father's regard and gave to the informer my rightful inheritance, together with the full secret of which I only got a part. But that part must help me now to the whole. I have seen the filigree ball many times; Veronica has it now. But its contents have never been shown me. If I knew what they were and why the master of this secret always left the library—"

Here the memorandum ceased with a long line straggling from the letter y as if the writer had been surprised at his task.

The effect upon me of these remarkable words was to heighten my interest and raise me into a state of renewed hope, if not of active expectation.

Another mind than my own had been at work along the only groove which held out any promise of success, and this mind, having at its command certain family traditions, had let me into a most valuable secret. Another mind! Whose mind? That was a question easily answered. But one man could have written these words; the man who was thrust aside in early life in favor of his younger brother, and who now, by the sudden death of that brother's daughter, had come again into his inheritance. Uncle David, and he only, was the puzzled inquirer whose self-communings I had just read. This fact raised a new problem far me to work upon, and I could but ask when these lines were written—before or after Mr. Pfeiffer's death and whether he had ever succeeded in solving the riddle he had suggested, or whether it was still a baffling mystery to him. I was so moved by the suggestion conveyed in his final and half-finished sentence, that I soon lost sight of these lesser inquiries in the more important one connected with the filigree ball. For I had seen this filigree ball. I had even handled it. From the description given I was very certain that it had been one of the many trinkets I had observed lying on the dressing table when I made my first hasty examination of the room on the evening of Mrs. Jeffrey's death. Why had no premonition of its importance as a connecting link between these tragedies and their mysterious cause come to me at the time when it was within reach of my hand? It was too late now. It had been swept away with the other loose objects littering the place, and my opportunity for pursuing this very promising investigation was gone for the night.

Yet it was with a decided feeling of triumph that I finally locked the door of this old mansion behind me. Certainly I had taken a step forward since my entrance there, to which I had but to add another of equal importance to merit the attention of the superintendent himself.

CHAPTER XXI

THE HEART OF THE PUZZLE

The next morning I swallowed my pride and sought out Durbin. He had superintended the removal of Mrs. Jeffrey's effects from the southwest chamber, and should know, if any one, where this filigree ball was now to be found. Doubtless it had been returned with the other things to Mr. Jeffrey, and yet, who knows? Durbin is sly and some inkling of its value as a clue may have entered his mind. If so, it would be anywhere but in Mr. Jeffrey's or Miss Tuttle's possession.

To test my rival's knowledge of and interest in this seemingly trivial object, I stooped to what I can but consider a pardonable subterfuge. Greeting him in the offhand way least likely to develop his suspicion, I told him that I had a great idea in connection with the Jeffrey case and that the clue to it lay in a little gold ball which Mrs. Jeffrey sometimes wore and upon which she set great store. So far I spoke the truth. It had been given her by some one—not Mr. Jeffrey—and I believed, though I did not know, that it contained a miniature portrait which it might be to our advantage to see.

I expected his lip to curl; but for a wonder it maintained its noncommittal aspect, though I was sure that I caught a slight, very slight, gleam of curiosity lighting up for a moment his calm, gray eye.

"You are on a fantastic trail," he sneered, and that was all.

But I had not expected more. I had merely wished to learn what place, if any, this filigree ball held in his own suspicions, and in case he had overlooked it, to jog his curiosity so that he would in some way betray its whereabouts.

That, for all its seeming inconsequence, it did hold some place in his mind was evident enough to those who knew him; but that it was within reach or obtainable by any ordinary means was not so plain. Indeed, I very soon became convinced that he, for one, had no idea where it was, or after the suggestive hint I had given him he would never have wasted a half-hour on me. What was I to do then? Tell my story to the major and depend on him to push the matter to its proper conclusion? "Not yet," whispered pride. "Durbin thinks you a fool. Wait till you can show your whole hand before calling attention to your cards." But it was hard not to betray my excitement and to act the fool they considered me when the boys twitted me about this famous golden charm and asked what great result had followed my night in the Moore house. But remembering that he who laughs last laughs best, and that the cause of mirth was not yet over between Durbin and myself, I was able to preserve an impassive exterior even when I came under the major's eye. I found myself amply repaid when one of the boys who had studiously avoided chaffing me dropped the following words in my ear:

"I don't know what your interest is in the small gold charm you were talking about, but you have done some good work in this case and I don't mind telling you what I know about it. That little gold ball has caused the police much trouble. It is on the list of effects found in the room where the candle was seen burning; but when all these petty belongings of Mrs. Jeffrey's were gathered up and carried back to her husband, this special one was not to be found amongst them. It was lost in transit, nor has it ever been seen since. And who do you think it was who called attention to this loss and demanded that the article be found? Not Mr. Jeffrey, who seems to lay little or no stress upon it, but the old man they call Uncle David. He who, to all appearance, possessed no interest in his niece's personal property, was on hand the moment these things were carried into her husband's house, with the express intention, it seems, of inquiring for this gold ball, which he declared to be a family heirloom. As such it belonged to him as the present holder of the property, and to him only. Attention being thus called to it, it was found to be missing, and as no one but the police seemed to be to blame for its loss the matter was hushed up and would have been regarded as too insignificant for comment, the trinket being intrinsically worthless, if Mr. Moore had not continued to make such a fuss about it. This ball, he declared, was worth as much to a Moore as all the rest of his property, which was bosh, you know; and the folly of these assertions and the depth of the passions he displayed whenever the subject was mentioned have made some of us question if he is the innocent inheritor he has tried to make himself out. At all events, I know for a certainty that the district attorney holds his name in reserve, if the grand jury fails to bring in an indictment against Miss Tuttle."

"The district attorney is wise," I remarked, and fell athinking.

Had this latent suspicion against Mr. Moore any solid foundation? Was he the guilty man? The memorandum I had come across in the book which had been lately pulled down from the library shelves showed that, notwithstanding his testimony to the contrary, he had been in that house close upon that fatal night, if not on the very night itself. It also showed his extreme interest in the traditions of the family. But did it show anything more? Had he interrupted his writing to finish his query in blood, and had one of his motives for this crime been the acquisition of this filigree ball? If so, why had he left it on the table upstairs? A candle had been lit in that room—could it have been by him in his search for this object? It would be a great relief to believe so. What was the reason then that my mind refused so emphatically to grasp this possibility and settle upon him as the murderer of Mrs. Jeffrey? I can not tell. I hated the man, and I likewise deeply distrusted him. But I could not, even after this revelation of his duplicity, connect him in my thoughts with absolute crime without a shock to my intuitions. Happily, my scruples were not shared by my colleagues. They had listed him. Here I felt my shoulder touched, and a newspaper was thrust into my hand by the man who had just addressed me.

"Look down the lost and found column," said he. "The third advertisement you will see there came from the district attorney's office; the next one was inserted by Mr. Moore himself."

I followed his pointing finer and read two descriptions of the filigree ball. The disproportion in the rewards offered was apparent. That promised by Uncle David was calculated to rouse any man's cupidity and should have resulted in the bauble's immediate return.

"He got ahead of the police that time," I laughed. "When did these advertisements appear?"

"During the days you were absent from Washington."

"And how sure are you that he did not get this jewel back?"

"Oh, we are sure. His continued anxiety and still active interest prove this, even if our surveillance had been less perfect."

"And the police have been equally unsuccessful?"

"Equally."

"After every effort?"

"Every."

"Who was the man who collected and carried out those things from the southwest chamber?"

He smiled.

"You see him," said he.

"It was you?"

"Myself."

"And you are sure this small ball was among them?"

"No. I only know that I have seen it somewhere, but that it wasn't among the articles I delivered to Mr. Jeffrey."

"How did you carry them?"

"In a hand-bag which I locked myself."

"Before leaving the southwest chamber?"

"Yes."

"Then it is still in that room?"

"Find it," was his laconic reply.

Here most men would have stopped, but I have a bulldog's tenacity when once I lay hold. That night I went back to the Moore house and, taking every precaution against being surprised by the sarcastic Durbin or some of his many flatterers, I ransacked the southwest chamber on my own behalf for what certainly I had little reason to expect to find there.

It seemed a hopeless cause from the first, but I acted as if no one had hunted for this object before. Moving every article, I sought first on the open floor and then in every possible cranny for the missing trinket. But I failed to find it and was about to acknowledge myself defeated when my eye fell on the long brocaded curtains which I had drawn across the several windows to hide every gleam of light from the street. They were almost free from folds, but I shook them well, especially the one nearest the table, and naturally with no effect.

"Folly," I muttered, yet did not quite desist. For the great tassels still hung at the sides and— Well! you may call it an impossible find or say that if the bauble was there it should have been discovered in the first search for it! I will not say no. I can only tell you what happened. When I took one of those tassels in my band, I thought, as it twirled under my touch, that I saw something gleam in its faded old threads which did not belong there. Startled, and yet not thoroughly realizing that I had come upon the object of my search, I picked at this thing and found it to be a morsel of gold chain that had become entangled in it. When I had pulled it out, it showed a small golden ball at one end, filigreed over and astonishingly heavy for its size and apparent delicacy.

How it came there—whether it rolled from the table, or was swept off inadvertently by the detective's hand, and how it came to be caught by this old tassel and held there in spite of the many shakings it must have received, did not concern me at this momentous instant. The talisman of this old family was found. I had but to discover what it held concealed to understand what had baffled Mr. Moore and made the mystery he had endeavored to penetrate so insolvable. Rejoicing in my triumph, but not wasting a moment in self-congratulation, I bent over the candle with my prize and sought for the clasp or fastening which held its two parts together. I have a knack at clasps and curious fastenings and was able at first touch to spring this one open. And what did I find inside? Something so different from what I expected, something so trivial and seemingly harmless, that it was not until I recalled the final words of Uncle David's memorandum that I realized its full import and the possibilities it suggested. In itself it was nothing but a minute magnifying glass; but when used in connection with—what? Ah, that was just what Uncle David failed to say, possibly to know. Yet this was now the important point, the culminating fact which might lead to a full understanding of these many tragedies. Could I hope to guess what presented itself to Mr. Moore as a difficult if not insolvable problem? No; guessing would not answer. I must trust to the inspiration of the moment which suggested with almost irresistible conviction:

The picture! That inane and seemingly worthless drawing over the fireplace in The Colonel's Own, whose presence in so rich a room has always been a mystery!

Why this object should have suggested itself to me and with such instant conviction, I can not readily say. Whether, from my position near the bed, the sight of this old drawing recalled the restless nights of all who had lain in face of its sickly smile, or whether some recollection of that secret law of the Moores which forbade the removal of any of their pictures from the time-worn walls, or a remembrance of the curiosity which this picture excited in every one who looked at it—Francis Jeffrey among the number—I no sooner asked myself what object in this house might possibly yield counsel or suggest aid when subjected to the influence of a magnifying glass, than the answer, which I have already given, sprang instantly into my mind: The picture!

Greatly excited, I sprang upon a chair, took down the drawing from the wall and laid it face up on the bed. Then I placed the glass over one of the large coils surrounding the insipid face, and was startled enough, in spite of all mental preparation, to perceive the crinkly lines which formed it, resolve themselves into script and the script into words, some of which were perfectly legible.

The drawing, simple as it looked, was a communication in writing to those who used a magnifying glass to read it. I could hardly contain my triumph, hardly find the self-control necessary to a careful study of its undulating and often conflicting lines and to the slow picking out of the words therein contained.

But when I had done this, and had copied the whole of the wandering scrawl on a page of my note book the result was of value.

Read, and judge for yourself.

"Coward that I am, I am willing to throw upon posterity the shadow of a crime whose consequences I dare not incur in life. Confession I must make. To die and leave no record of my deed is impossible. Yet how tell my story so that only my own heirs may read and they when at the crisis of their fate? I believe I have found the way by this drawing and the injunction I have left to the holders of the filigree ball.

"No man ever wished his enemy dead more than I did, and no man ever spent more cunning on the deed. Master in my own house, I contrived a device by which the man who held my fate in his hands fell on my library hearth with no one near and no sign by which to associate me with the act. Does this seem like the assertion of a madman? Go to the old chamber familiarly called "The Colonel's Own." Enter its closet, pull out its two drawers, and in the opening thus made seek for the loophole at the back, through which, if you stoop low enough, you can catch a glimpse of the library hearth and its great settle. With these in view, slip your finger along the wall on your right and when it touches an obstruction—pass it if it is a handle, for that is only used to rewind the apparatus and must be turned from you until it can be turned no farther; but if it is a depression you encounter, press, and press hard on the knob concealed within it. But beware when any one you love is seated in that corner of the settle where the cushion invites rest, lest it be your fate to mourn and wail as it is mine to curse the hour when I sought to clear my way by murder. For the doom of the man of blood is upon me. The hindrance is gone from my life, but a horror has entered it beyond the conception of any soul that has not yielded itself to the unimaginable influences emanating from an accomplished crime. I can not be content with having pressed that spring once. A mania is upon me which, after thirty years of useless resistance and superhuman struggle, still draws me from bed and sleep to rehearse in ghastly fashion that deed of my early manhood. I can not resist it. To tear out the deadly mechanism, unhinge weight and drum and rid the house of every evidence of crime would but drive me to shriek my guilt aloud and act in open pantomime what I now go through in fearsome silence and secrecy. When the hour comes, as come it must, that I can not rise and enter that fatal closet, I shall still enact the deed in dreams, and shriek aloud in my sleep and wish myself dead and yet fear to die lest my hell be to go through all eternity, slaying over and over my man, in ever growing horror and repulsion.

"Do you wish to share my fate? Try to effect through blood a release from the difficulties menacing you."

CHAPTER XXII

A THREAD IN HAND

There are moments which stand out with intense force and clearness in every man's life. Mine was the one which followed the reading of these lines which were meant for a warning, but which in more than one case had manifestly served to open the way to a repetition of the very crime they deplored. I felt myself under the same fascination. I wanted to test the mechanism; to follow out then and there the instructions given with such shortsighted minuteness and mark the result. But a sense of decorum prevented. It was clearly my duty to carry so important a discovery as this to the major and subject myself to his commands before making the experiment suggested by the scroll I had so carefully deciphered. Besides, it would be difficult to carry out this experiment alone, and with no other light than that afforded by my lantern. Another man and more lights were needed.

Influenced by these considerations, I restored the picture to its place, and left the building. As I did so, the first signs of dawn became visible in the east. I had expended three hours in picking out the meaning concealed in the wavy lines of the old picture.

I was early at headquarters that morning, but not so early as to find the superintendent alone. A group of men were already congregated about him in his small office, and when, on being admitted, I saw amongst them the district attorney, Durbin and another famous detective, I instinctively knew what matter was under discussion.

I was allowed to remain, possibly because I brought news in my face, possibly because the major felt more kindly toward me than I thought. Though Durbin, who had been speaking, had at first sight of me shut his mouth like a trap, and even went so far as to drum an impatient protest with his fingers on the table before which he stood, neither the major nor the district attorney turned an unkindly face toward me, and my amiable friend was obliged to accept my presence with what grace he could.

There was with them a fourth man, who stood apart. On him the general attention had been concentrated at my entrance and to him it now returned. He was an unpretentious person of kindly aspect. To any one accustomed to Washington residents, he bore the unmistakable signs of being one of the many departmental employees whose pay is inadequate to the necessities of his family. Of his personal peculiarities I noted two. He blinked when he talked, and stuttered painfully when excited. Notwithstanding these defects he made a good impression, and commanded confidence. This I soon saw was of importance, for the story he now entered upon was one calculated to make me forget my own errand and even to question my own convictions.

The first intimation I received of the curious nature of his communication was through the following questions, put to him by the major:

"You are sure this gentleman is identical with the one pointed out to you last night?"

"Very sure, sir. I can swear to it."

I omit all evidence of the defect in his speech above mentioned.

"You recognize him positively?"

"Positively. I should have picked him out with the same assurance, if I had seen him in some other city and in a crowd of as fine-looking gentlemen as himself. His face made a great impression on me. You see I had ample time to study it in the few minutes we stood so close together."

"So you have said. Will you be kind enough to repeat the circumstance? I should like the man who has just come in to hear your description of this scene. Give the action, please. It is all very interesting."

The stranger glanced inquisitively in my direction, and turned to obey the superintendent.

"I was returning to my home in Georgetown, on the evening of May the eleventh, the day of the great tragedy. My wife was ill, and I had been into town to see a physician and should have gone directly home; but I was curious to see how high the flood was running—you remember it was over the banks that night. So I wandered out on the bridge, and came upon the gentleman about whom you have been questioning me. He was standing all alone leaning on the rail thus." Here the speaker drew up a chair, and, crossing his arms over its back, bent his head down over them. "I did not know him, but the way he eyed the water leaping and boiling in a yellow flood beneath was not the way of a curious man like myself, but of one who was meditating some desperate deed. He was handsome and well dressed, but he looked a miserable wretch and was in a state of such complete self-absorption that he did not notice me, though I had stopped not five feet from his side. I expected to see him throw himself over, but instead of that, he suddenly raised his head and, gazing straight before him, not at the heavy current, but at some vision in his own mind, broke forth in these words, spoken as I had never heard words spoken before—"

Here the speaker's stuttering got the better of him and the district attorney had time to say:

"What were these words? Speak them slowly; we have all the time there is."

Instantly the man plucked up heart and, eying us all impressively, was able to say:

"They were these: 'She must die! she must die!' No name, but just the one phrase twice repeated, 'She must die!' This startled me, and hardly knowing whether to lay hands on him, or to turn about and run, I was moving slowly away, when he drew his arms from the rail, like this, and, still staring into space, added, in the same hard and determined voice, this one word more, 'To-night!'; and, wheeling about, passed me with one blank and wholly unconscious look and betook himself toward the city. As he went by, his lips opened for the third time. 'Which means—' he cried, between a groan and a shriek, 'a bullet for her and—' I wish I had heard the rest, but he was out of my hearing before his sentence was finished."

"What time was this?"

"As near half-past five as possible. It was six when I reached home a few minutes later."

"Ah, he must have gone to the cemetery after this."

"I am quite sure of it."

"Why didn't you follow the man?" grumbled Durbin.

"It wasn't my business. He was a stranger and possibly mad. I didn't know what to do."

"What did you do?"

"Went home and kept quiet; my wife was very ill that night and I had my own cause for anxiety."

"You, however, read the papers next morning?"

"No, sir, nor for many days. My wife grew constantly worse and for a week I didn't leave her, not knowing but that every breath would be her last. I was dead to everything outside the sick-room and when she grew better, which was very gradually, we had to take her away, so that I had no opportunity of speaking of this occurrence to any one till a week ago, when some remark, published in connection with Mrs. Jeffrey's death, recalled that encounter on the bridge. I told a neighbor that I believed the man I had seen there was Mr. Jeffrey, and we looked up the papers and ran over them till we came upon his picture. That settled it, and I could no longer—being free from home anxieties now—hold my tongue and the police heard—"

"That will do, Mr. Gelston," broke in the major. "When we want you again, we will let you know. Durbin, see Mr. Gelston out."

I was left alone with the major and the district attorney.

There was a moment's silence, during which my own heart beat so loud that I was afraid they would hear it. Since taking up Miss Tuttle's cause I had never really believed in Mr. Jeffrey's innocence in spite of the alibi he had brought forward, and now I expected to hear these men utter the same conviction. The major was the first to speak. Addressing the district attorney, he remarked: "This will strengthen your case very materially. We have proof now that Mrs. Jeffrey's death was actually determined upon. If Miss Tuttle had not shot her, he would. I wonder if it was a relief to him on reaching his door to find that the deed was done."

I could not suppress my surprise.

"Miss Tuttle!" I repeated. "Is it so unmistakably evident that Mr. Jeffrey did not get to the Moore house in time to do the shooting himself?"

The major gave me a quick look.

"I thought you considered Miss Tuttle the guilty one."

I felt that the time had come to show my colors.

"I have changed my mind," said I. "I can give you no good reason for this; something in the woman herself, I suppose. She does not look nor act like a criminal. While not desirous of raising myself in opposition to the judgment of those so greatly my superior in all respects, I have had this feeling, and I am courageous enough to avow it. And yet, if Mr. Jeffrey could not have left the cemetery gates and reached the Moore house in time to fulfil all the conditions of this tragedy, the case does look black against the woman. She admits to having been there when the pistol was fired, unless—"

"Unless what? You have something new to tell us. That I have seen ever since you entered the room. What is it?"

I cast a glance at the door. Should I be able to finish my story before Durbin returned? I thought it possible, and, though still upset by this new evidence, which I could now see was not entirely in Miss Tuttle's favor, I spoke up with what spirit I might.

"I have just come from spending another night in the Moore house. All the efforts heretofore made to exhaust its secrets have been founded upon a theory that has brought us nowhere. I had another in mind, and I was anxious to test it before resting from all further attempt to solve this riddle. And it has not failed me. By pursuing a clue apparently so trivial that I allowed it to go neglected for weeks, I have come upon the key to the many mysterious crimes which have defiled the library hearthstone. And where do you think it lies? Not in the hearthstone itself and not in the floor under the settle; not, in fact, in the library at all, but in the picture hanging upstairs in the southwest chamber."

"The picture! that faded-out sketch, fit only for the garret?"

"Yes. To you and to most people surveying it, it is just what you say and nothing more. But to the initiated few—pray Heaven they may have been few—it is writing, conveying secret instructions. The whole combination of curves which go to make up this sketch is a curious arrangement of words inscribed with the utmost care, in the smallest of characters. Viewed with a magnifying glass, the uncertain outlines of a shadowy face surmounted by a mass of piled-up hair resolve themselves into lines of writing, the words of which are quite intelligible and full of grim and unmistakable purpose. I have read those lines; and what is more, I have transcribed them into plain copy. Will you read them? They contain a most extraordinary confession; a confession that was manifestly intended as a warning, but which unfortunately has had very different results. It may explain the death of the man from Denver, even if it cast no light upon the other inexplicable features of the remarkable case we are considering."

As I spoke I laid open on the table before me the transcription of which I spoke. Instantly the two men bent over it. When they looked up again, their countenances showed not excitement only but appreciation; and in the one minute of triumph which I then enjoyed, all that had wounded or disturbed me in the past was forgotten.

"You are a man in a thousand," was the major's first enthusiastic comment; at which I was conscious of regretting, with very pardonable inconsistency, that Durbin had not returned in time to hear these words.

The major now proposed that we should go at once to the old house. "A family secret like this does not crop up every day even in a city so full of surprises as Washington. We will hunt for the spring under the closet drawers and see what happens, eh? And on our way there"—here he turned to me "I should like to hear the particulars concerning the little clue just mentioned. By the way, Mr. Jeffrey's interest in this old drawing is now explained. He knew its diabolical secret."

This was self-evident, and my heart was heavy for Miss Tuttle, who seemed to be so deep in her brother-in-law's confidence.

It grew still heavier when Durbin, joining us, added his incredulity to the air of suspicion assumed by the others. Through all the explanations I now entered into, I found myself inwardly repeating with somewhat forced iteration, "I will not believe her guilty under any circumstances. She carries the look of innocence, and innocent she must be proved, whatever the result may be to Francis Jeffrey."

To such an extent had I been influenced by the lofty expression which I had once surprised on her face.

Had Mr. David Moore been sitting open-eyed behind his vines that morning, he would have been much surprised to see so many of his natural enemies intrude on his property at so early an hour. But, happily, he had not yet risen, and we were able to enter upon our investigations without being watched or interrupted by him.

Our first move was to go in a body to the southwest chamber, take down the picture, examine it with a magnifying-glass and satisfy ourselves that the words I had picked out of its mazy lines were really to be found there. This done and my veracity established, we next proceeded to the closet where, according to the instructions embodied in this picture, the secret spring was to be found by which some unknown and devilish machinery would be released in the library below.

To my great satisfaction the active part in this experiment was delegated to me. Durbin continued to be a mere looker-on. Drawing out the two large drawers from their place at the end of this closet, I set them aside. Then I hunted for and found the small loophole which we had been told afforded a glimpse of the library hearthstone; but seeing nothing through it, I called for a light to be placed in the room below.

I heard Durbin go down, then the major, and finally, the district attorney. Nothing could stay their curiosity now, not even the possibility of danger, which as yet was a lurking and mysterious one. But when a light shot up from below, and the irregular opening before me became a loophole through which I could catch a very wide glimpse of the library beneath, I found that it was not necessary for me to warn them to keep away from the hearth, as they were all clustered very near the door—a precaution not altogether uncalled for at so hazardous a moment.

"Are you ready?" I called down.

"Ready!" rose in simultaneous response from below.

"Then look out!"

Reaching for the spring cleverly concealed in the wall at my right I vigorously pressed it.

The result was instantaneous. Silently, but with unerring certainty, something small, round, and deadly, fell plumb from the library ceiling to where the settle had formerly stood against the hearthstone. Finding nothing there but vacancy to expend itself upon, it swung about for a moment on what looked like a wire or a whip-cord, then slowly came to rest within a foot or so from the floor.

A cry from the horrified officials below was what first brought me to myself. Withdrawing from my narrow quarters I hastened down to them and added one more white face to the three I found congregated in the doorway. In the diabolical ingenuity we had seen displayed, crime had reached its acme and the cup of human depravity seemed full. When we had regained in some measure our self-possession, we all advanced for a closer look at the murderous object dangling before us. We found it to be a heavy leaden weight painted on its lower end to match the bosses of stucco-work which appeared at regular intervals in the ornamentation of the ceiling. When drawn up into place, that is, when occupying the hole from which it now hung suspended, the portion left to protrude would evidently bear so small a proportion to its real bulk as to justify any eye in believing it to be the mate, and the harmless mate, of all the others.

"It hangs just where the settle stood," observed Durbin, significantly.

"And just at the point where the cushions invite rest, as the colonel so suggestively puts it in his strange puzzle of a confession," added the district attorney.

"Replace the old seat," ordered the major, "and let us make sure of this."

Ready hands at once grasped it, and, with some effort, I own, drew it carefully back into position.

"You see!" quoth Durbin.

We did.

"Devilish!" came from the major's lips. Then with a glance at the ball which, pushed aside by the seat, now hung over its edge a foot or so from the floor, he added briskly: "The ball has fallen to the full length of the cord. If it were drawn up a little—"

"Wait," I eagerly interposed. "Let me see what I can do with it."

And I dashed back upstairs and into the closet of "The Colonel's Own."

With a single peep down to see if they were still on the watch, I seized the handle whose position I had made sure of when searching for the spring, and began to turn; when instantly—so quick was the response—the long cord stiffened and I saw the ball rise into sight above the settle top.

"Stop!" called out the major. "Let go and press the spring again."

I hastened to obey and, though the back of the settle hid the result from me, I judged from the look and attitude of those below that the old colonel's calculations had been made with great exactness, and that the one comfortable seat on the rude and cumbersome bench had been so placed that this leaden weight in descending would at the chosen moment strike the head of him who sat there, inflicting death. That the weight should be made just heavy enough to produce a fatal concussion without damaging the skull was proof of the extreme care with which this subtle apparatus had been contrived. An open wound would have aroused questions, but a mere bruise might readily pass as a result of the victim's violent contact with the furnishings of the hearth toward which the shocked body would naturally topple. The fact that a modern jury had so regarded it shows how justified he was in this expectation.

I was expending my wonder on this and on a new discovery which, with a very decided shock to myself I had just made in the closet, when the command came to turn the handle again and to keep on turning it till it would turn no farther.

I complied, but with a trembling hand, and though I did not watch the result, the satisfaction I heard expressed below was significant of the celerity and precision with which the weight rose, foot by foot, to the ceiling and finally slunk snugly and without seeming jar into its lair.

When, a few minutes later, I rejoined those below, I found them all, with eyes directed toward the cornice, searching for the hole through which I had just been looking. It was next to imperceptible, so naturally had it been made to fit in with the shadows of the scroll work; and even after I had discovered it and pointed it out to them, I found difficulty in making them believe that they really looked upon an opening. But when once convinced of this, the district attorney's remark was significant.

"I am glad that my name is not Moore."

The superintendent made no reply; his eye had caught mine, and he had become very thoughtful.

"One of the two candelabra belonging to the parlor mantel was found lying on that closet floor," he observed. "Somebody has entered there lately, as lately as the day when Mr. Pfeiffer was seated here."

"Pardon me," I impetuously cried. "Mr. Pfeiffer's death is quite explained." And, drawing forward my hand, which up to this moment I had held tight-shut behind my back, I slowly unclosed it before their astonished eyes.

A bit of lace lay in my palm, a delicate bit, such as is only worn by women in full dress.

"Where did you find that?" asked the major, with the first show of deep emotion I have ever observed in him.

My agitation was greater than his as I replied:

"In the rough boarding under those drawers. Some woman's arm and hand has preceded mine in stealthy search after that fatal spring. A woman who wore lace, valuable lace."

There was but one woman connected with this affair who rightly answered these conditions. The bride! Veronica Moore.

CHAPTER XXIII

WORDS IN THE NIGHT

Had I any premonition of the astounding fact thus suddenly and, I may say, dramatically revealed to us during the weeks I had devoted to the elucidation of the causes and circumstances of Mrs. Jeffrey's death? I do not think so. Nothing in her face, as I remembered it; nothing in the feeling evinced toward her by husband or sister, had prepared me for a disclosure of crime so revolting as to surpass all that I had ever imagined or could imagine in a woman of such dainty personality and unmistakable culture. Nor was the superintendent or the district attorney less confounded by the event. Durbin only tried to look wise and strut about, but it was of no use; he deceived nobody. Veronica Moore's real connection with Mr. Pfeiffer's death,—a death which in some inscrutable way had in so short a time led to her own,—was an overwhelming surprise to every one of us.

The superintendent, as was natural, recovered first.

"This throws quite a new light upon the matter," said he. "Now we can understand why Mr. Jeffrey uttered that extraordinary avowal overheard on the bridge: 'She must die!' She had come to him with blood on her hands."

It seemed incredible, nay more, unreal. I recalled the sweet refined face turned up to me from the bare boards of this same floor, the accounts I had read of the vivacity of her spirits and the wild charm of her manner till the shadow of this old house fell upon her. I marveled, still feeling myself in the dark, still clinging to my faith in womankind, still asking to what depths her sister had followed her in the mazes of crime we were forced to recognize but could not understand.

Durbin had no such feelings and no such scruples, as was shown by the sarcastic comment which now left his lips.

"So!" he cried, "we have to do with three criminals instead of two. Nice family, the Moore-Jeffreys!"

But no one paid any attention to him. Addressing the major, the district attorney asked when he expected to hear from Denver, adding that it had now become of the first importance to ascertain the exact relations existing between the persons under suspicion and the latest victim of this deadly mechanism.

The major's answer was abrupt. He had been expecting a report for days. He was expecting one yet. If it came in at any time, night or day, he was to be immediately notified. Word might be sent him in an hour, in a minute.

Were his remarks a prophecy? He had hardly ceased speaking when an officer appeared with a telegram in his hand. This the major eagerly took and, noting that it was in cipher, read it by means of the code he carried in his pocket. Translated, it ran thus:

Result of open inquiry in Denver.

Three brothers Pfeiffer; all well thought of, but plain in their ways and eccentric. One doing business in Denver. Died June, '97. One perished in Klondike, October, same year; and one, by name Wallace, died suddenly three months since in Washington.

Nothing further gained by secret inquiry in this place.

Result of open inquiry in Owosso.

A man named Pfeiffer kept a store in Owosso during the time V. M. attended school there. He was one of three brothers, home Denver, name Wallace. Simultaneously with V. M.'s leaving school, P. broke up business and at instigation of his brother William, who accompanied him, went to the Klondike. No especial relation between lady and this same P. ever noted. V. M. once heard to laugh at his awkward ways.

Result of secret inquiry in Owosso.

V. M. very intimate with schoolmate who has since died. Often rode together; once gone a long time. This was just before V. M. left school for good. Date same as that on which a marriage occurred in a town twenty miles distant. Bride, Antoinette Moore; groom, W. Pfeiffer of Denver; witness, young girl with red hair. Schoolmate had red hair. Had V. M. a middle initial, and was that initial A?

We all looked at each other; this last question was one none of us could answer.

"Go for Mr. Jeffrey at once," ordered the major, "and let another one of you bring Miss Tuttle. No word to either of what has occurred and no hint of their possible meeting here."

It fell to me to fetch Miss Tuttle. I was glad of this, as it gave me a few minutes by myself in which to compose my mind and adjust my thoughts to the new conditions opened up by the amazing facts which had just come to light. But beyond the fact that Mrs. Jeffrey had been answerable for the death which had occurred in the library at the time of her marriage—that, in the words of the district attorney, she had come to her husband with blood on her hands, my thoughts would not go; confusion followed the least attempt to settle the vital question of how far Miss Tuttle and Mr. Jeffrey had been involved in the earlier crime and what the coming interview with these two would add to our present knowledge. In my anxiety to have this question answered I hastened my steps and was soon at the door of Miss Tuttle's present dwelling place.

I had not seen this lady since the inquest, and my heart beat high as I sat awaiting her appearance in the dim little parlor where I had been seated by the person who held her under secret surveillance. The scene I had just been through, the uncertain nature of the relations held by this beautiful woman both toward the crime just discovered and the one long associated with her name, lent to these few moments of anticipation an emotion which poorly prepared me for the touching sight of the patient smile with which she presently entered.

But I doubt if she noticed my agitation. She was too much swayed by her own. Advancing upon me in all the unconscious pride of her great beauty, she tremulously remarked:

"You have a message for me. Is it from headquarters? Or has the district attorney still more questions to ask?"

"I have a much more trying errand than that," I hastened to say, with some idea of preparing her for an experience that could not fail to be one of exceptional trial. "For reasons which will be explained to you by those in greater authority than myself, you are wanted at the house where—" I could not help stammering under the light of her melancholy eyes—"where I saw you once before," I lamely concluded.

"The house in Waverley Avenue?" she objected wildly, with the first signs of positive terror I had ever beheld in her.

I nodded, dropping my eyes. What call had I to penetrate the conscience of this woman?

"Are they there? all there?" she presently asked again. "The police and—and Mr. Jeffrey?"

"Madam," I respectfully protested, "my duty is limited to conducting you to the place named. A carriage is waiting. May I beg that you will prepare yourself to go at once to Waverley Avenue?"

For answer she subjected me to a long and earnest look which I found it impossible to evade. Then she hastened from the room, but with very unsteady steps. Evidently the courage which had upborne her so long was beginning to fail. Her very countenance was changed. Had she recognized, as I meant she should, that the secret of the Moore house was no longer a secret confined to her own breast and to that of her unhappy brother-in-law?

When she returned ready for her ride this change in her spirits was less observable, and by the time we had reached the house in Waverley Avenue she had so far regained her old courage as to move and speak with the calmness of despair if not of mental serenity.

The major was awaiting us at the door and bowed gravely before her heavily veiled figure.

"Miss Tuttle," he asked, without any preamble, the moment she was well inside the house, "may I inquire of you here, and before I show you what will excuse us for subjecting you to the distress of entering these doors, whether your sister, Mrs. Jeffrey, had any other name or was ever known by any other name than that of Veronica?"

"She was christened Antoinette, as well as Veronica; but the person in whose memory the former name was given her was no honor to the family and she very soon dropped it and was only known as Veronica. Oh, what have I done?" she cried, awed and frightened by the silence which followed the utterance of these simple words.

No one answered her. For the first time in her presence, the minds of those who faced her were with another than herself. The bride! the unhappy bride—no maiden but a wife! nay, a wife one minute, a widow the next, and then again a newly-wedded bride before the husband lying below was cold! What wander that she shrank when her new-made bridegroom's lips approached her own! or that their honeymoon was a disappointment! Or that the shadow which fell upon her on that evil day never left her till she gave herself wholly up to its influence and returned to die on the spot made awful by her own crime.

Before any of us were quite ready to speak, a tap at the door told us that Durbin had arrived with Mr. Jeffrey. When they had been admitted and the latter saw Miss Tuttle standing there, he, too, seemed to realize that a turn had come in their affairs, and that courage rather than endurance was the quality most demanded from him. Facing the small group clustered in the dismal hall fraught with such unutterable associations, he earnestly prayed:

"Do not keep me in suspense. Why am I summoned here?"

The reply was as grave as the occasion warranted.

"You are summoned to learn the murderous secret of these old walls, and who it was that last made use of it. Do you feel inclined to hear these details from my lips, or are you ready to state that you already know the means by which so many persons, in times past as well as in times present, have met death here? We do not require you to answer us."

"I know the means," he allowed, recognizing without doubt that the crisis of crises had come, and that denial would be worse than useless.

"Then it only remains for us to acquaint you with the identity of the person who last pressed the fatal spring. But perhaps you know that, too?"

"I—" He paused; words were impossible to him; and in that pause his eyes flashed helplessly in the direction of Miss Tuttle.

But the major was quick on his feet and was already between him and that lady. This act forced from Mr. Jeffrey's lips the following broken sentence:

"I should—like—you—to—tell—me." Great gasps came with each heavily spoken word.

"Perhaps this morsel of lace will do it in a gentler manner than I could," responded the district attorney, opening his hand, in which lay the scrap of lace that, an hour or so before, I had plucked away from the boarding of that fatal closet.

Mr. Jeffrey eyed it and understood. His hands went up to his face and he swayed to the point of falling. Miss Tuttle came quickly forward.

"Oh!" she moaned, as her eyes fell on the little white shred. "The providence of God has found us out. We have suffered, labored and denied in vain."

"Yes," came in dreary echo from the man none of us had understood till now; "so great a crime could not be hid. God will have vengeance. What are we that we should hope to avert it by any act or at any cost?"

The major, with his eyes fixed piercingly on this miserable man, replied with one pregnant, sentence:

"Then you forced your wife to suicide?"

"No," he began; but before another word could follow, Miss Tuttle, resplendent in beauty and beaming with new life, broke in with the fervid cry:

"You wrong him and you wrong her by such a suggestion. It was not her husband but her conscience that forced her to this retributive act. What Mr. Jeffrey might have done had she proved obdurate and blind to the enormity of her own guilt, I do not know. But that he is innocent of so influencing her is proved by the shock he suffered at finding she had taken her punishment into her own hands."

"Mr. Jeffrey will please answer the question," insisted the major. Whereupon the latter, with great effort, but with the first appearance of real candor yet seen in him, said earnestly:

"I did nothing to influence her. I was in no condition to do so. I was benumbed—dead. When first she told me,—it was in some words muttered in her sleep—I thought she was laboring under some fearful nightmare; but when she persisted, and I questioned her, and found the horror true, I was like a man turned instantly into stone, save for one intolerable throb within. I am still so; everything passes by me like a dream. She was so young, seemingly so innocent and light-hearted. I loved her! Gentlemen, you have thought me guilty of my wife's death,—this young fairy-like creature to whom I ascribed all the virtues! and I was willing, willing that you should think so, willing even to face the distrust and opprobrium of the whole world,—and so was her sister, the noble woman whom you see before you—rather than that the full horror of her crime should be known and a name so dear be given up to execration. We thought we could keep the secret—we felt that we must keep the secret—we took an oath—in French—in the carriage with the detectives opposite us. She kept it—God bless her! I kept it. But it was all useless—a tiny bit of lace is found hanging to a lifeless splinter, and all our efforts, all the hopes and agony of weeks are gone for naught. The world will soon know of her awful deed—and I—"

He still loved her! That was apparent in every look, in every word he uttered. We marveled in awkward silence, and were glad when the major said:

"The deed, as I take it, was an unpremeditated one on her part. Is that why her honor was dearer to you than your own, and why you could risk the reputation if not the life of the woman who you say sacrificed herself to it?"

"Yes, it was unpremeditated; she hardly realized her act. If you must know her heart through all this dreadful business, we have her words to show you—words which she spent the last miserable day of her life in writing. The few lines which I showed the captain and which have been published to the world was an inclosure meant for the public eye. The real letter, telling the whole terrible truth, I kept for myself and for the sister who already knew her sin. Oh, we did everything we could!" And he again moaned: "But it was in vain; quite in vain."

There were no signs of subterfuge in him now, and we all, unless I except Durbin, began to yield him credence. Durbin never gives credence to anybody whose name he has once heard associated with crime.

"And this Pfeiffer was contracted to her? A man she had secretly married while a school-girl and who at this very critical instant had found his way to the house."

"You shall read her letter. It was meant for me, for me only—but you shall see it. I can not talk of him or of her crime. It is enough that I have been unable to think of anything else since first those dreadful words fell front her lips in sleep, thirty-six hours before she died." Then with the inconsistency of great anguish he suddenly broke forth into the details he shrank from and cried "She muttered, lying there, that she was no bigamist. That she had killed one husband before she married the other. Killed him in the old house and by the method her ancestors had taught her. And I, risen on my elbow, listened, with the sweat oozing from my forehead, but not believing her, oh, not believing her, any more than any one of you would believe such words uttered in a dream by the darling of your heart. But when, with a long-drawn sigh, she murmured, 'Murderer!' and raised her fists—tiny fists, hands which I had kissed a thousand times—and shook them in the air, an awful terror seized me, and I sought to grasp them and hold them down, but was hindered by some nameless inner recoil under which I could not speak, nor gasp, nor move. Of course, it was some dream-horror she was laboring under, a nightmare of unimaginable acts and thoughts, but it was one to hold me back; and when she lay quiet again and her face resumed its old sweetness in the moonlight, I found myself staring at her almost as if it were true—what she had said—that word—that awful word which no woman could use with regard to herself, even in dreams, unless—Something, an echo from the discordant chord in our two weeks' married life, rose like the confirmation of a doubt in my shocked and rebellious breast. From that hour till dawn nothing in that slowly brightening room seemed real, not her face lying buried in its youthful locks upon the pillow, not the objects well-known and well-prized by which we were surrounded—not myself—most of all, not myself, unless the icy dew oozing from the roots of my lifted hair was real, unless that shape, fearsome, vague, but persistent, which hovered in the shadows above us, drawing a line of eternal separation between me and my wife, was a thing which could be caught and strangled and— Oh! I rave! I chatter like a madman; but I did not rave that night. Nor did I rave when, in the bright, broad sunlight, her eye slowly unclosed and she started to see me bending so near her, but not with my usual kiss or glad good morning. I could not question her then; I dared not. The smile which slowly rose to her lips was too piteous—it showed confidence. I waited till after breakfast. Then, while she was seated where she could not see my face, I whispered the question: 'Do you know that you have had a horrible dream?' She shrieked and turned. I saw her face and knew that what she had uttered in her sleep was true.'

"I have no remembrance of what I said to her. She tried to tell me how she had been tempted and how she had not realized her own act, till the moment I bent down to kiss her lips as her husband. But I did not stop to listen—I could not. I flew immediately to Miss Tuttle with the violent demand as to whether she knew that her sister was already a wife when she married me, and when she cried out 'No!' and showed great dismay, I broke forth with the dreadful tale and cowered in unmanly anguish at her feet, and went mad and lost myself for a little while. Then I went back to my wretched wife and asked her how the awful deed had been done. She told me, and again I did not believe her and began to look upon it all as some wild dream or the distempered fancies of a disordered brain. This thought calmed me and I spoke gently to her and even tried to take her hand. But she herself was raving now, and clung about my knees, murmuring words of such anguish and contrition that my worst fears returned and, only stopping to take the key of the Moore house from my bureau, I left the house and wandered madly—I know not where.

"I did not go back that day. I could not face her again till I knew how much of her confession was fancy and how much was fact. I roamed the streets, carrying that key from one end of the city to the other, and at night I used it to open the house which she had declared contained so dreadful a secret.

"I had bought candles on my way there but, forgetting to take them from the store, I had no light with which to penetrate the horrible place that even the moon refused to illumine. I realized this when once in, but would not go back. All I have told about using matches to light me to the southwest chamber is true, also my coming upon the old candelabrum there, with a candle in one of its sockets. This candle I lit, my sole reason for seeking this room being my desire to examine the antique sketch for the words which she had said could be found there.

"I had failed to bring a magnifying-glass with me, but my eyes are phenomenally sharp. Knowing where to look, I was able to pick out enough words here and there in the lines composing the hair, to feel quite sure that my wife had neither deceived me nor been deceived as to certain directions being embodied there in writing. Shaken in my last lingering hope, but not yet quite convinced that these words pointed to outrageous crime, I flew next to the closet and drew out the fatal drawer.

"You have been there and know what the place is, but no one but myself can ever realize what it was for me, still loving, still clinging to a wild inconsequent belief in my wife, to grope in that mouth of hell for the spring she had chattered about in her sleep, to find it, press it, and then to hear, down in the dark of the fearsome recess, the sound of something deadly strike against what I took to be the cushions of the old settle standing at the edge of the library hearthstone.

"I think I must have fainted. For when I found myself possessed of sufficient consciousness to withdraw from that hole of death, the candle in the candelabrum was shorter by an inch than when I first thrust my head into the gap made by the removed drawers. In putting back the drawers I hit the candelabrum with my foot, upsetting it and throwing out the burning candle. As the flames began to lick the worm-eaten boarding of the floor a momentary impulse seized me to rush away and leave the whole place to burn. But I did not. With a sudden frenzy, I stamped out the flame, and then finding myself in darkness, griped my way downstairs and out. If I entered the library I do not remember it. Some lapses must be pardoned a man involved as I was."

"But the fact which you dismiss so lightly is an important one," insisted the major. "We must know positively whether you entered this room or not."

"I have no recollection of doing so"

"Then you can not tell us whether the little table was standing there, with the candelabrum upon it or—"

"I can tell you nothing about it."

The major, after a long look at this suffering man, turned toward Miss Tuttle.

"You must have loved your sister very much," he sententiously remarked.

She flushed and for the first time her eyes fell from their resting-place on Mr. Jeffrey's face.

"I loved her reputation," was her quiet answer, "and—" The rest died in her throat.

But we all—such of us, I mean, who were possessed of the least sensibility or insight, knew how that sentence sounded as finished in her heart "and I loved him who asked this sacrifice of me."

Yet was her conduct not quite clear.

"And to save that reputation you tied the pistol to her wrist?" insinuated the major.

"No," was her vehement reply. "I never knew what I was tying to her. My testimony in that regard was absolutely true. She held the pistol concealed in the folds of her dress. I did not dream—I could not— that she was contemplating any such end to the atrocious crime—to which she had confessed. Her manner was too light, too airy and too frivolous—a manner adopted, as I now see, to forestall all questions and hold back all expressions of feeling on my part. 'Tie these hanging ends of ribbon to my wrist,' were her words. 'Tie them tight; a knot under and a bow on top. I am going out— There, don't say anything— What you want to talk about will keep till tomorrow. For one night more I am going to make merry—to—to enjoy myself.' She was laughing. I thought her horribly callous and trembled with such an unspeakable repulsion that I had difficulty in making the knot. To speak at all would have been impossible. Neither did I dare to look in her face. I was touching the hand and she kept on laughing— such a hollow laugh covering up such an awful resolve! When she turned to give me that last injunction about the note, this resolve glared still in her eyes."

"And you never suspected?"

"Not for an instant. I did not do justice either to her misery or to her conscience. I fear that I have never done her justice in anyway. I thought her light, pleasure-loving. I did not know that it was assumed to hide a terrible secret."

"Then you had no knowledge of the contract she had entered into while a school-girl?"

"Not in the least. Another woman, and not myself, had been her confidante; a woman who has since died. No intimation of her first unfortunate marriage had ever reached me till Mr. Jeffrey rushed in upon me that Tuesday morning with her dreadful confession on his lips."

The district attorney, who did not seem quite satisfied on a certain point passed over by the major, now took the opportunity of saying:

"You assure us that you had no idea that this once lighthearted sister of yours meditated suicide when she left you?"

"And I repeat it, sir."

"Then why did you immediately go to Mr. Jeffrey's drawer, where you could have no business, unless it was to see if she had taken his pistol with her?"

Miss Tuttle's head fell and a soft flush broke through the pallor of her cheek.

"Because I was thinking of him. Because I was terrified for him. He had left the house the morning before in a half-maddened condition and had not come back to sleep or eat since. I did not know what a man so outraged in every sacred feeling of love and honor might be tempted to do. I thought of suicide. I remembered the old house and how he had said, 'I don't believe her. I don't believe she ever did so cold-blooded an act, or that any such dreadful machinery is in that house. I never shall believe it till I have seen and handled it myself. It is a nightmare, Cora. We are insane.' I thought of this, sirs, and when I went into her room, to change the place of the little note in the book, I went to his bureau drawer, not to look for the pistol—I did not think of that then,—but to see if the keys of the Moore house were still there. I knew that they were kept in this drawer, for I had been present in the room when they were brought in after the wedding. I had also been short-sighted enough to conclude that if they were gone it was he who had taken them. They were gone, and that was why I flew immediately from the house to the old place in Waverley Avenue. I was concerned for Mr. Jeffrey! I feared to find him there, demented or dead."

"But you had no key."

"No. Mr. Jeffrey had taken one of them and my sister the other. But the lack of a key or even of a light—for the missing candles were not taken by me[1]—could not keep me at home after I was once convinced that he had gone to this dreadful house. If I could not get in I could at least hammer at the door or rouse the neighbors. Something must be done. I did not think what; I merely flew."

"Did you know that the house had two keys?"

"Not then."

"But your sister did?"

"Probably."

"And finding the only key, as you supposed, gone, you flew to the Moore house?"

"Immediately."

"And now what else?"

"I found the door unlocked."

"That was done by Mrs. Jeffrey?"

"Yes, but I did not think of her then."

"And you went in?"

"Yes; it was all dark, but I felt my way till I came to the gilded pillars."

"Why did you go there?"

"Because I felt—I knew—if he were anywhere in that house he would be there!"

"And why did you stop?"

Her voice rose above its usual quiet pitch in shrill protest:

"You know! you know! I heard a pistol-shot from within, then a fall. I don't remember anything else. They say I went wandering about town. Perhaps I did; it is all a blank to me—everything is a blank till the policeman said that my sister was dead and I learned for the first time that the shot I had heard in the Moore house was not the signal of his death, but hers. Had I been myself when at that library door," she added, after a moment of silence, "I would have rushed in at the sound of that shot and have received my sister's dying breath."

"Cora!" The cry was from Mr. Jeffrey, and seemed to be quite involuntary. "In the weeks during which we have been kept from speaking together I have turned all these events over in my mind till I longed for any respite, even that of the grave. But in all my thinking I never attributed this motive to your visit here. Will you forgive me?"

There was a new tone in his voice, a tone which no woman could hear without emotion.

"You had other things to think of," she said, and her lips trembled. Never have I seen on the human face a more beautiful expression than I saw on hers at that moment; nor do I think Mr. Jeffrey had either, for as he marked it his own regard softened almost to tenderness.

The major had no time for sentimentalities. Turning to Mr. Jeffrey, he said:

"One more question before we send for the letter which you say will give us full insight into your wife's crime. Do you remember what occurred on the bridge at Georgetown just before you came into town that night?"

He shook his head.

"Did you meet any one there?"

"I do not know."

"Can you remember your state of mind?"

"I was facing the future."

"And what did you see in the future?"

"Death. Death for her and death for me! A crime was on her soul and she must die, and if she, then myself. I knew no other course. I could not summon the police, point out my bride of a fortnight and, with the declaration that she had been betrayed into killing a man, coldly deliver her up to justice. Neither could I live at her side knowing the guilty secret which parted us; or live anywhere in the world under this same consciousness. Therefore, I meant to kill myself before another sun rose. But she was more deeply stricken with a sense of her own guilt than I realized. When I returned home for the pistol which was to end our common misery I found that she had taken her punishment into her own hands. This strangely affected me, but when I found that, in doing this, she had remembered that I should have to face the world after she was gone, and so left a few lines for me to show in explanation of her act, my revolt against her received a check which the reading of her letter only increased. But the lines she thus wrote and left were not true lines. All her heart was mine, and if it was a wicked heart she has atoned—"

He paused, quite overcome. Others amongst us were overcome, too, but only for a moment. The following remark from the district attorney soon recalled us to the practical aspects of the case.

"You have accounted for many facts not hitherto understood. But there is still a very important one which neither yourself nor Miss Tuttle has yet made plain. There was a candle on the scene of crime; it was out when this officer arrived here. There was also one found burning in the upstairs room, aside from the one you professedly used in your tour of inspection there. Whence came those candles? And did your wife blow out the one in the library herself, previous to the shooting, or was it blown out afterward and by other lips?"

"These are questions which, as I have already said, I have no means of answering," repeated Mr. Jeffrey. "The courage which brought her here may have led her to supply herself with light; and, hard as it is to conceive, she may even have found nerve to blow out the light before she lifted the pistol to her breast:"

The district attorney and the major looked unconvinced, and the latter, turning toward Miss Tuttle, asked if she had any remark to make on the subject.

But she could only repeat Mr. Jeffrey's statement.

"These are questions I can not answer either. I have said that I stopped at the library door, which means that I saw nothing of what passed within."

Here the major asked where Mrs. Jeffrey's letter was to be found. It was Mr. Jeffrey who replied:

"Search in my room for a book with an outside cover of paper still on it. You will probably find it on my table. The inner cover is red. Bring that book here. Our secret is hidden in it."

Durbin disappeared on this errand. I followed him as far as the door, but I did not think it necessary to state that I had seen this book lying on the table when I paid my second visit to Mr. Jeffrey's room in company with the coroner. The thought that my hand had been within reach of this man's secret so many weeks before was sufficiently humiliating without being shared.

[1] We afterwards found that these candles were never delivered at the house at all; that they had been placed in the wrong basket and left in a neighboring kitchen.

CHAPTER XXIV

TANTALIZING TACTICS

I made my way to the front door, but returned almost immediately. Drawing the major aside, I whispered a request, which led to a certain small article being passed over to me, after which I sauntered out on the stoop just in time to encounter the spruce but irate figure of Mr. Moore, who had crossed from the opposite side.

"Ah!" said I. "Good morning!" and made him my most deferential bow.

He glared and Rudge glared from his place on the farther curb. Evidently the police were not in favor with the occupants of the cottage that morning.

"When is this to cease?" he curtly demanded. "When are these early-morning trespasses upon an honest citizen's property coming to an end? I wake with a light heart, expecting that my house, which is certainly as much mine as is any man's in Washington, would be handed over this very day for my habitation, when what do I see—one police officer leaving the front door and another sunning himself in the vestibule. How many more of you are within I do not presume to ask. Some half-dozen, no doubt, and not one of you smart enough to wind up this matter and have done with it."

"Ah! I don't know about that," I drawled, and looked very wise.

His curiosity was aroused.

"Anything new?" he snapped.

"Possibly," I returned, in a way to exasperate a saint.

He stepped on to the porch beside me. I was too abstracted to notice; I was engaged in eying Rudge.

"Do you know," said I, after an instant of what I meant should be one of uncomfortable suspense on his part, "that I have a greater respect than ever for that animal of yours since learning the very good reason he has for refusing to cross the street?"

"Ha! what's that?" he asked, with a quick look behind him at the watchful brute straining toward him with nose over the gutter.

"He sees farther than we can. His eyes penetrate walls and partitions," I remarked. Then, carelessly and with the calm drawing forth of a folded bit of paper which I held out toward him, I added: "By the way, here is something of yours."

His hand rose instinctively to take it; then dropped.

"I don't know what you mean," he remarked. "You have nothing of mine."

"No? Then John Judson Moore had another brother." And I thrust the paper back into my pocket.

He followed it with his eye. It was the memorandum I had found in the old book of memoirs plucked from the library shelf within, and he recognized it for his and saw that I did also. But he failed to show the white feather.

"You are good at ransacking," he observed; "pity that it can not be done to more purpose."

I smiled and made a fresh start. With my hand thrust again into my pocket, I remarked, without even so much as a glance at him:

"I fear that you do some injustice to the police. We are not such bad fellows; neither do we waste as much time as you seem to think." And drawing out my hand, with the little filigree ball in it, I whirled the latter innocently round and round on my finger. As it flashed under his eye, I cast him a penetrating look.

He tried to carry the moment off successfully; I will give him so much credit. But it was asking too much of his curiosity, and there was no mistaking the eager glitter which lighted his glance as he saw within his reach this article which a moment before he had probably regarded as lost forever.

"For instance," I went on, watching him furtively, though quite sure from his very first look that he knew no more now of the secret of this little ball than he knew when he jotted down the memorandum I had just pocketed before his eyes, "a little thing—such a little thing as this," I repeated, giving the bauble another twist—"may lead to discoveries such as no common search would yield in years. I do not say that it has; but such a thing is possible, you know: who better?"

My nonchalance was too much for him. He surveyed me with covert dislike, and dryly observed "Your opportunities have exceeded mine, even with my own effects. That petty trinket which you have presumed to flaunt in my face—and of whose value I am the worst judge in the world since I have never had it in my hand—descended to me with the rest of Mrs. Jeffrey's property. Your conduct, therefore, strikes me in the light of an impertinence, especially as no one could be supposed to have more interest than myself in what has been for many years recognized as a family talisman."

"Ah," I remarked. "You own to the memorandum then. It was made on the spot, but without the benefit of the talisman."

"I own to nothing," he snapped. Then, realizing that denial in this regard was fatal, he added more genially: "What do you mean by memorandum? If you mean that recapitulation of old-time mysteries and their accompanying features with which I once whiled away an idle hour, I own to it, of course. Why shouldn't I? It is only a proof of my curiosity in regard to this old mystery which every member of my family must feel. That curiosity has not been appeased. If it would not be indiscreet on your part, may I now ask if you have found out what that little golden ball of mine which you sport so freely before my eyes is to be used in connection with?"

"Read the papers," I said; "read tomorrow's papers, Mr. Moore; or, better still, tonight's. Perhaps they will inform you."

He was as angry as I had expected him to be, but as this ire proved conclusively that his strongest emotion had been curiosity rather than fear, I felt assured of my ground, and turned to reenter the house. Mr. Moore did not accompany me.

The major was standing in the hall. The others had evidently retreated to the parlor.

"The man opposite knows what he knows," said I; "but this does not include the facts concerning the picture in the southwest chamber or the devilish mechanism."

"You are sure?"

"As positive as one of my inexperience can be. But, Major, I am equally positive that he knows more than he should of Mrs. Jeffrey's death. I am even ready to state that in my belief he was in the house when it occurred."

"Has he acknowledged this?"

"Not at all."

"Then what are your reasons for this belief?"

"They are many"

"Will you state them?"

"Gladly, if you will pardon the presumption. Some of my conclusions can not be new to you. The truth is that I have possibly seen more of this old man than my duty warranted, and I feel quite ready to declare that he knows more of what has taken place in this house than he is ready to avow. I am sure that he has often visited it in secret and knows about a certain broken window as well as we do. I am also sure that he was here on the night of Mrs. Jeffrey's suicide. He was too little surprised when I informed him of what had happened not to have had some secret inkling of it beforehand, even if we had not the testimony of the lighted candle and the book he so hurriedly replaced. Besides, he is not the man to drag himself out at night for so simple a cause as the one with which he endeavored to impose upon us. He knew what we should find in this house."

"Very good. If Mr. Jeffrey's present explanations are true, these deductions of yours are probably correct. But Mr. Moore's denial has been positive. I fear that it will turn out a mere question of veracity."

"Not necessarily," I returned. "I think I see a way of forcing this man to acknowledge that he was in or about this house on that fatal night."

"You do?"

"Yes, sir; I do not want to boast, and I should be glad if you did not oblige me to confide to you the means by which I hope to bring this out. Only give me leave to insert an advertisement in both evening and morning papers and in two days I will report failure or success."

The major eyed me with an interest that made my heart thrill. Then he quickly said: "You have earned the privilege; I will give you two days."

At this moment Durbin reappeared. As I heard his knock and turned to open the door for him, I cast the major an entreating if not eloquent look.

He smiled and waved his hand with friendly assurance. The state of feeling between Durbin and myself was evidently well known to him.

My enemy entered with a jaunty air, which changed ever so slightly when he saw me in close conference with the superintendent.

He had the book in his pocket. Taking it out, he handed it to the major, with this remark:

"You won't find anything there; the gent's been fooling you."

The major opened the book, shook it, looked under the cover, found nothing, and crossed hastily to the drawing-room. We as hastily followed him. The district attorney was talking with Miss Tuttle; Mr. Jeffrey was nervously pacing the floor. The latter stopped as we all entered and his eyes flashed to the book.

"Let me take it," said he.

"It is absolutely empty," remarked the major. "The letter has been abstracted, probably without your knowledge."

"I do not think so," was Mr. Jeffrey's unexpected retort. "Do you suppose that I would intrust a secret, for the preservation of which I was ready to risk life and honor, to the open pages of a book? When I found myself threatened with all sorts of visits from the police and realized that at any moment my effects might be ransacked, I sought a hiding place for this letter, which no man without superhuman insight could discover. Look!"

And, pulling off the outside wrapper, he inserted the point of his penknife under the edge of the paper lining the inside cover and ripped it off with a jerk.

"I pasted this here myself," he cried, and showed us where between this paper and the boards, in a place thinned out to hold it, there lay a number of folded sheets, which, with a deep sigh, he handed over to the major's inspection. As he did so he remarked:

"I had rather have died any natural death than have had my miserable wife's secret known. But since the crime has come to light, this story of her sin and her repentance may serve in some slight degree to mitigate public opinion. She was sorely tempted and she succumbed; the crime of her ancestors was in her blood."

He again walked off. The major unfolded the sheets.

CHAPTER XXV

WHO WILL TELL THE MAN INSIDE THERE

Later I saw this letter. It was like no other that has ever come under my eye. Written at intervals, as her hand had power or her misery found words, it bore on its face all the evidences of that restless, suffering spirit which for thirty-six hours drove her in frenzy about her room, and caused Loretta to say, in her effort to describe her mistress' face as it appeared to her at the end of this awful time: "It was as if a blight had passed over it. Once gay and animated beyond the power of any one to describe, it had become a ghost's face, with the glare of some awful resolve upon it." I give this letter just as it was written-disjointed paragraphs, broken sentences, unfinished words and all. The breaks show where she laid down her pen, possibly for that wild pacing of the floor which left such unmistakable signs behind it. It opens abruptly:

"I killed him. I am all that I said I was, and you can never again give me a thought save in the way of cursing and to bewail the day I came into your life. But you can not hate me more than I hate myself, my wicked self, who, seeing an obstacle in the way to happiness, stamped it out of existence, and so forfeited all right to happiness forever.

"It was so easy! Had it been a hard thing to do; had it been necessary to lay hand on knife or lift a pistol, I might have realized the act and paused. But just a little spring which a child's hand could manage— Who, feeling for it, could help pressing it, if only to see—

"I was always a reckless girl, mad for pleasure and without any thought of consequences. When school bored me, I took all my books out of my desk, called upon my mates to do the same, and, stacking them up into a sort of rostrum in a field where we played, first delivered an oration from them in which reverence for my teachers had small part, then tore them into pieces and burned them in full sight of my admiring school-fellows. I was dismissed, but not with disgrace. Teachers and scholars bewailed my departure, not because they liked me, or because of any good they had found in me, but because my money had thrown luster on them and on the whole establishment.

"This was when I was twelve, and it was on account of this reckless escapade that I was sent west and kept so long from home and all my flatterers. My guardian meant well by this, but in saving me from one pitfall he plunged me into another. I grew up without Cora and also without any idea of the requirements of my position or what I might anticipate from the world when the time came for me to enter it. I knew that I had money; so did those about me; but I had little or no idea of the amount, nor what that money would do for me when I returned to Washington. So, in an evil day, and when I was just eighteen, I fell in love, or thought I did, with a man—(Oh, Francis, imagine it, now that I have seen you!)—of sufficient attraction to satisfy one whose prospects were limited to a contracted existence in some small town, but no more fitted to content me after seeing Washington life than if he had been a common farm hand or the most ordinary of clerks in a country store. But I was young, ignorant and self-willed, and thought because my cheek burned under his look that he was the man of men, and suited to be my husband. That is, if I thought at all, which is not likely; for I was in a feverish whirl, and just followed the impulse of the moment, which was to be with him whenever I could without attracting the teacher's attention. And this, alas! was only too often, for he was the brother of one of our storekeepers, a visitor in Owosso, and often in the store where we girls went. Why the teachers did not notice how often we needed things there, I do not know. But they did not, and matters went on and—

"I can not write of those days, and you do not want to hear about them. They seem impossible to me now, and almost as if it had all happened to some one else, so completely have I forgotten the man except as the source and cause of an immeasurable horror. Yet he was not bad himself; only ordinary and humdrum. Indeed, I believe he was very good in ways, or so his brother once assured me. We would not have been married in the way we were if he had not wanted to go to the Klondike for the purpose of making money and making it quickly, so that his means might match mine.

"I do not know which of us two was most to blame for that marriage. He urged it because he was going so far away and wanted to be sure of me. I accepted it because it seemed to be romantic and because it pleased me to have my own way in spite of my hard old guardian and the teachers, who were always prying about, and the girls, who went silly over him—for he was really handsome in his way—and who thought, (at least many of them did,) that he cared for them when he cared only for me.

"I have hated black eyes for a year. He had black eyes.

"I forgot Cora, or, rather, I did not let any remembrance of her hinder me. She was a very shadowy person to me in those days. I had not seen her since we were both children, and as for her letters—they were almost a bore to me; she lived such a different life from mine and wrote of so many things I had no interest in. On my knees I ask her pardon now. I never understood her. I never understood myself. I was light as thistledown and blown by every breeze. There came a gust one day which blew me into the mouth of hell. I am hovering there yet and am sinking, Francis, sinking—Save me! I love you—I—I—

"It was all planned by him—I have no head for such things. Sadie helped him—Sadie was my friend—but Sadie had not much to say about it, for he seemed to know just how to arrange it all so that no one at the seminary should know or even suspect what had occurred till we got ready to tell them. He did not even take his brother into his confidence, for Wallace kept store and gossiped very much with his customers. Besides, he was very busy just then selling out, for he was going to the Klondike with William, and he had too much on his mind to be bothered, or so William said. All this I must tell you or you will never understand the temptation which assailed me when, having returned to Washington, I awoke to my own position and the kind of men whom I could now hope to meet. I was the wife—oh, the folly of it—but this was known to so few, and those were so far removed, and one even—my friend

Sadie—being dead— Why not ignore the miserable secret ceremony and cheat myself into believing myself free, and enjoy this world of pleasure and fashion as Cora was enjoying it and—trust. Trust what? Why the Klondike! That swallower-up of men. Why shouldn't it swallow one more— Oh, I know that it sounds hateful. But I was desperate; I had seen you.

"I had one letter from him after he reached Alaska, but that was before I left Owosso. I never got another. And I never wrote to him. He told me not to do so until he could send me word how and where to write; but when these directions came my heart had changed and my only wish was to forget his existence. And I did forget it—almost. I rode and danced with you and went hither and yon, lavishing money and time and heart on the frivolities which came in my way, calling myself Veronica and striving by these means to crush out every remembrance of the days when I was known as Antoinette and Antoinette only. For the Klondike was far and its weather bitter, and men were dying there every day, and no letters came (I used to thank God for this), and I need not think—not yet—whither I was tending. One thing only made me recall my real position. That was when your eyes turned on mine—your true eyes, so bright with confidence and pride. I wanted to meet them full, and when I could not, I suddenly knew why, and suffered.

"Do you remember the night when we stood together on the balcony at the Ocean View House and you laid your hand on my arm and wondered why I persisted in looking at the moon instead of into your expectant face? It was because the music then being played within recalled another night and the pressure of another hand on my arm—a hand whose touch I hoped never to feel again, but which at that moment was so much more palpable than yours that I came near screaming aloud and telling you in one rush of maddened emotion my whole abominable secret.

"I did not accept your attentions nor agree to marry you, without a struggle. You know that. You can tell, as no one else can, how I held back and asked for time and still for time, thus grieving you and tearing my own breast till a day came—you remember the day when you found me laughing like a mad woman in a circle of astonished friends? You drew me aside and said words which I hardly waited for you to finish, for at last I was free to love you, free to love and free to say so. The morning paper had brought news. A telegraphic despatch from Seattle told how a man had struggled into Nome, frozen, bleeding and without accouterments or companion. It was with difficulty he had kept his feet and turned in at the first tent he came to. Indeed, he had only time to speak his name before he fell dead. This name was what made this despatch important to me. It was William Pfeiffer. For me there was but one William Pfeiffer in the Klondike—my husband—and he was dead! That was why you found me laughing. But not in mirth. I am not so bad as that; but because I could breathe again without feeling a clutch about my throat. I did not know till then how nearly I had been stifled.

"We were not long in marrying after that. I was terrified at delay, not because I feared any contradiction of the report which had given this glorious release, but because I dreaded lest some hint of my early folly should reach you and dim the pride with which you regarded me. I wanted to feel myself yours so closely and so dearly that you would not mind if any one told you that I had once cared, or thought I had cared, for another. The week of our marriage came; I was mad with gaiety and ecstatic with hope. Nothing had occurred to mar my prospects. No letter from Denver—no memento from the Klondike, no word even from Wallace, who had gone north with his brother. Soon I should be called wife again, but by lips I loved, and to whose language my heart thrilled. The past, always vague, would soon be no more than a forgotten dream—an episode quite closed. I could afford from this moment on to view life like other girls and rejoice in my youth and the love which every day was becoming more and more to me.

"But God had His eye upon me, and in the midst of my happiness and the hurry of our final preparations His bolt fell. It struck me while I was at the—don't laugh; rather shudder—at the dressmaker's shop in Fourteenth Street. I was leaning over a table, chattering like a magpie over the way I wanted a gown trimmed, when my eye fell on a scrap of newspaper in which something had come rolled to madame. It was torn at the edge, but on the bit lying under my eyes I saw my husband's name, William Pfeiffer, and that the paper was a Denver one. There was but one William Pfeiffer in Denver—and he was my husband. And I read—feeling nothing. Then I read again, and the world, my world, went from under my feet; for the man who had fallen dead in the camp at Nome was Wallace, William's brother, and not William himself. William had been left behind on the road by his more energetic brother, who had pushed on for succor through the worst storm and under the worst conditions possible even in that God-forsaken region. With the lost one in mind, the one word that Wallace uttered in sight of rescue, was William. A hope was expressed of finding the latter alive and a party had started out—Did I read more? I do not think so. Perhaps there was no more to read; here was where the paper was torn across. But it was no matter. I had seen enough. It was Wallace who had fallen dead, and while William might have perished also, and doubtless had, I had no certainty of it. And my wedding day was set for Thursday.

"Why didn't I tell Cora; why didn't I tell you? Pride held my tongue; besides, I had had time to think before I saw either of you, and to reason a bit and to feel sure that if Wallace had been spent enough to fall dead on reaching the camp, William could never have survived on the open road. For Wallace was the stronger of the two and the most hardy every way. Free I certainly was. Some later paper would assure me of this. I would hunt them up and see—but I never did. I do not think I dared. I was afraid I should see some account of his rescue. I was afraid of being made certain of what was now but a possibility, and so I did nothing. But for three nights I did not sleep.

"The caprice which had led me to choose the old Moore house to be married in led me to plan dressing there on my wedding morning. It was early when we started, Cora and I, for Waverley Avenue, but not too early for the approaches to that dreadful house to be crowded with people, eager to see the daring bride. Why I should have shrunk so from that crowd I can not say. I trembled at sight of their faces and at the sound of their voices, and if by chance a head was thrust forward farther than the rest I cowered back instinctively and nearly screamed. Did I dread to recognize a too familiar face? The paper I had seen bore a date six months back. A man could arrive here from Alaska in that time. Or was my conscience aroused at last and clamoring to be heard when it was too late? On the corner of N Street the carriage suddenly stopped. A man had crossed in front of it. I caught one glimpse of this man and instantly the terrors of a lifetime were concentrated into one instant of agonizing fear. It was William Pfeiffer. I knew the look; I knew the gait. He was gone in a moment and the carriage rolled on. But I knew my doom as well that minute as I did an hour later. My husband was alive and he was here. He had escaped the perils of the Klondike and wandered east to reclaim his recreant wife. There had been time for him to do this since the rescue party left home in search of him; time for him to recover, time for him to reach home, time for him to reach the east. He had heard of my wedding; it was in all the papers, and I should find him at the house when I got there, and you would know and Cora would know, and the wedding would stop and my name be made a by-word the world over. Instead of the joy awaiting me a moment since, I should have to go away with him into some wilderness or distant place of exile where my maiden name would never be heard, and all the memories of this year of stolen delights be effaced. Oh, it was horrible! And all in a minute! And Cora sat there, pale, calm and beautiful as an angel, beaming on me with tender eyes whose expression I have never understood! Hell in my heart,— and she, in happy ignorance of this, brooding over my joy and smiling to herself while the soft tears rose!

"You were waiting at the curb when I arrived, and I remember how my heart stood still when you laid your hand on the carriage door and confronted me with that light on your face I had never seen disturbed since we first pledged ourselves to marry. Would he see it, too, and come forward from the secret place where he held himself hidden? Was I destined to behold a struggle in the streets, an unseemly contest of words in sight of the door I had expected to enter so joyously? In terror of such an event, I seized the hand which seemed my one refuge in this hour of mortal trouble, and hastened into the house which, for all its doleful history, had never received within its doors a heart more burdened or rebellious. As this thought rushed over me, I came near crying out, 'The house of doom! The house of doom!' I had thought to brave its terrors and its crimes and it has avenged itself. But instead of that, I pressed your hand with mine and smiled. O God! if you could have seen what lay beneath that smile! For, with my entrance beneath those fatal doors a thought had come. I remembered my heritage. I remembered how I had been told by my father when I was a very little girl,—I presume when he first felt the hand of death upon him,—that if ever I was in great trouble,—very great trouble, he had said, where no deliverance seemed possible—I was to open a little golden ball which he showed me and take out what I should find inside and hold it close up before a picture which had hung from time immemorial in the southwest corner of this old house. He could not tell me what I should encounter there this I remember his saying—but something that would assist me, something which had passed with good effect from father down to child for many generations. Only, if I would be blessed in my undertakings, I must not open the golden ball nor endeavor to find out its mystery unless my trouble threatened death or some great disaster. Such a trouble had indeed come to me, and—startling coincidence—I was at this moment in the very house where this picture hung, and—more startling fact yet—the golden ball needed to interpret its meaning was round my neck—for with such jealousy was this family trinket always guarded by its owner. Why then not test their combined effect? I certainly needed help from some quarter. Never would William allow me to be married to another while he lived. He would yet appear and I should need thus great assistance (great enough to be transmitted from father to son) as none of the Moores had needed it yet; though what it was I did not know and did not even try to guess.

"Yet when I got to the room I did not drag out the filigree ball at once nor even take more than one fearful side-long look at the picture. In drawing off my glove I had seen his ring—the ring you had once asked about. It was such a cheap affair; the only one he could get in that obscure little town where we were married. I lied when you asked me if it was a family jewel; lied but did not take it off, perhaps because it clung so tightly, as if in remembrance of the vows it symbolized. But now the very sight of it gave me a fright. With his ring on my finger I could not defy him and swear his claim to be false the dream of a man maddened by his experiences in the Klondike. It must come off. Then, perhaps, I should feel myself a free woman. But it would not come off. I struggled with it and tugged in vain; then I bethought me of using a nail file to sever it. This I did, grinding and grinding at it till the ring finally broke, and I could wrench it off and cast it away out of sight and, as I hoped, out of my memory also. I breathed easier when rid of this token, yet choked with terror whenever a step approached the door. I was clad in my bridal dress, but not in my bridal veil or ornaments, and naturally Cora, and then my maid, came to assist me. But I would not let them in. I was set upon testing the secret of the filigree ball and so preparing myself for what my conscience told me lay between me and the ceremony arranged for high noon.

"I did not guess that the studying out of that picture would take so long. The contents of the ball turned out to be a small magnifying-glass, and the picture a maze of written words. I did not decipher it all; I did not decipher the half. I did not need to. A spirit of divination was given me in that awful hour which enabled me to grasp its full meaning from the few sentences I did pick out. And that meaning! It was horrible, inconceivable. Murder was taught; but murder from a distance, and by an act too simple to awake revulsion. Were the wraiths of my two ancestors who had played with the spring hidden in the depths of this old closet, drawn up in mockery beside me during the hour when I stood spellbound in the middle of the floor, thinking of what I had just read, and listening—listening for something less loud than the sound of carriages now beginning to roll up in front or the stray notes of the band tuning up below?—less loud, but meaning what? A step into the empty closet yawning so near—an effort with a drawer—a—a— Do not ask me to recall it. I did not shudder when the moment came and I stood there. Then I was cold as marble. But I shudder now in thinking of it till soul and body seem separating, and the horror which envelopes me gives me such a foretaste of hell that I wonder I can contemplate the deed which, if it releases me from this earthly anguish, will only plunge me into a possibly worse hereafter. Yet I shall surely take my life before you see me again, and in that old house. If it is despair I feel, then despair will take me there. If it is repentance, then repentance will suffice to drive me to the one expiation possible to me—to perish where I caused an innocent man to perish, and so relieve you of a wife who was never worthy of you and whom it would be your duty to denounce if she let another sun rise upon her guilt.

"I did not stand there long between the wraiths of my murderous ancestors. A message was shouted through the door—the message for which my ears had been strained in dreadful anticipation for the last two hours. A man named Pfeiffer wanted to see me before I went down to be married. A man named Pfeiffer!

"I looked closely at the boy who delivered this message. He showed no excitement, nor any feeling greater than impatience at being kept waiting a minute or so at the door. Then I glanced beyond him, at the people chatting in the hall. No alarm there; nothing but a very natural surprise that the bride should keep so big a crowd waiting. I felt that this fixed the event. He who had sent me this quiet message was true to himself and to our old compact. He had not published below what would have set the house in an uproar in a moment. He had left his secret to be breathed into my ear alone. I could recall the moment he passed me his word, and his firm look as he said, with his hand lifted to Heaven 'You have been good to me and given me your precious self while I was poor and a nobody. In return, I swear to keep our marriage a secret till great success shows me to be worthy of you or till you with your own lips express forgiveness of my failure and grant me leave to speak. Nothing but death or your permission shall ever unseal my lips.' When I heard that he was dead I feared lest he might have spoken, but now that I had seen him alive, I knew that in no other breast, save his, my own and that of the unknown minister in an almost unknown town, dwelt any knowledge of the fact which stood between me and the marriage which all these people had come here to see. My confidence in his rectitude determined me. Without conscious emotion, without fear even,—the ending of suspense had ended all that,—I told the boy to seat the gentleman in the library. Then "I am haunted now, I am haunted always, by one vision, horrible but persistent. It will not leave me; it rises between us now; it has stood between us ever since I left that house with the seal of your affection on my lips. Last night it terrified me into unconscious speech. I dreamed that I saw again, and plainly, what I caught but a shadowy glimpse of in that murderous hour: a man's form seated at the end of the old settle, with his head leaning back, in silent contemplation. His face was turned the other way—I thanked God for that—no, I did not thank God; I never thought of God in that moment of my blind feeling about for a chink and a spring in the wall. I thought only of your impatience, and the people waiting, and the pleasure of days to come when, free from this intolerable bond, I could keep my place at your side and bear your name unreproved and taste to the full the awe and delight of a passion such as few women ever feel, because few women were ever loved by a man like you. Had my thoughts been elsewhere, my fingers might have forgotten to fumble along that wall, and I had been simply wretched to-day,—and innocent. Innocent! O, where in God's universe can I be made innocent again and fit to look in your face and to love—heart-breaking thought—even to love you again?

"To turn and turn a miserable crank after those moments of frenzied action and silence that was the hard part-that was what tried my nerve and first robbed me of calmness. But I dared not leave that fearful thing dangling there; I had to wind. The machinery squeaked, and its noise seemed to fill the house, but no one came nor did the door below open. Sometimes I have wished that it had. I should not then have been lured on and you would not have become involved in my ruin.

"I have heard many say that I looked radiant when I came down to be married. The radiance was in their thoughts. Or if my face did shine, and if I moved as if treading on air, it was because I had triumphed over all difficulties and could pass down to the altar without fear of that interrupting voice crying out: 'I forbid! She is mine! The wife of William Pfeiffer can not wed another!' No such words could be dreaded now. The lips which might have spoken them were dumb. I forgot that fleshless lips gibber loudest, and that a lifetime, long or short, lay before me, in which to hear them mumble and squeak their denunciation and threats. Oh, but I have been wretched! At ball and dinner and dance those lips have been ever at my ear, but most when we have sat alone together; most then; Oh, most then!

"He is avenged; but you! Who will avenge you, and where will you ever find happiness?

"To blot myself from your memory I would go down deeper into the vale of suffering than ever I have gone yet. But no, no! do not quite forget me. Remember me as you saw me one night—the night you took the flower out of my hair and kissed it, saying that Washington held many beautiful women, but that none of them save myself had ever had the power to move your inmost heart-strings. Ah, low was your voice and eloquent your eyes that hour, and I forgot,—for a moment I forgot—everything but this pure love; and the heartbeat it called up and the hope, never to be realized—that I should live to hear you repeat the same sweet words in our old age, in just such a tone and with just such a look. I was innocent at that moment, innocent and good. I am willing that you should remember me as I was that night.

"When I think of him lying cold and dead in the grave I myself dug for him, my heart is like stone, but when I think of you—

"I am afraid to die; but I am more afraid of failing in courage. I shall have the pistol tied to me; this will make it seem inevitable to use it. Oh! that the next twenty-four hours could be blotted out of time! Such horror can not be. I was born for joy and gaiety; yet no dismal depth of misery and fear has been spared me! But all on account of my own act. I do not accuse God; I do not accuse man; I only accuse myself, and my thoughtless grasping after pleasure.

"I want Cora to read this as well as you. She must know me dead as she never knew me living. But I can not tell her that I have left a confession behind me. She must come upon it unexpectedly, just as I mean you to do. Only thus can it reach either of you with any power. If I could but think of some excuse for sending her to the book where I propose to hide it! that would give her a chance of reading it before you do, and this would be best. She may know how to prepare or comfort you—I hope so. Cora is a noble woman, but the secret which kept my thoughts in such a whirl has held us apart.

"You did what I asked. You found a place for Rancher's waiter in the volunteer corps. Surprised as you were at the interest I expressed in him, you honored my first request and said nothing. Would you have shown the same anxious eagerness if you had known why I whispered those few words to him from the carriage door? Why I could neither rest nor sleep till he and the other boy were safely out of town?

"I must leave a line for you to show to people if they should wonder why I killed myself so soon after my seemingly happy marriage. You will find it in the same book with this letter. Some one will tell you to look in the book—I can not write any more.

"I can not help writing. It is all that connects me now with life and with you. But I have nothing more to say except, forgive—forgive—

"Do you think that God looks at his wretched ones differently from what men do? That He will have tenderness for one so sorry—that He will even find place—But my mother is there! my father! Oh, that makes it fearful to go—to meet—But it was my father who led me into this—only he did not know—There! I will think only of God.

"Good by—good by—good—"

That was all. It ended, as it began, without name and without date,—the final heart-throbs of a soul, awakened to its own act when it was quite too late. A piteous memorial which daunted each one of us as we read it, and when finished, drew us all together in the hall out of the sight and hearing of the two persons most intimately concerned in it.

Possibly because all had one thought—a thrilling one, which the major was the first to give utterance to.

"The man she killed was buried under the name of Wallace. How's that, if he was her husband, William?"

An officer we had not before noted was standing near the front door. He came forward at this and placed a second telegram in the superintendent's hand. It was from the same source as the one previously received and appeared to settle this very question.

"I have just learned that the man married was not the one who kept store in Owosso, but his brother William, who afterward died in Klondike. It is Wallace whose death you are investigating."

"What snarl is here?" asked the major.

"I think I understand," I ventured to put in. "Her husband was the one left on the road by the brother who staggered into camp for aid. He was a weak man—the weaker of the two she said—and probably died, while Wallace, after seemingly collapsing, recovered. This last she did not know, having failed to read the whole of the newspaper slip which told about it, and so when she saw some one with the Pfeiffer air and figure and was told later that a Mr. Pfeiffer was waiting to see her, she took it for granted that it was her husband, believing positively that Wallace was dead. The latter, moreover, may have changed to look more like his brother in the time that had elapsed."

"A possible explanation which adds greatly to the tragic aspects of the situation. She was probably a widow when she touched the fatal spring. Who will tell the man inside there? It will be his crowning blow."

CHAPTER XXVI

RUDGE

I never saw any good reason for my changing the opinion just expressed. Indeed, as time went on and a further investigation was made into the life and character of these two brothers, I came to think that not only had the unhappy Veronica mistaken the person of Wallace Pfeiffer for that of her husband William, but also the nature of the message he sent her and the motives which actuated it; that the interview he so peremptorily demanded before she descended to her nuptials would, had she but understood it properly, have yielded her an immeasurable satisfaction instead of rousing in her alarmed breast the criminal instincts of her race; that it was meant to do this; that he, knowing William's secret—a secret which the latter naturally would confide to him at a moment so critical as that which witnessed their parting in the desolate Klondike pass—had come, not to reproach her with her new nuptials, but to relieve her mind in case she cherished the least doubt of her full right to marry again, by assurances of her husband's death and of her own complete freedom. To this he may have intended to add some final messages of love and confidence from the man she had been so ready to forget; but nothing worse. Wallace Pfeiffer was incapable of anything worse, and if she had only resigned herself to her seeming fate and consented to see this man—

But to return to fact and leave speculation to the now doubly wretched Jeffrey.

On the evening of the day which saw our first recognition of this crime as the work of Veronica Moore, the following notice appeared in the Star and all the other local journals:

"Any person who positively remembers passing through Waverley Avenue between N and M Streets on the evening of May the eleventh at or near the hour of a quarter past seven will confer a favor on the detective force of the District by communicating the same to F. at the police headquarters in C street."

I was "F.," and I was soon deep in business. But I was readily able to identify those who came from curiosity, and as the persons who had really fulfilled the conditions expressed in my advertisement were few, an evening and morning's work sufficed to sift the whole matter down to the one man who could tell me just what I wanted to know. With this man I went to the major, and as a result we all met later in the day at Mr. Moore's door.

This gentleman looked startled enough when he saw the number and character of his visitors; but his grand air did not forsake him and his welcome was both dignified and cordial. But I did not like the way his eye rested on me.

But the slight venom visible in it at that moment was nothing to what he afterwards displayed when at a slight growl from Rudge, who stood in an attitude of offense in the doorway beyond, I drew the attention of all to the dog by saying sharply:

"There is our witness, sirs. There is the dog who will not cross the street even when his master calls him, but crouches on the edge of the curb and waits with eager eyes but immovable body, till that master comes back. Isn't that so, Mr. Moore? Have I not heard you utter more than one complaint in this regard?"

"I can not deny it," was the stiff reply, "but what—"

I did not wait for him to finish.

"Mr. Correan," I asked, "is this the animal you gassed between the hours of seven and eight on the evening of May the eleventh, crouching in front of this house with his nose to the curbstone?"

"It is; I noted him particularly; he seemed to be watching the opposite house."

Instantly I turned upon Mr. Moore.

"Is Rudge the dog to do that," I asked, "if his master were not there? Twice have I myself seen him in the self-same place and with the self-same air of expectant attention, and both times you had crossed to the house which you acknowledge he will approach no nearer than the curb on this side of the street."

"You have me," was the short reply with which Mr. Moore gave up the struggle. "Rudge, go back to your place. When you are wanted in the court-room I will let you know."

The smile with which he said this was sarcastic enough, but it was sarcasm directed mainly against himself. We were not surprised when, after some sharp persuasion on the part of the major, he launched into the following recital of his secret relation to what he called the last tragedy ever likely to occur in the Moore family.

"I never thought it wrong to be curious about the old place; I never thought it wrong to be curious about its mysteries. I only considered it wrong, or at all events ill judged, to annoy Veronica, in regard to them, or to trouble her in any way about the means by which I might effect an entrance into its walls. So I took the one that offered and said nothing.

"I have visited the old house many times during my sojourn in this little cottage. The last time was, as one of your number has so ably discovered on the most memorable night in its history; the one in which Mrs. Jeffrey's remarkable death occurred there. The interest roused in me by the unexpected recurrence of the old fatality attending the library hearthstone reached its culmination when I perceived one night the glint of a candle burning in the southwest chamber. I did not know who was responsible for this light, but I strongly suspected it to be Mr. Jeffrey; for who else would dare to light a candle in this disused house without first seeing that all the shutters were fast? I did not dislike Mr. Jeffrey or question his right to do this. Nevertheless I was very angry. Though allied to a Moore he was not one himself and the difference in our privileges affected me strongly. Consequently I watched till he came out and upon positively recognizing his figure vowed in my wrath and jealous indignation to visit the old house myself on the following night and make one final attempt to learn the secret which would again make me the equal of this man, if not his superior.

"It was early when I went; indeed it was not quite dark, but knowing the gloom of those old halls and the almost impenetrable nature of the darkness that settles over the library the moment the twilight set in, I put in my pocket two or three candles, sirs, about which you have made such a coil. My errand was twofold. I wanted first to see what Mr. Jeffrey had been up to the night before, and next, to spend an hour over a certain book of old memoirs which in recalling the past might explain the present. You remember a door leading into the library from the rear room. It was by this door I entered, bringing with me from the kitchen the chair you afterwards found there."

I knew where the volume of memoirs I speak of was to be found—you do, too, I see—for it was my hand which had placed it in its present concealment. Quite determined to reread such portions of it, as I had long before marked as pertinent to the very attempt I had in mind, I brought in the candelabrum from the parlor and drew out a table to hold it. But I waited a few moments before taking down the book itself. I wanted first to learn what Mr. Jeffrey had been doing upstairs the night before. So leaving the light burning in the library, I proceeded to the southwest chamber, holding an unlit candle in my hand, the light feebly diffused through the halls from some upper windows being sufficient for me to see my way. But in the chamber itself all was dark.

The wind had not yet risen and the shutter which a half-hour later moved so restlessly on its creaking hinges, hugged the window so tightly that I imagined Mr. Jeffrey had fastened it the night before. Looking for some receptacle in which to set the candle I now lit, I failed to find anything but an empty tumbler, so I made use of that. Then I glanced about me, but seeing nothing worth my attention—Mrs. Jeffrey's wedding fixings did not interest me, and everything else about the room looking natural except the overturned chair, which struck me as immaterial. I hurried downstairs again, leaving the candle burning behind me in case I should wish to return aloft after I had refreshed my mind with what had been written about this old room.

"Not a sound disturbed the house as I seated myself to my reading in front of the library shelves. I was as much alone under that desolate roof as mortal could be with men anywhere within reach of him. I enjoyed the solitude and was making a very pretty theory for myself on a scrap of paper I tore from another old book when a noise suddenly rose in front, which, slight as it was, was quite unmistakable to ears trained in listening. Some one was unlocking the front door.

"Naturally I thought it to be Mr. Jeffrey returning for a second visit to his wife's house, and knowing what I might expect if he surprised me on the premises, I restored the book hastily to its place and as hastily blew out the candle. Then, with every intention of flight, I backed toward the door by which I had entered. But some impulse stronger than that of escape made me stop just before I reached it. I could see nothing; the place was dark as Tophet; but I could listen. The person—Mr. Jeffrey, or some other— was coming my way and in perfect darkness. I could hear the faltering steps—the fingers dragging along the walls; then a rustle as of skirts, proving the intruder to be a woman—a fact which greatly surprised me—then a long drawn sigh or gasp.

"The last determined me. The situation was too intense for me to leave without first learning who the woman was who in terror and shrinking dared to drag her half resisting feet through these empty halls and into a place cursed with such unwholesome memories. I did not think of Veronica. No one looks for a butterfly in the depths of a dungeon. But I did think of Miss Tuttle—that woman of resolute will. Without attempting to imaging the reason for her presence, I stood my ground and harkened till the heavy mahogany door at the other end of the room began to swing in by jerks under the faint and tremulous push of a terrified hand. Then there came silence—a long silence—followed by a moan so agonized that I realized that whatever was the cause of this panting woman's presence here, it was due to no mere errand of curiosity. This whetted my purpose. Anything done in this house was in a way done to me; so I remained quiet and watched. But the sounds which now and then came from the remote corner upon which my attention was concentrated were very eloquent.

"I heard sighs and bitter groans, with now and then a murmured prayer, broken by a low wailing, in which I caught the name of Francis. And still, possibly on account of the utterance of this name, I thought the woman near me to be Miss Tuttle, and even went so far as to imagine the cause of her suffering if not the nature of her retribution. Words succeeded cries and I caught phrases expressive of fear and some sort of agonized hesitation. Once these broken ejaculations were interrupted by a dull sound. Something had dropped to the bare floor. We shall never know what it was, but I have no doubt that it was the pistol, and that the marks of dust to be found on the connecting ribbon were made by her own fingers in taking it again in her hand. (You will remember that these same fingers had but a few minutes previous groped their way along the walls.) For her voice soon took a different tone, and such unintelligible phrases as these could be heard issuing from her partly paralyzed lips:

"'I must!—I can never meet his eye again alive. He would despise— Brave enough to—to—another's blood—coward—when—own. Oh, God! forgive!' Then another silence during which I almost made up my mind to interfere, then a loud report and a flash so startling and unexpected that I recoiled, during which the room leaped into sudden view—she too—Veronica—with baby face drawn and set like a woman's—then darkness again and a heavy fall which shook the floor, if not my hard old heart. The flash and that fall enlightened me. I had just witnessed the suicide of the last Moore saving myself; a suicide for which I was totally unprepared and one which I do not yet understand."

I did not go over to her. She was as dead when she fell as she ever would be. In the flash which lit everything, I had seen where her pistol was pointed. Why disturb her then? Nor did I return upstairs. I had small interest now in anything but my own escape from a situation more or less compromising.

"Do you blame me for this? I was her heir and I was where I had no legal right to be. Do you think that I was called upon to publish my shame and tell how I lingered there while my own niece shot herself before my eyes? That shot made me a millionaire. This certainly was excitement enough for one day— besides, I did not leave her there neglected. I notified you later—after I had got my breath and had found some excuse. That wasn't enough? Ah, I see that you are all models of courage and magnanimity. You would have laid yourselves open to every reproach rather than let a little necessary perjury pass your lips. But I am no model. I am simply an old man who has been too hardly dealt with for seventy long years to possess every virtue. I made a mistake—I see it now—trusted a dog when I shouldn't—but if Rudge had not seen ghosts—well, what now?"

We had, one and all, with an involuntary impulse, turned our backs upon him.

"What are you doing?" he hotly demanded.

"Only what all Washington will do to-morrow, and afterwards the whole world," gravely returned the major. Then, as an ejaculation escaped the astonished millionaire, he impressively added: "A perjury which allows an innocent man and woman to remain under the suspicion of murder for five weeks is one which not only the law has a right to punish, but which all society will condemn. Henceforth you will find yourself under a ban, Mr. Moore."[1]

My story ends here. The matter never came before the grand jury. Suicide had been proved, and there the affair rested. Of myself it is enough to add that I sometimes call in Durbin to help me in a big case.

[1] Time amply verified this prophecy. Mr. Moore is living in great style in the Moore house, and drives horses which are conspicuous even in Washington. But no one accepts his invitations, and he is as much

of a recluse in his present mansion as he ever was in the humble cottage in which his days of penury were spent.

CHAPTER XXVII

"YOU HAVE COME! YOU HAVE SOUGHT ME!"

These are some words from a letter written a few months after the foregoing by one Mrs. Edward Truscott to a friend in New York:

"Edinburgh, May 7th, 1900.

"Dear Louisa:—You have always accused me of seeing more and hearing more than any other person of your acquaintance. Perhaps I am fortunate in that respect. Certainly I have been favored today with an adventure of some interest which I make haste to relate to you.

"Being anxious to take home with me some sketches of the exquisite ornamentation in the Rosslyn chapel about which I wrote you so enthusiastically the other day, I took advantage of Edward's absence this morning to visit the place again and this time alone. The sky was clear and the air balmy, and as I approached the spot from the near-by station I was not surprised to see another woman straying quietly about the exterior of the chapel gazing at walls which, interesting as they are, are but a rough shell hiding the incomparable beauties within. I noticed this lady; I could not help it. She was one to attract any eye. Seldom have I seen such grace, such beauty, and both infused by such melancholy. Her sadness added wonderfully to her charm, and I found it hard enough to pass her with the single glance allowable to a stranger, especially as she gave evidence of being one of my own countrywomen:

"However, I saw no alternative, and once within the charmed edifice, forgot everything in the congenial task I had set for myself. For some reason the chapel was deserted at this moment by all but me. As the special scroll-work I wanted was in a crypt down a short flight of steps at the right of the altar, I was completely hidden from view to any one entering above and was enjoying both my seclusion and the opportunity it gave me of carrying out my purpose unwatched when I heard a light step above and realized that the exquisite beauty which had so awakened my admiration had at last found its perfect setting. Such a face amid such exquisite surroundings was a rare sight, and interested as I always am in artistic effects I was about to pocket pencil and pad and make my way up to where she moved among the carved pillars when I heard a soft sigh above and caught the rustle of her dress as she sat down upon a bench at the head of the steps near which I stood. Somehow that sigh deterred me. I hesitated to break in upon a melancholy so invincible that even the sight of all this loveliness could not charm it away, and in that moment of hesitation something occurred above which fixed me to my place in irrepressible curiosity.

"Another step had entered the open door of the chapel—a man's step—eager and with a purpose in it eloquent of something deeper than a mere tourist's interest in this loveliest of interiors. The cry which escaped her lips, the tone in which he breathed her name in his hurried advance, convinced me that this was a meeting of two lovers after a long heart-break and that I should mar the supreme moment of their lives by intruding into it the unwelcome presence of a stranger. So I lingered where I was and thus heard what passed between them at this moment of all moments ire their lives.

"It was she who spoke first.

"Francis, you have come! You have sought me!"

"To which he replied in choked accents which yet could not conceal the inexpressible elation of his heart:

"'Yes I have come, I have sought you. Why did you fly? Did you not see that my whole soul was turning to you as it never turned even to—to her in the best days of our unshaken love; and that I could never rest till I found you and told you how the eyes which have once been blind enjoy a passion of seeing unknown to others—a passion which makes the object seem so dear—so dear—'

"He paused, perhaps to look at her, perhaps to recover his own self-possession, and I caught the echo of a sigh of such utter content and triumph from her lips that I was surprised when in another moment she exclaimed in a tone so thrilling that I am sure no common circumstances had separated this pair:

"'Have we a right to happiness while she— Oh, Francis, I can not! She loved you. It was her love for you which drove her—'

"'Cora!' came with a sort of loving authority, 'we have buried our erring one and passionately as I loved her, she is no more mine, but God's. Let her woeful spirit rest. You who suffered, supported—who sacrificed all that woman holds dear to save what, in the nature of things, could not be saved—have more than right to happiness if it is in my power to give it to you; I, who have failed in so much, but never in anything more than in not seeing where true worth and real beauty lay. Cora, there is but one hand which can lift the shadow from my life. That hand I am holding now—do not draw it away—it is my anchor, my hope. I dare not confront life without the promise it holds out. I should be a wreck—'

"His emotion stopped him and there was silence; then I heard him utter solemnly, as befitted the place: 'Thank God!' and I knew that she had turned her wonderful eyes upon him or nestled her hand in his clasp as only a loving woman may.

"The next moment I heard them draw away and leave the place.

"Do you wonder that I long to know who they are and what their story is and whom they meant by 'the erring one?'"

Anna Katharine Green – A Concise Bibliography

The Leavenworth Case (1878)
A Strange Disappearance (1880)
The Sword of Damocles: A Story of New York Life (1881)
The Defence of the Bride, and other Poems (1882)
X Y Z: A Detective Story (1883)
Hand and Ring (1883)
The Mill Mystery (1886)
7 to 12: A Detective Story (1887)

Risifi's Daughter, A Drama (1887)
Behind Closed Doors (1888)
Forsaken Inn (1890)
A Matter of Millions (1891)
The Old Stone House and Other Stories (1891)
Cynthia Wakeham's Money (1892)
Marked "Personal" (1893)
Miss Hurd: An Enigma (1894)
The Doctor, His Wife, and the Clock (1895)
Doctor Izard (1895)
That Affair Next Door (1897)
Lost Man's Lane: A Second Episode in the Life of Amelia Butterworth (1898)
Agatha Webb (1899)
The Circular Study (1900)
A Difficult Problem (1900)
One of my Sons (1901)
The Filigree Ball: Being a Full and True Account of the Solution of the Mystery Concerning the Jeffrey-Moore Affair (1903)
The Amethyst Box (1905)
The House in the Mist (1905)
The Millionaire Baby (1905)
The Chief Legatee' (1906)
The Woman in the Alcove (1906)
The Mayor's Wife (1907)
The House of the Whispering Pines (1910)
Three Thousand Dollars (1910)
Initials Only (1911)
Masterpieces of Mystery (1913)
Dark Hollow (1914)
The Golden Slipper, and Other Problems for Violet Strange (1915)
To the Minute; Scarlet and Black: Two Tales of Life's Perplexities (1916)
The Mystery of the Hasty Arrow (1917)
The Step on the Stair (1923)